DARK QUASAR IGNITES

FRIENDS OF A FORMER SPACE JANITOR
BOOK 2

JULIA HUNI

IPH MEDIA, LLC

Cover designed by German Creative
Editing by Paula Lester at Polaris Editing

Julia Huni
Visit my website at juliahuni.com

IPH Media, LLC

For the robots who don't want to take over the world. The ones who just want to follow their programming and leave the humans to deal with themselves.

CHAPTER ONE

THE ALERT KLAXON rings through the ship, startling me out of my meditation. I blank the screen on my reader, so no unsuspecting crewmates stumble across my current text. Not that an unsuspecting crewmate should be prowling through my cabin unaccompanied. Not if they want to live to see another planetfall.

Except Elodie, of course. She does whatever the heck she wants, and no amount of arguing, pleading, or threatening on my part has succeeded in changing her behavior. Even the lock on the door doesn't deter her. And honestly, if Elodie saw that cover, she'd probably demand a copy of the book.

On my way out the door, I debate grabbing the kitten snoozing on my bunk but leave her there. Hadriana Caats have an extra sense—if we were truly in danger, she would know. I swing my arm through the huge "alert" icon, silencing the klaxon. My footfalls on the companionway decking thud into the sudden quiet, interrupted by a door sliding open on my right.

Elodie emerges, rubbing her eyes. "What's going on?"

"Nothing threatening the ship. Go back to bed." I seize the next doorframe to pivot through it and bolt up the steep steps—or "ladder" as Arun insists we call it—to the upper deck. At the top, three long strides take me to the bridge's hatch.

Which won't open.

I slap the heel of my hand against the metal. "Arun, open up!" Not waiting for a response, I flick my holo-ring to open a call to the bridge. "Let me in!"

Elodie appears at my back, wrapping her gauzy, floaty robe around a ridiculous nightgown. Semi-sheer pink chiffon drifts over a silky spaghetti-strap babydoll gown that ends well above her knees. The tiny ribbon roses along the plunging neckline look itchy, and the whole outfit makes me wonder who she's dressing up for. She, Arun, and I are the only ones aboard. Well, us and cats.

The hatch pops and I shove it wide, the thick metal thudding against the bulkhead. "What's happening?"

Arun, focused on the screens before him, waves a casual hand at the co-pilot's chair but doesn't respond.

Elodie follows me onto the small bridge. An enormous black cat appears at her side, then leaps to the back of my chair. He shoves his smooshed-in face next to my ear, his purr stuttering like a poorly tuned engine. I give his left ear—the one with a chunk missing—a good scratch. When I stop, his claws pop out and he swipes a huge paw at my head, pulling half my hair from its updo without touching my skull. Apawllo demonstrates impressive accuracy.

Arun glances over his shoulder, his eyes widening when they land on Elodie's elaborate lingerie. He returns to his screens without commenting on her appearance or presence. "I'm vetting another potential co-pilot."

My shoulders relax a fraction, and I hide a yawn behind my hand. "Why the ship-wide klaxon if this is just an evaluation? I thought someone had crashed."

"We almost did. Suffice it to say I will not be hiring this particular candidate." He pokes a green icon, then swipes it off the screen. Casting another look at Elodie, he pulls a communications app from the ether and flicks the green "transmit" button. "I've got the shuttle on autopilot. It will return you to Station Crippen-Hauck. Thanks for coming to see us today."

The prospective employee starts to say something, but Arun bats the comm app away, cutting him off. "That's the third candidate they've sent, and each has been worse than the one before. I can't believe any of them passed their exams. I miss Helva."

Elodie leans against the side of my chair, her attention focused on the huge cat draped over my headrest. "Apawllo wants to know why you're bothering. We don't need another qualified pilot. Interstellar law only requires two for a ship this size."

"True, but you've threatened to leave five times since Leo relocated. With Helva gone—" A shadow crosses his face. "If you're going to leave the ship, I need someone else. And cats don't talk."

"Finish training Vanti." She flips her hand at me. Unlike Apawllo, she hits the side of my head, and one of my hairpins falls to my shoulder. "Sorry."

"You might have forgotten this, but I work for you." I pull the remaining pins from my hair and gather the copper mass together. "At least that's what my last paycheck said." I don't mention that my last paycheck was five weeks ago. She knows she owes me, and her vid views—thus her income—have been low this month.

She sighs, then takes the pins from my hand. "Let me do that. Since I can't afford to pay you, the least I can do is take care of your hair. But if you pass the pilot exams, Arun can hire you."

"No!" Arun and I say together, our gazes locking in surprise.

"Why not?" I ask him.

"You go first. Why don't you want to work for me?"

"I have a job." I tip my head at Elodie.

She grabs my skull with both hands and turns it to face front again. "Hold still. And I just told you, I can't afford you anymore."

"That's temporary. I understand how vid celebrity works. Followers come and go. Videos spike and drop. You just need another viral series. Maybe it's time to resurrect one of the old ones. A new take on Gagarin?"

"You would rather go back to Gagarin than work for me?" Arun asks.

"No. Yes. Not exactly. I don't want to go back to Gagarin. I meant she could remix the old vids." I shake my head, but Elodie grabs it again, her fingernails biting into my skin. "We could try Lewei. Now that we don't have a deposed dictator's kid riding along."

"As far as we know." Elodie slides the pins into my hair, anchoring whatever she's creating back there. Knowing her, it's not a simple twist.

"Is there something you aren't telling us about your past?" Arun gives up on his holo-screens and turns in his seat to look at her. "I know who my parents are. Not a despot among them."

She laughs. "How many parents you got? I wasn't talking about either of us. My parents both grew up poor on Kaku. But we don't know anything about your past, Vanti."

My shoulders tighten again. I don't talk about my past. Even Griz doesn't know much, and I've been friends with him longer than anyone else. "My roots are deeply planted in the swamps of Grissom."

"The swamps?" Elodie pulls the jump seat down and drops onto it, leaning forward so far I'm afraid her flimsy bodice will not withstand the pressure. "Tell me more."

"Nope."

Arun gives me a long look, then something that might be pity passes through his expression, quickly banished when his nose wrinkles. "Back to the matter at hand. Why don't you want to work for me?"

I flick a look at Elodie, but she's settled in as if she's watching her favorite vid. I can almost see popcorn in her hand as her eyes ping-pong between us. "Could you give us a moment?"

She sighs, and her whole body droops. "I guess. But let me know what the final outcome is. If you're staying with me, I need to get my numbers up." She rises, and the jump seat snaps vertical with a thwap. With a snap of her fingers, she turns toward the door. Apawllo gets to his feet, stretching and arching in leisurely fashion, as if to counter his quick response to her summons. Then he leaps to the deck, his paws barely making a sound despite his twelve kilos, and paces out the door behind her.

When the hatch thuds shut, I turn back to Arun, focusing on his shoulder to avoid his gaze. "I don't want to work for you because I don't want it to be weird." I gesture between us. "Our… *association* is awkward enough. Having you as my boss? No. Besides, I have a job."

"You mean the CCIA thing? I thought Elodie knew about that." He flinches when my hand flies up in protest. "What? Am I not allowed to say it?"

I surreptitiously flick my holo-ring and activate my jammer. "I don't talk about my employer. Ever. And Elodie knows I have income from another source and occasionally have to do jobs for them. We don't discuss the… origin of that income."

Arun's head snaps around to his control screen. "Did you seriously just turn on a jammer? Don't you trust me?"

"I don't trust anyone." I lift my hand to exhibit the red winking icon.

He reaches into the ether and pulls out another flashing red three-dimensional image. "I've always got one running."

"Don't you think that will draw unwanted attention?"

"Less than turning one on and off. You want the bad guys to know when you're talking classified stuff?"

I roll my eyes. "Please. My system is much more sophisticated than that. It cycles randomly, so anyone paying attention will not know when I'm using it. Not only that, but anyone who doesn't know who I am will think it's simply a glitch in their data collection system." I cross my arms and lean back as far as the co-pilot's chair will allow. "Your turn. Why don't you want me working for you?"

His face goes pink, and he looks away.

I don't want to have a "define the relationship" discussion—now or probably ever—but I'm not going to let him get away with telling someone else he won't hire me. Even if that someone else is technically my boss and she just begged him to take me on. In fact, maybe especially in that case. "Well?"

He sighs heavily. “I don’t want to hire you because…. Well, the truth is you’re a terrible pilot.”

CHAPTER TWO

HUMILIATION FLOODS THROUGH ME. I know my flying skills are still improving, but am I bad enough to be unemployable? I rise and lift my chin, keeping my hard-earned poker face in play. "Thank you for telling me."

Arun jumps to his feet, touching my forearm hesitantly. "No, I don't mean you're that bad. It's just—"

"You said 'terrible,' so I think that's exactly what you meant." I pull away, moving toward the hatch. "No problem. I have a very particular set of skills. Skills I have acquired over the years. Flying is not one of them. I don't always have to be exceptional." I don't actually believe that. I work hard to be well above the curve on *everything*. And I thought I was better than terrible. I've worked as hard at flying as I have at any other skill. I should be well above average.

"Vanti. Please listen. Even though you haven't taken your exam, you're still an exceptional student. But new pilots are *all* terrible. No matter how good they are. You simply don't have the breadth of experience I require in a co-pilot. We fly into some unusual circumstances, and I need to be able to trust my co with my life."

"You trust Elodie!" I swing around, anger burning in me. Elodie is —she's a fabulous friend, but she's an *airhead*. The idea that she's better than me at anything— No that's not it. I don't deny she's better than me at many things. Just not the things I care about being good at.

He puts his hands on my upper arms. I want to pull away in anger, but the bridge is small. And some tiny part of me wants the comfort of his touch. "Vanti, listen to me. Elodie has been flying a long time. She started as a kid. Sure, she took a lot of years off when she was raising a family, but she spent a long time redeveloping her skills. And she's very good at flying. She has an ability to focus that is remarkable. And completely surprising, knowing how hare-brained she can be in the rest of life." He shrugs. "She kind of turns off the distractions and zeroes in on the flying. It's truly remarkable. And I won't put my ship—or the lives of my passengers—into the hands of anyone less capable. You *are* an exceptional student, but you need a few more years of practice to reach that level." He squeezes my arms gently. "Knowing you, you'll get there faster than average."

I scoff. "Faster than average? I've never been 'average' at anything."

"That's what I mean." He gives me a quick shake, then lets me go. As he turns away, he mutters something else, something I don't quite catch.

"What?"

He tosses his smooth, top-lev smile over his shoulder. "Nothing. Gotta look at new applicants."

I hide a smirk as I head back to my cabin. He doesn't want to hire me for my flying skills, but I heard what he said. "I can't date the help." I might not want to have a DTR talk, but it's nice to know he wants me.

A FEW DAYS LATER, my comm system pings with Griz's tone. I turn down the intensity on the FlexTrainer and connect. "Hey, Griz."

Ty O'Neill grins up at me. "You swimming? How far?"

The FlexTrainer allows the user to swim without water. I'm not a fan of getting wet, but swimming is an excellent workout, so I use it frequently. "Today's a full-body medley. Not going for distance. You've got about two minutes before my two-hundred-meter sprint."

"I can call you back when you're done."

"Talk fast, and you won't have to."

"Triana and I are planning our honeymoon. Finally."

"You did that already." I check the readout. Forty meters left on this easy interval.

"Until we ended up in another reality."

"Alternate universe," I reply, because I know he's expecting it.

"Right. Anyway, this time we're going to Moghbeli Luna Major. There's a high-end resort, but also some other fun extras that Triana will enjoy."

"You didn't call me across the galaxy to tell me you're going on vacation. Twenty meters."

He looks around, as if he's worried someone is listening, then leans closer to the camera. "I have exciting news, but I'm not supposed to—"

"Ten meters." I make a get-on-with-it gesture.

"I'm going to be a father."

My arms and legs stop working. "What?" I hang suspended in the FlexTrainer, my mouth open. The simulated water pushes me to the end of the tank, and I end up with my butt against the wall.

He grins, clearly thrilled with the effect his news has had on me. "Yup. Triana doesn't want anyone to know yet. She's only six weeks. But she agreed I could tell you. Because we both know you won't tell anyone. And she's convinced you'd find out anyway."

The system pings, reminding me I should be swimming. I swipe a hand through the display and turn it off. The artificial gravity gives me a five-second count-down, and I manage to get my feet beneath me before I drop to the floor. Leaning against the side of the tank, I try to get my breathing under control. "Congratulations."

He smiles, glowing with joy.

We chat a little longer, then sign off. Interstellar calls are ridiculously expensive, but Triana can afford them once in a while. The perks of being a top-lev.

As I finish my swim, I mull over Griz's news. I'm not a very introspective person. All those feelings. Yeesh! But this is life-changing news from my closest friend. I'd be lying if I said it didn't get me thinking about relationships and children. But while I wouldn't mind a real relationship—someday, when my life settles down—I have no plans to bring little Fioravantis into the world. I don't have the patience for that. You have to feed them and interact with them. And change their dirty diapers—or have enough credits to buy a baby-bot.

I'll stick with secret agenting, thank you very much.

When I'm done with my workout—not my personal best, but I did have a legitimate interruption—I hit the sonic shower then grab a protein bar from my secret stash. Arun buys only top-shelf macronutrients for the Autokich'n and even brings fresh produce on board when we're near a station, but I like the consistent familiarity of my protein bars. I guess they're my comfort food, and I need that after Griz's announcement.

Ugh, more feelings.

Even playing with Noelle, my Hadriana kitten, brings me no peace. Leaving her in the cabin, I bound up the ladder to the bridge level and poke my head through the open hatch, but no one is inside. We're currently docked at Station Crippen-Hauck, orbiting Sally Ride. Arun is still trying to find a new pilot, although Elodie has decided to stay at least until we go back to Kaku. If she leaves, I'll have to come up with another reason to stay aboard. Or find a new highly flexible travel gig. I suppose I could just wander the galaxy like a space bum, but that doesn't appeal to my need for order and control.

The rest of the ship is strangely empty. I vaguely remember Elodie muttering something about shopping this morning. And Arun mentioned another trip dirtside. Sally Ride is his home planet, and he has a nice place in the hills outside New Sydney. I connect to the ship's comm system and check the logs. Sure enough, he left a few hours ago.

I pace the corridors, restless but unsure what I want to do. I don't like this aimless feeling. I need a mission. Returning to my stateroom, I send a message to my CCIA handler. She's on Grissom, but unlike Griz and Triana, I can't afford a real-time call.

I'm in the middle of my tenth set of pushups when my audio implant pings. I switch to one-handed pushups and use my free hand to flick my connections—incoming call from Grissom. Wow, it's my day for high-end communications. I roll to my butt and hit accept. "Fioravanti."

Aretha O'Neill, my CCIA handler and Griz's sister, appears in my holo and nods gravely. "Dark Quasar. You're ready for your first mission?"

I frown, puzzled. "I've been on the active list since we finished the last one. And this is hardly my first."

Noelle leaps from the bed, landing on my shoulder. She and Aretha exchange a long, mutually unfriendly glare, then ignore each other. Aretha's lips purse. "This will be your first since we changed your status from deep undercover to crisis intervention."

What is she on about? I've done a dozen jobs since we discovered my identity had been leaked. True, most of them were little things: package retrieval, minor weapons bust, small hostage negotiation. I wave off her categorization. "What's up?"

"Your message came at an opportune time. We need a team to investigate an anomaly on the edge of Leweian space."

"A team? I work solo."

"Not anymore. That's why I called this your first mission. Your first as team lead."

"I was team lead on that bust on SK2."

She snorts. It might have been a laugh, but Aretha doesn't really have a sense of humor—at least not at work. "That was a long time ago. And your partner claims *he* was team lead."

"Yeah, well, he's a man. They always think they're in charge."

Her stony expression makes me wonder if I've gone too far. My partner on that job was Griz, and he's her little brother, after all. Maybe she's more sensitive to slights on his behalf. Or maybe she doesn't like me bashing half the population. After years of working for her, I still can't read Aretha most of the time. Finally, she shrugs. "True."

I suck in a breath of relief. "Who are you sending?"

"I'll forward their details to you." She swipes something, and my ring vibrates with an incoming file alert. "You'll be well outside the usual shipping lanes, so there should be zero interaction with the local populace, but having a native speaker would help."

"I don't speak Leweian."

"No, but you know someone who does."

I paw through my mental catalog of agents I've worked with in the past, but none of them spoke more than a few words of Leweian. "I'm coming up blank."

She swipes another file to me. "Ervin Lewei."

I flick the new icon and an image of Ervin Lewei, aka Ervin Zhang, aka Leonidas, pops up. "Leo's a civilian. And Lewei isn't safe for him."

"He speaks the language. Knows the culture."

"I don't think he's going to want to go to Lewei. You remember what happened to him when we went to Gagarin." And I'm not sure I trust him after that adventure, but I don't say that. Aretha expects me to distrust everyone.

"I've already sent him an invitation he can't refuse. And as I mentioned, you won't be anywhere near the planet. Even if you were, your translator should be sufficient to communicate with the locals. Ervin will be more valuable as a cultural translator should you need one. The target is supposed to be Commonwealth, but it's possible the Leweians put it there. Having a local might give you insight into their intentions. Send me a message when the team is assembled and you're ready to depart."

"I'll have to convince Arun to make the trip. Or hire a ship myself." I flip to the mission brief. "Interstellar conveyance isn't cheap, and you didn't give me much of a budget."

"You don't want to draw attention by hiring a ship. You are no longer strictly 'undercover,' but we prefer you stay under the radar as much as possible." Aretha's eyelids drop halfway over her eyes. "Convince Arun. I'm sure you can." The comm bubble pops as she signs off.

CHAPTER THREE

I PROWL THE SHIP, scanning through the documents Aretha sent me. Noelle paces beside me for a while, then wanders away. I consider going after her, but she's a Hadriana Caat—an alien species that, according to the rumors, is sapient and sentient. Some of them even talk, but Noelle has not yet exhibited that behavior. Either way, she's safe on the ship and smart enough to stay out of trouble.

According to the files, an abandoned ship has been located on the edge of Leweian space. It's a civilian ship, standard Commonwealth design, and the Leweians don't appear to have noticed it. Yet. Our mission is to determine what happened to the ship and crew, retrieve anything of value, and leave Leweian space without being detected.

A simple in-and-out.

The crew she's assigned me is small. We shouldn't need to physically search the ship—logs will tell us if anything of interest is aboard. Aretha's team includes a cargo specialist, a communications expert, and a demolitions guy.

I puzzle over that last one. Blowing things up isn't a good way to stay under the radar. Maybe she thinks we'll need to blow open some internal bulkheads. That might be fun.

My comm system pings, and the bright pink flash tells me it's

Elodie. I skip the greetings. "I can't believe you left the ship without your security team."

"Good morning, sleepy head." She beams at me through the camera. "I was going to take you, but you looked so peaceful I didn't want to wake you."

My blood runs cold. "You saw me? Sleeping? In my cabin?"

"Nope." She laughs merrily. "I knew that would set you off. I had a meeting with a new contact at *CelebVid*."

"They want you back? Didn't we kind of burn that bridge when we refused to—"

"Fortenoy has been replaced. The board didn't like a lot of the things he was doing, so they voted him off the island." She laughs again, this time triumphantly. "They took out all of his transdimensional gear. Decided he was a lunatic."

We exchange a smug smile. While Ser Fortenoy's fascination with flying to other dimensions sounds crazy, we both know his experimental equipment was successful. And highly dangerous. "So, are we going back to the *Solar Reveler*?" My heart sinks. I don't want to leave the *Ostelah Veesta*—or her owner. But Elodie is still my boss. At least on record.

"Nebulas, no! I like the flexibility Arun gives us. Not to mention the safety. He's not going to willingly fly us into something dangerous just to get good vid." She glances over her shoulder. "I'll be back on the ship in a tick. See you then." And she's gone.

I head for the lounge at the stern of the ship and grab a bottle of water, then settle into one of the comfy couches to call the surface. My call goes through quickly, but Leo doesn't answer. I'm about to hang up when the call connects.

"Vanti?"

"Leo."

His brows draw down. "Why did you get me fired?"

"Fired? What are you talking about?"

Leo works at a high-end restaurant on Sally Ride, in one of the few human-run kitchens on the planet. His face goes darker, the bright orange turban clashing with his reddened countenance. "I was let go this morning."

"Why would you think I have anything to do with that?" I try to sound innocent, but I'm sure Aretha set this up. That woman has no qualms about messing with civilians' lives. I understand why she does it —she's responsible for the safety of the Commonwealth. Maybe not completely, but part of it. But that's no reason to be so cavalier about peoples' livelihoods. She grew up in an upper-lev family on Grissom, so the idea that someone might *need* their job to survive is foreign to her.

"I don't know." He lifts a finger, jabbing it at the ceiling. "My boss says he has to let me go but won't say why." He sticks up another finger. "You call not ten minutes later. I haven't heard from you since the whole Gagarin thing. Now you show up the day I get canned." A third finger goes up, then he flings his hand down. "I don't have a third thing, but those two alone are enough."

I lift both hands. "It was not my doing. But since you're at loose ends…"

He crosses his arms and leans back in his chair. "What?"

"How'd you like to take a little jaunt on the *Ostelah*? With me and Elodie?" I give him my best "Lindsay the recruiter" smile. And realize with a tiny twinge of surprise that I'll probably never play that role again. Not that I miss pretending to be perky and bubbly, but living in Pacifica City was nice. There were lots of good restaurants around the Techno-Inst. And I kind of miss Triana, although if anyone else suggested that, I'd deny it in a heartbeat.

He sighs and uncrosses his arms to pull off his turban. Shoving his hand through his short curly hair, he looks away from the camera for a long moment. I've never asked him why he wears the traditional Leweian robe and turban since he dislikes his home planet so much, but it's odd to see him so casual. I guess he feels comfortable with me. "To be honest, I was getting kind of bored here. You and Triana have ruined me for a normal, quiet life."

I suppress an exultant cheer and give him a small nod instead. "Some of us are not cut out for a boring existence. Although to be fair, you can't blame us for all of it. You were the runaway son of a deposed dictator when we met you."

A smile finally lightens his dark features. "Not to mention classically trained chef and surf instructor."

"Not quite in the same league, but the combination is unusual for sure." I raise my brows. "When can we expect you?"

He looks around the room. The corner I can see looks utilitarian—as if he's living in a long-term temporary apartment and hasn't bothered decorating. Or even unpacking much. But maybe the rest of the place is all gauzy draperies and neon lights. "I don't have a lot of stuff. I can probably get upstairs by tomorrow. Give me your docking berth—I'll need to ship a few small crates."

I send him the info. "Arun is down at his place—he might be able to pick you up. You want me to ask?"

Leo's smile returns. "I'll give him a call. I missed one from him a few minutes before yours came through."

I frown. Why did Arun call Leo? "Do you talk to him often?"

He snaps his fingers. "I knew there was a third thing! I haven't heard anything since I left the ship. Then I get a call from you and him the same day?" He points at me. "I'm still suspicious. But I'll see you soon." He waves and closes the connection.

I drum my fingers on the arm of the couch. Why did Arun call Leo? He doesn't know about the mission. It could be a coincidence, but I don't believe in those.

Aretha met Arun when I used him as cover for a pickup on Tereshkova. Could she have recruited him for this mission before assigning it to me? I wouldn't put it past her. Aretha does whatever it takes to complete the objective.

I heave another sigh, then give up trying to figure it all out. I can ask them when they arrive. And I'll have adult beverages ready, so they're more likely to talk.

CHAPTER FOUR

TURNS out preparing lunch that will sweet-talk a team into being friendly is not as easy as Elodie makes it look. When she arrives and finds me in the galley, I've got a stack of sliced meat on a plate, a loaf of bread, and a pile of apples. I heave a sigh. "It would be easier to just let everyone order what they want from the Autokich'n."

Elodie laughs as she pulls a few slices of bread from the package. "Easier for you. But if you're trying to butter someone up, you don't start with, 'make yourself some lunch.' You gotta show them the love." She pulls out a knife and bottles of condiments and starts building sandwiches. "Slice those apples. And rinse the berries I brought. Who are we buttering and why?"

I step out of her way, folding my arms as I lean against the counter. "What makes you think I'm trying to butter anyone? And why would you want to do that anyway? Sounds… greasy."

Elodie gives an outrageous wink, then grabs the berries and thrusts the package at me. "Get to work. I recognize a soft-soap when I see one. Besides, when have you ever made lunch for anyone?"

I pull an offended face and slap my hand against my chest. "I've made lunch before." I try to come up with an example but draw a blank.

"If you call handing out those disgusting protein bars 'making lunch' you might have done it once. Or twice. You're not exactly good at sharing them." She flourishes a knife at me, then swipes it across a slice of bread.

I open the berry container and run it under the faucet. "I believe in being prepared. And if I'm sharing my resources with those who are less prepared, then we're all unready."

"Like the foolish bridesmaids?"

"Is that *Ancient TēVē*?" I give the container a shake, then dump the berries into a bowl.

"Biblical reference. Never mind." She takes the fruit and sets it on the counter dividing the galley and the lounge, next to a platter full of delicious-looking sandwiches.

I point at the stack. "How did you do that so quickly?"

She smirks. "Hospitality is one of my superpowers." The Auto-kich'n pings, and she pulls a second plate from it, this one full of cookies. "Knowing what to outsource to technology is key." The sweet, buttery aroma wraps around us, making my mouth water.

"Who all's coming to this low-key arm-twisting?" She pulls glasses from a cupboard and arranges them on the table.

"I'm not actually sure." I frown as I pull up the notes Aretha sent me. "Leo, for one."

"Leo!" She grabs both my arms and shakes me, bouncing on her toes in excitement. "When did you talk to him? How long is he staying? How'd you get him to come back? Why didn't you tell me? Wait... isn't using food to butter up a chef kind of risky?"

I pull away. "I told you I'm not buttering anyone. I contacted him because I—" How much should I tell Elodie? Nothing classified, obviously. And nothing even remotely sensitive, because Elodie has no ability to keep secrets. "I heard he might be between jobs, so I called him and invited him to come."

Elodie's eyes narrow. "You heard he might be—how exactly did you hear that? Wait, don't tell me. It was that 'handler' of yours. And she probably engineered the whole thing." She does air quotes around the word "handler."

I do a double take. "How do you know about my handler?" Frowning, I sort through my memories, trying to pinpoint a discussion in which I might have let the term slip.

"Ha! So you do have one! I knew it!" Elodie does a little victory dance, knocking over one of the glasses with her flailing arms. She catches it before it falls off the counter and sets it upright.

"Very clever." I frown, deploying my death glare, but it's never been effective on Elodie.

She fills one of the glasses with sparkling Frooti-Sweet and perches on the stool beside the counter. "Tell me everything."

"If you know I have a handler, you know I can't tell you anything."

"Don't try that inscrutable stuff on me. I've been your cover long enough to be let in on the loop. Or whatever the saying is." She waves a hand dismissively, then takes a sip of her drink. "Give it up."

"Let's wait until everyone gets here, okay? Then I don't have to explain it all again."

"When will that be?" She looks at the sandwiches, then at her chrono.

"Soon." I tip a finger at the door.

It slides open.

Elodie squeaks in surprise. "How'd you do that?"

I give her my blank stare then raise a brow.

Leo walks in. Elodie deserts me with another squeal and throws herself at the tall Leweian. He's abandoned the robe and turban and sports slim, dark pants, a gray shirt with an indecipherable logo, and a trendy blue jacket. He's almost unrecognizable.

Arun follows him through the door wearing similar garb. The look is so consistent, I suspect Leo borrowed clothes from Arun's closet. They're about the same height and build—tall and muscular without being bulky. For some reason, Arun has always looked less physically intimidating than the Leweian. I blame the turban.

Arun stops in the doorway. "What's going on?"

I give him an innocent look. "Lunch?"

"You invited me to join you for lunch. And now there are two—" He breaks off as a short, blocky woman enters the room, holding two grubby duffle bags. "There are three other people here. Who are you?" He thrusts a finger at the woman.

Noelle appears beside Arun, gives the newcomer a death glare, and darts out the open hatch.

The woman watches the kitten leave, then turns to Arun, giving his hand a thoughtful look. She drops the bags, dusts her palms on her worn pants, and bumps her knuckles against his, avoiding the still outstretched pointer finger. "Zwanilda Serevdoba. Blaster. Call me Zwani." She glances past us. "Ooh, lunch. Excellent."

Arun watches her walk away, a strained look on his face. "Why is there a 'blaster'—whatever that is—named Zwani on my ship? And how did she get aboard?" He turns to me as he asks that last question.

I lift my shoulders. "I might have given her access."

"You *might* have let her in?" He flicks his holo-ring and pulls up the security files. "And let her wander through my ship on her own? Did it ever occur to you there might be things on board I don't want strangers messing with?"

I put a hand on his arm. The muscles are tense under my fingertips, like he's made of titanium. I glance around and lower my voice. "Aretha sent her. We have a—there's a thing she'd like us to check out, and Zwani's expertise might be necessary. And no, of course I didn't let her wander through the ship untracked."

He glares at me for a long moment, then glances at the others, filling their plates at the counter. "Excuse us." He grabs my arm and pulls me into the corridor. As soon as the door shuts, he releases me, his hand remaining open as if he can't wait to end the contact. "Aretha does not own this ship. She hasn't contracted with me to use this ship. What the—" He swallows what was surely going to be an expletive and takes a deep breath. "Why is Zwani here and what does she do?"

This is not going the way I planned. "I guess I should have called you before—"

"You think?" He throws both hands in the air then stomps away from me down the corridor. Before I can follow, he spins and stalks back. "Explain."

"There's a ship on the edge of Leweian space. It appears to have been abandoned. The distress beacon indicates it's a Commonwealth freighter, but there's no record of it in any transportation databases. Aretha has asked me—us—to check it out."

"Why us? Why not a CTA ship?"

"They want to keep it 'unofficial.' Sending a Commonwealth ship—even a Transportation Authority vessel—that close to Leweian space might precipitate unwanted political effects."

"You're saying she didn't want to cause an international incident?" He hunches his shoulders and crosses his arms. "What happens if we get caught nosing around?"

I pick at an imaginary thread on my sleeve, so I don't have to meet his eyes. "We're just tourists. Elodie's vid career gives us the perfect excuse. Vid stars bumble into things all the time. The Leweians won't want the negative publicity that would come with interfering with a vid starlet broadcasting live."

"She won't be able to broadcast live from Lewei. They keep their comm beacons clamped down tight. No signals get in or out unless they approve."

"I'm sure we can get the signal out."

"Another hidden relay, like at Gagarin?" His mouth twists. "For all the good that did us."

"We were very successful on Gagarin." I look up, and our eyes meet. His burn into mine, like a stunner at short range. I pull my gaze away with an almost audible snap. "I need to brief the team."

His hand falls on my shoulder as I turn away. I freeze, barely restraining the instinctive urge to flip him over my shoulder onto his back in the middle of the corridor. I turn slowly. "Yes?"

He snatches his hand away as if I burned him. "Nothing."

CHAPTER FIVE

ARETHA'S other two recruits show up as we finish loading our plates. I approve their credentials, which opens the airlock between us and the station, and tell them to leave their gear by the hatch. Then I watch them via the security system as they follow a code slip to the lounge.

The door slides open, and two men enter. The first one, a ridiculously tall, slender man wearing a baggy coverall, nods at us and makes a beeline for the food. His companion, a short, broad guy dressed in a shiny business suit, ignores the sandwiches and helps himself to one of the bottles of craft beer on the end of the counter. They join us at the table.

I stand and move to the end of the room. "Good afternoon and thank you for coming. I'm Agent Fioravanti. You may call me Vanti. Our captain, Arun Kinduja, and I welcome you to the *Ostelah Veesta*." I don't look at Arun, but I can feel his displeasure burning into me. "We have been tasked with investigating an apparently abandoned Commonwealth ship near Lewei."

The short man launches to his feet. "Hang on! No one said anything about going to Lewei! That place is not on my bucket list."

I lift my hand. "Don't worry, we aren't going to the planet. The ship is orbiting the Leweian system but it's nowhere near the planet."

Arun shoves his chair away from the table, his food untouched, and gives me a narrow-eyed glare. "Before we go any further, maybe we can do introductions? I'd like to know who I'm welcoming to my ship." His faint emphasis on "my" is not lost on me.

"Of course." I gesture to the short guy still standing in front of his chair. "This is Steve Jones. He's a freight specialist. He will review the ship's manifests, match them to the cargo on board, and report back any salvageable materials."

Jones spreads both arms and bows, the beer sloshing in its bottle with the expansive gesture. "At your service."

Arun grunts.

"Vladimir Kerovsky-Martinez is a communications tech. He'll help us locate the ship, then retrieve the black box and download and examine any communications in an attempt to determine why the ship was abandoned." The skinny guy—who hasn't stopped shoveling food into his mouth since he arrived—waves his fork without looking up from his plate.

I nod at the woman. "Zwanilda Serevdoba is our blaster. She's a demolitions expert and will facilitate our entry to any inaccessible areas of the ship."

"Call me Zwani. Pleased to meet you all." She raises her sandwich at us. "And thanks for the grub. This is good eatin'."

I point at Elodie. "You can thank Elodie for that."

Zwani frowns, then shakes her sandwich at Elodie. "I know you. You run that deli over on third street?"

Elodie giggles. "Nope. I'm strictly amateur when it comes to sandwich creation."

"But I seen you before. Work at the grocery?" Zwani waves the sandwich more, bits of meat and pickled peppers flying loose. One lands in Arun's salad. He picks it out with a fork but doesn't say anything. He doesn't need to—his closed expression says it all.

"She's Elodie-Oh," Vladimir says through a mouthful, spraying crumbs across his own plate but thankfully not on anyone else's.

"Who?" Zwani takes another bite.

"I've watched your vids. Loved the TechnoTropolis one." Vlad points a pickle at Elodie, then shoves it into his mouth.

Elodie preens. "Thank you!"

Jones gives Elodie a long, dead-eyed stare as he finishes off his beer. With a loud belch, he stomps across the room to get another one.

I cough and gesture to Leo. "This is Leonidas. He's our Leweian culture expert."

"I thought you said we aren't going to the planet." Jones stops with the second beer halfway to his mouth. "If you're goin' to Lewei, I'm out."

"We are not going to Lewei," I say firmly. "But I prefer to be prepared for any contingency."

"Like what? You expectin' the Leweians to show up on this ship? I don't want no truck with Leweians."

"You have made that very clear." I frown at the little man. Why did Aretha send him to us? Surely she could have found a cargo specialist without an anti-Leweian bias?

Aretha doesn't do anything capriciously. Jones was selected for a reason. I just need to figure out what that reason is.

"Again, we have no plans to go to Lewei." I flick my holo-ring and a display appears beside me showing the Shenzhou system. That's the official name of the star Lewei circles, but everyone calls it Lewei. Just like everyone calls the Baekdu system after the planet encircling it—Sally Ride. I'm not sure why the ancients bothered naming both star and planet, but just because we're stuck with the names doesn't mean we have to use them.

Another flick sets a pinpoint flashing on the edge of the display. "This is the location of the ship. As you can see, it's several astronomical units outside Lewei's orbit. And at this time, it's on the opposite side of Shenzhou. With the star between us and the planet, we should be able to get in and out without the Leweians even noticing us."

"Then why do we need him?" Jones points his beer bottle at Leo.

"It's possible we'll need his expertise in communications with the jump node. As you know, Commonwealth-Leweian relations are strained. Official communication all goes through Tereshkova and has for decades. The same goes for physical visits to Lewei—ships jump to Tereshkova, then from there to Lewei. We're circumventing that process and may need someone who reads Leweian to help with hijacking the comm node."

Vlad looks up, his third sandwich halfway between his plate and his mouth, his jaw still for the first time since he arrived. His gaze travels from me to Leo to Jones, then back again. After a long, pregnant pause, he grunts and resumes eating. I'm not sure if he agrees or is mocking my fabricated explanation, but he doesn't contribute anything else to the conversation.

Leo watches the skinny comm tech for a long moment, then turns to me, his brows raised. I widen my eyes at him, and he snorts a tiny huff of air.

Elodie, completely oblivious to any tension, jumps up to retrieve the fruit. "Anyone want dessert?"

AFTER SHOWING Jones and Vlad to their shared stateroom next door to Leo's, I open the door across the passageway and gesture for Zwani to enter. "You'll be in here." I grab my duffle bag and Noelle's pillow from the floor.

"Is this your place?" She drops her case by the door and takes a quick tour of the compartment. "This is nice. Way nicer than I usually get. There's two bunks. We can share." She winks at me, then peeks into the small sanitation cubicle. "Very nice. I don't want to kick you out of your regular room."

"I'm moving to a crew cabin on the upper deck." I look around to make sure I haven't missed anything. "We're down one, so there's plenty of space. Elodie is next door." I nod at the forward bulkhead.

"Down one crew member? Hope it isn't anything important, like a pilot or engineer." She laughs. "This ship don't carry much more than what, two crew?"

"Two or three. But we have all of the required positions

covered." I give the room another quick look. "Make yourself comfortable. We should be departing Station Crippen-Hauck shortly."

"Don't forget this." Zwani waves my reader at me, then she takes a look at the cover image and whistles soundlessly. "*Captive Brides of the Atlantean Nebula*? That's some spicy reading!"

I snatch the device from her hand—I thought I shut that off. "Must be Elodie's book," I mutter, willing my cheeks not to flush. "She's always leaving her things lying around."

"Hey, no judgment here." She gives me a knowing smirk, then hefts her suitcase onto one of the bunks. "Girl's gotta have her vices."

Back stiff, I stalk out of the room. Noelle hisses at the woman and follows me out. I haven't had her long enough to know if she's like this with all strangers or if she senses something about Zwani. I file the behavior away as I blank the reader's screen. Shoving it into my bag, I head for the ladder. The kitten trots along behind.

At the top, I make my way to the second officer's compartment. It's smaller than the passenger suite I just vacated, but I don't need a lot of space. And with this many strangers aboard, being away from the passenger deck appeals to me.

The door across from me opens, and Arun emerges, stopping short when he catches sight of me. "Just, uh, going to the bridge so we can depart." He waves at the hatch, as if I don't know where it is.

"I'm moving in. That's okay, right?"

"Of course. I told you before—as long as we don't have an official co-pilot, you're welcome to it. And you can use the office if you need more space." He tips his head at the door beyond mine. The captain's cabin takes up as much space as the conference room and second officer's cabin together

I nod and step inside the compartment. It contains a comfortable bunk and a tiny but useable sanitation module. I toss my gear on the bed and turn to find Arun crouched in the doorway, petting Noelle. "Good kitty."

"Did you need something?"

He rises and takes a step back. "Nope. Just making sure the

cleaning bots did their job. Don't have a maintenance tech here to oversee that stuff."

"It's fine. No one has lived here in months." I run a finger along the edge of the tiny desk. "And look, no dust."

He gives me a jerky nod. "Perfect. You coming to the bridge for departure?"

"If you don't mind." Since we got back from Gagarin—months ago—every interaction has been tense. Of course I know the reason—Arun started to show his feelings for me, and I deflected. As I always do, because being involved with a coworker makes things messy. No matter how much I might want it to happen.

CHAPTER SIX

Our first hurdle is the jump. Two days after picking up the crew, we approach the jump belt. Normally, ships and beacons communicate seamlessly, feeding the coordinates and timing to the jump engines. But in this case, there is no direct jump to Lewei. Not that it can't be done, but it isn't politically acceptable. All traffic between the Commonwealth and Lewei goes through the Tereshkovan system.

But if we go through Tereshkova, they'll have a record of our transit, and Aretha told me to stay under the radar. Plus, after our last visit there, I'm not sure they'd be happy to see us. Luckily, the CCIA has a tool for this.

I ask Leo and Vlad to join me on the bridge, then head there myself. Arun sits in the left-hand seat, ready for jump. This ship has an excellent autopilot program, but Arun likes to have a hand on the tiller at key moments. In this particular case, it's necessary. He looks back when the hatch opens, gives me a grunt, then returns to swiping through news feeds.

We haven't been actively avoiding each other, but everyone on the ship seems to have spent more time in their cabins than normal. We've staggered our mealtimes, whether unintentionally or by design, I'm not sure, and even the tiny gym has been empty every time I've gone. It's been refreshing for an introvert like me, but also a little worrisome. Shouldn't we be bonding as a team or something? That's what I remember from my decade-old leadership training.

I slide into the right seat. "Vlad will need to load a module before we jump."

Arun's eyes snap to mine. "What sort of module?"

I flick my ring and swipe a file to him. "An 'important to our jump' module."

"And by that, you mean an illicit coordinate bender." He crosses his arms, as if he's getting ready to argue with me.

"I'm not sure what that is, but it sounds about right." Shutting down my holo, I turn to stare at the forward display. "I don't know how it works, but it'll make sure we arrive in the place we want to be instead of in the place the normal beacon would send us."

He scrolls through the informational file in his palm. "We call them jump benders. They take the coordinates from the beacon and calculate a new destination, then feed that to the jump engines. They're illegal and potentially dangerous."

The hatch opens and Leo enters, followed by Vlad. They're both wearing common Leweian garb: an ankle-length robe and matching turban. Leo's robe is covered in monochromatic embroidery. The light on the bridge is too dim to see, but I recognize the outfit. The elegant embroidery is all Sachmos—characters from a children's game which has a huge adult following as well. Leo had it made as a kind of parody of traditional high-end Leweian fashion.

Vlad's robe is unadorned dark blue—a working Leweian's kaftan with a high collar and shoulder pads. Perfect, if our jump was going to take us back in time fifty years. These days, most Leweians—except the top-level politicians and their families who use their expensive, traditional clothing to reinforce their importance—wear fashions indistinguishable from ours.

I can't resist a bland dig. "I see you dressed for the occasion."

Vlad blinks at me, then makes a shooing motion. "Outta the way. If we're flying into Leweian space, I wanna be ready to chat with anyone who hails us. This makes me look like a local."

I rise and move away from the seat. "That makes you look like a cos-player. No one wears those things on Lewei anymore."

Vlad drops into the chair, his slender frame dwarfed by the wide seat back. "You been to Lewei recently?"

"I was there about three years ago."

"Huh." He nods at Arun and accepts a link the pilot swipes to him. "Well, I was there two weeks ago. Trust me, this is what I need to wear."

Leo clears his throat. "If you're capable of chatting with the locals, what do you need me for?" He takes a slow step backward toward the hatch.

I grab his arm and shake my head.

"I do the techy stuff." Vlad flicks through screens so fast I can't read more than a word or two here and there. "As such, I speak what you might call 'flying Leweian.' Flight instructions, coordinates, docking details. You're here in case we gotta have an actual discussion, right Vanti?"

I nod. "We probably won't need you today. The whole point is we're supposed to insert without attracting attention. But if we're noticed, you two are going to get us out of trouble."

"How will we do that?" Leo slides back another step, pulling me with him.

I yank hard on his arm, then fold down a jump seat and point at it. "Sit."

He sits.

I take the one across the aisle and buckle in. "If we're contacted, Vlad will respond. We've experienced a technical failure—"

Vlad cranes his neck and looks back at us. "I'm going to tell them the flux chromera winlette has failed and—"

I wave him off. "I don't care about the technical details. There's no reason Leo would know those. He's a passenger." I wave at his fancy dress and hat. "Trying to get home to Lewei."

"No!" Leo jumps up.

"You're as touchy as Jones. Relax." I grab his arm again before he can bolt from the bridge. "I've got a PVD for you, so you won't look like you. And that code slip—"

Arun interrupts. "Jump bender."

"The jump bender hides our entry stats." I ignore Arun's fake gasp and focus on Leo. "No one will know you—the real you—are here."

"Why *are* you here?" Vlad asks over his shoulder as he watches the data running across his holo. "If I escaped from Lewei, I sure as hell wouldn't be heading back."

"Escaped?" Leo repeats faintly as he drops into his seat. "What makes you think I've ever been to Lewei?"

Vlad throws a smirking grin at us, then returns to his work. "You're here as the cultural liaison. That implies intimate knowledge of the target culture, which requires boots on the ground. You've got a Leweian accent, even when speaking Standard, although you've tried to eradicate it, so it's my guess you grew up there. I've met a lot of 'cultural liaisons' in my time, and none of them are natives. They're all Commonwealth citizens—that gives them a golden ticket to get back out if things go wrong."

"I'm a Commonwealth citizen!" Leo glares at Vlad, straightening his robe, suppressed anger evident in every movement. "I'm not afraid to go back. I've got that golden ticket."

"Do you?" The question is mild, inoffensive, bland. But waves of avid curiosity roll off Vlad like water off a pod of swamp whales.

"Why wouldn't I? As you say, I'd be stupid to return if I didn't."

"Huh." Vlad swipes an icon. "Coming up on jump in two minutes. The bender is installed and communicating with the beacon. All systems green."

Arun raises a hand for silence, then flicks the ship-wide announcement icon. "Attention. Jump in two minutes. Please find a seat. Auto restraints will engage at the one-minute mark. Bridge out." He flicks the green holo and swipes it away, then fastens a belt across his lap.

Vlad follows suit. "Ninety seconds to jump. All systems nominal."

I jerk my head at Leo. "Better buckle up."

"I thought this boat had auto restraints." He slides his butt away from the wall and peers over his shoulder, then fumbles with the buckles recessed in the fold-down seat compartment.

"The passenger spaces do. But up here on the bridge, we prefer the security of real straps and buckles." Arun yanks on the end of his lap belt to tighten it, then pulls the shoulder straps over his head.

Vlad chuckles as he loops his loosely across his body. "Typical pilot. Tell everyone else it's safe, then take extra precautions."

"I know what can go wrong. Not my fault if your average passenger is too ignorant to be careful."

I glare at Arun, even though I can only see his shoulder and the side of his head. "I've flown on this ship for a long time, and this is the first I'm hearing of a need for additional precautions."

"We've always jumped using legit beacon coordinates." He flips his hand at Vlad. "I don't know what he's done to my navigation. We could end up in an alternate universe."

From here I can't tell for sure, but I think he's hiding a grin. We were involved in an experiment that sent our friends Ty and Triana into another dimension, but that ship had a lot more modifications than a simple jump bender.

"Sixty seconds to jump," Vlad says as he throws a countdown clock to the top of the screen. The big red numbers blink hypnotically.

We wait out the final minute in silence. Leo's fingers drum against his thighs, slapping out a nervous pattern. Vlad hums under his breath, a song that sounds familiar but which I can't quite place. I focus on my breathing, trying to appear relaxed and calm. I have years of practice and have become an expert.

Vlad's humming cuts out, and he counts us down. "Jumping in five, four, three, two, one, jump."

The usual weird tremor goes down my spine as we jump. I shake it off. "Are we there yet?"

Arun scans his data stream and nods once. "Arrival in Shenzhou system confirmed. We're heading south from the entrance ring at a distance of two AU. All systems nominal. Vlad?"

"No one hailing us. In fact, there's no one within hailing distance. We're on the far side of Shenzhou from the planet, and well outside normal communications range. Looks like the bender did its job. Scanning for our target."

As we wait for Vlad to find the ship, I unfasten my harness and motion for Leo to do the same. "You're off the hook for now, Leo. But please keep your comm system open. If we need you, we'll need you fast."

Leo unsnaps his buckles and throws the straps off his shoulders. "You don't have to tell me twice. I need to go bake something." He surges to his feet and whirls out the hatch before anyone has a chance to respond.

CHAPTER SEVEN

WHILE THE COMPUTER continues to scan for the mysterious ship—and Vlad babysits it on the bridge—the rest of us meet in the lounge. I haven't seen Jones or Zwani since lunch on the first day. I suspect Jones has been avoiding the rest of us. My surveillance data shows he's used the gym at regular times—four sessions in the two days we've been together. He likes to lift heavy weights and avoids cardio.

Vlad has apparently been living in the lounge. He sleeps on the couch, rising early and going to bed late so the rest of us won't notice. If I had to guess, I'd say Jones kicked him out of their shared cabin. During the day, he stashes his belongings in the cargo hold. I've toyed with locking him out just to see what he'll do, but that seems mean, even for me.

Zwani hasn't left her room. There are no cameras in the passenger cabins, so I don't know what she's been doing in there, but between the high-end entertainment suite and the luxury Autokich'n Arun has provided, a person could comfortably live there for months.

Am I nosy? Maybe, but I believe in knowing your team.

For today's meal, however, I've called them together. Leo, Arun, and Elodie join us, not because I invited them, but because it's lunch time. And because they're nosy too. Plus, technically, Leo is a member of the team, although I have no plans to put his particular skills to use. If we have to talk to Leweian authorities, I'd rather trust my auto-translator rather than put Leo at risk.

As I take my seat, I wonder again why Aretha insisted Leo join us. He's a skilled chef. I have no doubt he could have found a new job at a top-lev resort or in the home of a wealthy foodie. We first met when he was caretaker for Dame Morgan, and I'm sure she's given him a stellar reference. If he's looking for adventure, there are much safer places for him to visit. I make a mental note to corner him when this mission is over and find out what's going on in that unturbaned head of his.

Once everyone has food—or in Jones's case beer—in front of them, I flick my holo-ring to make sure the bridge is looped into the conversation. A holo of Vlad lounging in the co-pilot's seat with his feet propped on the pilot's armrest pops up in the center of the table. Apawllo looks up from the back of the pilot's seat, blinks his golden eyes at the camera, then goes back to sleep. I knock my knuckles against the table. "Time to talk tactics."

The quiet chatter dies out, and five pairs of eyes turn to me. Vlad waves an arm, peering around the bridge as if he isn't sure where the camera is. I don't believe that for a second.

"Vlad is on the bridge, trying to find the target. He'll alert us as soon as the system pinpoints it." I glare at the holo. "Can't you do that from here?"

"I could." Vlad scoots back in the chair and lets his boots drop to the floor. "But I'm less likely to be distracted on my own."

"You're not really doing anything that requires that level of concentration." Jones scowls. "The computer will alert you when it finds the ship."

Vlad swings around and stares directly at the camera, as if he can see Jones through it. "This is my area of expertise, Jones. And if I say I need to be here to do it—" He stabs a finger at the deck. "Then that's where I'll be."

All eyes swivel to Jones. He raises both hands. "Just trying to support the team."

"Riiiiiight." Vlad leans back and puts his feet up again.

Arun winces and looks away from the holo, surreptitiously rubbing the arm rest of his chair as if he can wipe out any smudges from Vlad's boots.

I turn to Zwani and Jones. "Once Vlad locates the ship, we'll dock. Will you be able to get us inside?"

Zwani rubs her hands together. "Definitely."

I lift a finger. "Without blowing a hole in the hatch? Or hull?"

Her head drops back with a dramatic groan, and she stares up at the overhead. "You people are no fun."

"If this ship is registered in the Commonwealth, I have the means to activate the unlock sequence." Jones lifts his beer with a smug smile and toasts himself.

"Even an older ship? Based on the intel, it's a Fenstron hull. None of those have been reported missing in the last ten years."

"Fenstrons are the most common hull in the Commonwealth. And yeah, I have the ability to get into 'em. Even an old one." Jones crooks his fingers at me. "Ya got the scan data?"

"There was no scan data. Everything we have came from local assets."

Jones's eyes narrow and he jumps to his feet. "You mean we're heading out here on the say-so of a Leweian double agent? I'm not going near that ship. Take me home. Now." He crosses his arms and glares at Arun.

Our captain gives him a flat stare, then looks away as if bored.

I point at the short man's chair. "Sit down, Jones. As a CCIA operative, you should have a clear understanding of how our intelligence works. The chances that this informant was a 'double agent' is extremely unlikely. And even if they were, our intel department assessed the data and declared it extremely reliable."

"That's what they told you."

I lift my chin. "That's what the report said. You think they lied?"

"Well, if they told you I'm a CCIA operative, then yes, they lied. I am a civilian recruit, not a professional agent." With a smug grin, he drops into his chair.

Leo's head snaps up. His gaze cuts to Jones and then to me.

I put on my poker face and give Leo a reassuring nod. Leo doesn't look reassured.

I turn back to Jones. "You're a civilian?" Aretha didn't tell me that. I flick my holo-ring and scan through the files, keeping them opaqued so the others can't read the data.

"That's what I said. I have a skill set that is useful to this mission. The agency is paying me a large number of credits to assist you. They even sent me scan data. Data you said doesn't exist." He flicks his own ring and pulls up a file.

I make a grabby motion at him. "*You* got scan data?" Why would Aretha have neglected to give me the data?

He opens a file, flings it onto the projector long enough for me to read the first couple of lines, then pulls it back. "You don't need this—it's essential only to my part of the mission."

Zwani, who has been working her way through her meal silently, pushes back from the table. "I might need it." She throws me a glare. "If I ever get to blow anything up."

"It's a standard Fenstron." Jones's hand clenches around his ring, as if he's afraid she'll rip it from his finger. "Regular hull, normal hatches, no modifications, boring as can be. Neither of you need to know more than that."

"You *will* share that data with the team." I put my hands on my hips and give Jones my most intimidating glare.

He rubs the tips of his thumb and first two fingers together in the ancient sign for money. "Make it worth my while."

"Excuse me?" I draw myself up and glare harder. "Are you seriously putting the safety of this team at risk in an attempt to extort credits?"

"No, of course not." He smiles. "I told you, there's nothing dangerous in this file. I'm trying to save you time and energy." He shows me his palms, as if to demonstrate the total lack of important information, then walks across the room to get another beer.

Noelle appears seemingly from nowhere and hisses at Jones. He ignores her.

Leo stands. "I have bread to shape." He slips away before I can stop him, with the kitten on his heels.

"Where's he making bread?" Elodie waves at the cabinets along the wall that hold the Autokich'n and galley. "Shouldn't it be here?"

"He took a bowl to the engine room." Arun rearranges the veggies on his plate for probably the fifteenth time. "Muttered something about the temperature and humidity."

"That tracks." Elodie goes back to her soup, apparently not interested in the safety of the team due to lack of data. "I hope he does the one with rosemary and olives."

Time to regain control of the meeting. "Jones, I want your data. Now. Or I will confine you to your cabin and report you to my superiors when we return."

"Works for me. I agreed to fly out here with you and access the ship's inventory logs. I can do that from my cabin if Vlad gives me access." He pulls a third beer from the chiller and heads to the door. "You know where to find me."

CHAPTER EIGHT

I STOMP out of the room and head for my cabin. Normally when I'm this mad, a swim in the FlexTrainer device is the best way to chill, but I'm not ready to release my anger. I need to send a message to Aretha now while I'm in the heat of the moment. I want her to feel my fury.

Locking the door behind me, I pull up my communications app. I mentally lay out my arguments, then turn on the recording. "I don't know why you sent Jones, but he's seriously sabotaging this mission." I enumerate the problems he's caused in the two short days he's been aboard, including alienating his teammates and refusing to share information vital to the mission.

Someone knocks on my door. I shut down the recording. "Just a minute." Then I set my system to send as soon as we're within range of the hidden relays the CCIA has planted around the Leweian system. Aretha probably won't see it until we're finished here, but I want her to understand what happened if it all goes to heck.

"Come in."

The door opens and Arun steps into my tiny compartment. "I've got it."

"You have what?" I drop onto the bunk and cross my arms defensively.

"A copy of Jones's file. I made a copy when he put it on the projector."

I stare at Arun in disbelief. "You got it that quickly?"

A little smile slides across his lips and vanishes as he pulls the chair away from the narrow desk and straddles it. My cabin is so small our knees brush.

The door opens again, this time without warning, and Elodie peeks in. "Can I join the party?" Noelle prowls past her and jumps to my lap. Apawllo slinks in, as if he's trying to make it clear he wasn't following the kitten.

I scoot down the bunk, leaving space for Elodie at the top. She grabs my pillow, folds it behind her, and leans against the bulkhead. "Did you tell her?"

"He just told me he has a copy of Jones's report. Based on what he didn't say, I assume he has the system set to automatically record any data thrown to it. I'm not sure that's legal, without an explicit, signed waiver." I raise my brow at Arun.

He smirks and raises a finger. "One, it's not legal in the Commonwealth, but we aren't in the Commonwealth. Two." He raises his middle finger. "Everyone who enters this ship signs the waiver when they agree to the conditions of entry. Three. I got what you want, so why are you fighting me?"

"The conditions of entry?" Elodie sits upright, her eyes sparkling. "Are you telling us you put a data privacy release in the welcome packet?"

I look from Arun to Elodie and back, then flick my holo-ring and open the file that is automatically sent to anyone who comes through the ship's hatch. I read it thoroughly the first time I came aboard, of course, and didn't see anything granting permission to copy my data. But the ship delivers the same file every time you walk through the hatch, so I stopped reading it. I flip through the pages and find the relevant paragraph. "It didn't use to say this!"

"Nope." Arun nods at Elodie. "It was her idea to add it when we found out you were a CCIA agent."

I stare at them, dumbfounded. I've taken great pains to ensure my data is never at risk. I don't share it to common-use systems, even on a private ship like this one. My mistrust has been validated, but that doesn't stop the little tremor of betrayal that runs through me. "You—"

Arun raises a hand. "I don't copy any of yours. Either of you." He wags a finger between me and Elodie. "But after Grigori, and the doubts we had about Leo, it seemed prudent to be proactive."

"Do you still distrust Leo?" Elodie stops fussing with the pillow and pins her bright gaze on Arun. "That whole thing in Gagarin—he didn't betray us. He was playing Grigori."

"Maybe. Probably." Arun sighs. "No, I don't really doubt Leo. But I knew we'd likely run into other... guests... who might wish us harm. Or who might be willing to hold us hostage for a few extra credits, like Jones." He juts a thumb toward the stern of the ship, then flicks his holo and brings up a file. "This is it."

My holo-ring buzzes as the file arrives. I slide it open and discover Jones was telling the truth. The rudimentary scan shows a standard Fenstron hull with no modifications. The cargo area appears to be shielded, so the scan shows only a blank return, which means they could be carrying anything. Well, anything not radioactive. Particle emissions would be evident, even on a long-distance scan like this one. Noelle rises to her feet and bats a paw through the holo, then loses interest when it doesn't react.

"He was right. It's useless." I close the file and scratch the kitten's head. She purrs.

Elodie looks at Arun. "You didn't tell her, did you?"

He shrugs. "It's speculation. Wild speculation."

"It's not. We got a positive face match." She turns to me. "She needs to know."

I cross my arms. "I always need to know everything. What's going on?"

"Jones is not who he says he is."

I sigh. "That was pretty obvious. I mean, Steve Jones is about as generic a name as you can come up with. And now that I know he's not an agent..."

"He's not just 'not an agent.' He's a gangster."

"Not again." We dealt with Gagarian criminals on our last trip outside the Commonwealth. "Who's he work for?" And why did Aretha send him?

"He doesn't work *for* anyone." Elodie scoots sideways, leaning against the head of the bunk and wrapping her arms around my pillow. "He's Vinnie Sondre, the head of the Sondre family."

I frown as I try to remember who the Sondre family is. My expertise is mostly with foreign crime syndicates, and none of the Gagarian or Leweian organizations use that name. "Who?"

"Fairly small-time syndicate out of Sarvo Six. They were in on that scam the dirty Academy commandant was running a few years back. They got slapped down pretty well, the organization got shaken up, and Vinnie—aka Steve Jones—came out on top."

"How do you know all of this? You're a vid star, not an intelligence operative."

Arun barks a laugh. "That's what I said."

"I keep my eyes open. My head up. My ear to the ground." Elodie widens her eyes in her familiar poker tell. Then her lips twitch and she gives up with a snicker. "I snuck a picture of him and did some research. Thought he might be competition. Did you know he wears a distorter?"

"I noticed when he arrived. For some undercover operatives, it's standard procedure. But he should feel safe enough on the ship to drop it." I glance at Arun, and he shakes his head. Distortion devices and makeup prevent surveillance cams from getting a clear image of the wearer. "Of course, now that we know he's a criminal, it makes sense. How'd you get a picture?"

"I wandered into the gym when he was there." She smirks again. "Right at the end of his workout. I'd taken a picture of the group at lunch, for my private scrap book."

"You really shouldn't take pictures of operatives on a mission—"

"If they don't want their picture taken, they shouldn't travel with a vid celebrity." She lifts her chin in mock arrogance. With a giggle she goes on. "Anyway, when I took the lunch picture, I noticed the distorter. So, I just happened to swing by the gym at the end of his workout, figuring his distortion makeup would be less effective when he was all sweaty."

"Plus, you like looking at sweaty men."

She smacks me with my own pillow. "Ew. I mean, sure, the super fit ones. But Jones is little. And kind of uneven. He has that massive chest, but have you noticed how scrawny his legs are? He's built like a barrel on sticks."

Arun clears his throat and rolls his hand in a "get on with it" motion.

"I snuck more vid while I chatted with him, but it's all distorted too. So, I mentioned it to Arun." She looks at him and lets him take over the story.

"It struck me as odd that he would conceal his identity while inside the ship." Arun rubs the back of his neck. "I might have glitched his distorter."

"You can do that?" I stare at him, aghast. I often use distortion makeup and Personal Video Disruptors, or PVDs, while undercover. If they can be "glitched," I need to reconsider my techniques.

"Turns out it was harder than I expected. But you know I like a technical challenge. I had to hit him with a tiny, super-focused, interval-distorted electro-magnetic pulse at the exact time Elodie took the image. It only crapped out for a second—those things are robust." He flicks his holo-ring and tosses an image at me.

This man looks like someone drew Jones with their eyes closed. He's similar in appearance, but a little rougher. Crooked nose, uneven eyes, lopsided chin. He's different enough to confound facial recognition software. "And you ran this image through your search? What engine did you use?"

Elodie coughs. "I used FindaFriend, and it brought up nothing." Her gaze cuts to Arun.

"Lemme guess." I point at him. "You wrote your own."

He ducks his head and shrugs in mock bashfulness, but he can't hide the grin. "Of course I did." His smile fades. "As Elodie said, he's Vinnie Sondre, head of the Sondre crime syndicate, and he's trying to make a name for himself. We need to watch him like a hawk. He's dangerous."

CHAPTER NINE

After Elodie and Arun leave, I record an addendum to my previous message and send it. If Aretha sent a member of the Sondre family on my mission, I want to know why.

A second possibility has occurred to me—maybe she didn't send Jones. Or rather, maybe she sent the real Jones but Sondre intercepted him and infiltrated us. That would imply Sondre knew we were coming to Lewei. Is he interested in the ship, or was he merely looking for a covert entry to the system? If it's the latter, we'll need to keep a lock on the shuttle and watch for anyone attempting to pick him up. If it's the former—well, I want to know what he's looking for.

I spare a thought for the real Jones—if he existed, he's likely dead. We all know death is a hazard of the job, but it doesn't make the eventuality any less final. In a weird, anti-social back corner of my mind, I rationalize that Jones getting killed means one less possibility of it happening to me. I *know* this line of reasoning is completely ridiculous, but it makes me feel better.

WHEN VLAD finally finds the ship, he calls us to the bridge. I already knew he'd found it—I'd set an alert on the bridge computer to notify me in the event of a positive acquisition, but I wait in my cabin until Vlad sends the message. Any delay in notifying us will make me suspect him as well.

Who am I kidding? I already suspect both he and Zwani are not who they claim to be. But Vlad notifies the rest of us promptly, so he gets one more tick in the "trustworthy" category of my mental score sheet. Or rather, the "not completely untrustworthy" category.

I open my cabin door and am overwhelmed by the warm, yeasty aroma of baking bread. Leo must be working off his stress. I suck in a deep, appreciative breath, then head for the bridge.

Arun sits in the left seat, Vlad in the right. The forward screen shows the image of a large cargo ship with an overlay of information including estimated mass, identification data from the transponder, current direction and speed, and projected flight path to reach this location including possible point of origination.

I squint at the screen, then reach out and stretch the data field. "You think they jumped in with a bender like we did?"

Arun nods. "Yeah, but not recently. This thing has been drifting closer to Lewei over the last five or six months. I'm shocked we found it first. Based on the trajectory, about four weeks ago, it passed close enough to Luna to be detected. If they were scanning the right direction at the right time."

I hum under my breath. "It's possible they did detect it. They could have already done what we're going to do. Might even have set booby traps. We'll need to be very careful. When can we go aboard?"

Arun throws a surprised look over his shoulder. "I thought you were going to analyze from here first."

"We will. In fact, get Jones up here to interface with the—"

"He's already accessing the ship from his—our cabin." Vlad points at a flashing light on his screen. "I forwarded the link as soon as he responded to my call."

I frown at Arun and raise my brows. He gives me a tiny nod.

Vlad intercepts the look and laughs. "We're recording his interactions. Twice. I've got an official audit running, and I can see your sneaky one running in the background."

"Not as sneaky as I'd like, obviously." Arun frowns. "Not sure I'm a fan of having another comm expert on my ship."

Ignoring the argument, I flick my holo-ring and contact Jones. "Status?"

"This is going to take time, boss." Jones shoves a hand through his immaculate hair, but it feels rehearsed. As if he knows harried people do this, and he wants me to feel his stress.

"I'm sure it will. I'm not expecting you to be done. I just want to know where we're at. And an estimate of how long it might take." I press my lips together, holding back my inclination to call out his obvious subterfuge.

"I'm running a cracker on their system right now. It could take anywhere from seconds to years. Depends on how good their security is. I had hopes I could just walk in through a back door, but those appear to have been locked. Doesn't bode well for our timeline."

Arun turns to look at me, peering through Jones's hologram. He gives a tiny nod, then lifts a hand and rocks it back and forth. I interpret this to mean Jones is not one hundred percent honest in his assessment. Closing the connection, I swipe it away so I can see Arun clearly. "What?"

Vlad answers. "Technically, Jones is correct. The system has good security—for an older ship. But there've been a lot of advances since that thing was built. And I doubt they've stayed current on updates." He waves his hands through his holo like a conductor at a symphony, sweeping and swooping, then bats a file to me.

A login screen materializes in front of me. Vlad does a few more hand-waves and data populates in the screen, then it dissolves and is replaced with a "Welcome to the *HCS Fairwell*" banner. I look over the screen at Vlad. "We're in?"

He smirks and nods, then lowers his voice in a mocking imitation of Jones. "Yeah, boss, we're in."

We move to the conference room, leaving Vlad on the bridge where he's watching for approaching ships. Not that he couldn't do that from anywhere else, but he seems to enjoy the private space. And since Jones tossed him out of their stateroom, I can't blame him. I close the conference door behind me and engage my jammer.

Arun cracks a smile as he takes a seat and shows me his holo. He's running a security layer under mine. No one is going to listen in on this conversation unless they know way more about communications than Arun. And since he's a certified genius, I'm not worried.

At least not much.

"Should we call Leo?" Arun throws another holo to the tabletop projector and stretches it to cover half the table. In the bottom corner, there's a real-time image of the bridge. Good to know he doesn't trust Vlad completely, either.

"Not yet. The target is a Commonwealth ship, so we don't need a native Leweian for this." I throw my own data to the other half of the table. Now that I'm logged in, the ship's system is surprisingly easy to use, and a few swipes takes me to a cargo manifest. "According to this, they're empty."

Arun frowns. "No cargo at all?"

I shrug and point to a section of data. "Nope. Nothing listed."

His scowl deepens. "That's not normal. Interstellar distances are expensive to cross—jump beacon charges are based on ship size, not mass, so you pay the same, empty or full. Anyone traveling in a cargo ship is going to take *something* to help pay bills. And let's face it, almost any Commonwealth cargo is going to sell like hotcakes in Lewei."

"Is that legal?" I pull up the ship's history files. "Doesn't everything have to be sold to the government in Tereshkova, then approved for transport to Lewei?"

"Officially, yeah. If you're going to Lewei, you register your cargo in Tereshkova and offer to transport at a good rate. Technically, the Tereshkovans could buy your shipment and move it to another ship, but they don't usually bother. Anyone brave—or crazy—enough to ship to Lewei knows which palms to grease and how to get tapped with a ship-through approval. Tereshkova doesn't have to pay for moving the stuff between ships. It's a win-win, except when they're flexing."

"Is that the officially approved method?" I drag my gaze away from Arun and try to focus on the files while he talks. The man's voice is so smooth, and he's so pretty to look at, it's hard to concentrate.

"That's the official under-the-table method. I'm not sure there is a strictly-by-the-book method that allows Commonwealth ships into Lewei. There's also the black-market option."

"Which is?"

"Pay off the Tereshkovan officials. They don't register your cargo at all, and you sail to Lewei unsanctioned. It's usually more lucrative, but you have to be willing to take bigger risks. If something goes wrong, Tereshkova won't go to bat for you. Not that they'd stick their necks out for anyone, but at least if you register, you have a document trail to prove you're quasi-legit."

I tap a finger on the table. "So, we're black-market?"

"Oh, no, what we did was *completely* off the charts. Thanks to the bender, Tereshkova doesn't know we exist. If we get caught here, both Tereshkova and the Commonwealth will deny any knowledge of us. We'll be at the mercy of the Leweians, which means we'd probably end up in Xinjianestan prison."

"High stakes. Just the way I like it."

His sharp eyes lock on mine. "Really?"

I look away. "No. But that's what a CCIA agent is supposed to say."

CHAPTER TEN

I CHECK THE EXTERNAL FEED. The *Fairwell* looks no closer than it did last time I checked.

"It's only been three minutes, Vanti." Elodie looks over the top of her ezine reader, her eyes huge thanks to the massive eyelashes and expert makeup.

"Three minutes since what?" I swipe the feed away and settle back in the couch as if I have nothing better to do than gossip.

The truth is, I don't actually have anything better to do, and it's driving me crazy. I'm an agent. I like to investigate, snoop, spy. Sitting on my butt waiting for the ship to dock is not my strong suit. I've learned to fake a level of calm over the years, of course, but I've also begun to let my guard down a little around Elodie.

They say admitting to a problem is the first step toward recovery. Time to stop being so transparent.

"Three minutes since you checked the feed the last time." She turns a page with a dramatic flourish. "Arun said we're still twenty-five minutes out. Or twenty-two, now, I guess."

"I was… reassessing the ingress options."

She snickers. "That means you were looking at the door again."

"It's called a hatch. You're a pilot; you should know that."

Her gaze flicks to me, then back to her reader. "I do know it. I just like to make you squirm."

"I don't squirm!" I suck in a deep breath. I've always been known for my unflappable calm under pressure. It's one of the traits that makes me a good agent. I can make calm, reasonable decisions in a calm and cool manner.

I've thought the word "calm" so many times it no longer has any meaning.

Elodie smirks again, then heaves a little sigh and puts her device aside. She leans forward to put a hand on my knee. "Do you want to talk about it?"

"Talk about what? How long docking takes? No, thank you. I understand the physics."

She squeezes my leg. "No, about your relationship problems. You should talk them out with Arun, but I'm here if you want to bounce them off me first."

I take her wrist between my thumb and middle finger, as if I'm afraid she'll contaminate me, and remove her hand from my leg, dropping it into her lap. "We aren't having relationship problems because we don't have a relationship. At least, nothing more than ship's captain and crew. Not even crew, since I work for you, not him. It's a captain to passenger's staff... *association,* which is barely a connection at all. There is no problem."

"Suit yourself." She shrugs and picks up her reader. "I've never seen you this... antsy... so something must be bothering you. And it's clearly not the mission because you never let those concerns show. Plus you and Arun have been mega weird around each other."

Definitely time to stop being so transparent. "I'm fine. The mission is fine. My relationships are fine."

She shakes her head sadly. "No one wants a 'fine' relationship."

Before I can respond, the lounge door opens. Zwani stands in the doorway, almost unrecognizable in a thick padded suit.

"What are you wearing?" Elodie rises and moves closer. "That is—well, I hate to use the word 'hideous,' but when the shoe fits..." Her gaze travels to the bulky white boots covering Zwani's feet.

The shorter woman fiddles with the latch at her throat, then folds her transparent face shield up. Her puffy white suit bears a strong resemblance to the early space suits from *Ancient TēVē*. It covers her from neck to toes, complete with articulated joints at the elbows and knees, and bulky pads that cover over the backs of her hands to protect her fingers.

"This is my PPE—personal protective equipment." She flips the hand-guards back, and they snap around her wrists like puffy bracelets. The gloves beneath are thin and flexible.

"Why not use a force shield?" I ask. "Less restrictive and much easier to pack."

Zwani carries two cases into the room and sets them beside the doorway. "Less restrictive, but not nearly as effective. They give you a false sense of security. I've had friends lose fingers thinking a force shield would protect them from shrapnel. Of course, if you're doing the job right, the blast goes away from you, but PPE is designed to protect you from the mistakes."

"What's in these?" Elodie nudges one of the cases with a toe.

"Those are my tools."

"You mean the dynamite?"

"Dynamite." Zwani laughs. "That's ancient history. And crazy dangerous. No, I use directional impulse blasters. Extremely precise. I can blow a hole smaller than your—" She breaks off, as if realizing Elodie might not appreciate crass humor. "Smaller than a pinhole."

Elodie looks impressed. "Then why do you need the suit?"

"I told you—the PPE protects me from mistakes. Not that I make many, but no one is one hundred percent perfect. Fingers are expensive to regrow. My insurance doesn't cover that."

"Good insurance might be less expensive—and much less effort—than that get up." I nod at her.

She laughs again. "Maybe. But you ever blown off a finger? Even knowing it can be regrown don't make it fun. And regrowing hurts like a—" She breaks off again, her gaze darting to Elodie and back to me.

"I think Elodie's heard worse."

Elodie looks upward and raises her brows. "I appreciate the courtesy."

"Anyway." Zwani clears her throat. "What do you need me to blow?"

Elodie and I exchange a look.

"Nothing," I say.

She throws her hands in the air. "Nothing? But I got all my gear! And you brought me along, so you must need something blown."

"Not at this time." I'm still not sure why Aretha sent a demolitions expert on this mission, but I'm not going to admit that to Zwani. Or Elodie, for that matter. "I'll let you know when your expertise is needed."

"Nothing to blow? What's the point of all this, then?" She flings herself onto the couch, the force of her descent shoving the sofa back a few centimeters. "My handler warned me this mission would be a bust."

"You still get paid, though, right?" Elodie drops beside her and puts a hand on her arm. "Why not just enjoy the trip?"

Zwani sniffs and nods. "Yeah, I'm a salaried employee. But I like my job."

"I get that." Elodie turns to me. "Can't we find her something to explode?"

"We're trying to keep a low profile." I close my eyes for a second to block out Elodie's sincere yet mischievous face. Taking a deep breath, I count to ten, then open my eyes. "I'll do what I can, but no promises."

CHAPTER ELEVEN

IN THE AIRLOCK, I don my pressure suit. It's restrictive, which I don't like, but carries enough oxygen to keep me alive for a full day, and I like being alive. The material will protect me from the vacuum of space as well as radiation, which our ship claims to be free of, but I'm not above taking precautions. And it's nowhere near as ugly as Zwani's.

The hatch beeps, then slides open, revealing Arun, glowering. "We should send a drone."

I raise a brow. "Already done."

He looks around the small space, as if he can visually inventory the ship's complement of drones and find one missing. "When?"

"As soon as we locked onto the ship, I sent one." I pull the thick fabric over my shoulders and shrug my arms into the sleeves. This suit was custom built for me, so it fits like a glove—once I've got it on. I give a little wiggle, and it kind of snaps into place. My range of motion in this thing is limited but it's worth the tradeoff.

"I didn't see a drone launch on my system." Arun gestures to his holo-ring, as if I don't know what he's talking about.

I puff out a sigh and raise my fishbowl helmet over my head. "I attached a drone pod to the exterior of the ship before we left Crip so

I could launch without opening any of the *Ostelah's* airlocks. Three buzzing the exterior—I'll send those inside as soon as we get the hatch open. But there aren't any life signs on the ship." Tucking my braid into my suit, I slide the flexible, transparent sphere over my head and lock it into place.

"You could have shared that information." Arun's words are muffled, so I engage the exterior mics. "I still think you shouldn't go alone."

"I'd rather go alone than have one of our new friends at my back. Leo's deep in his bread baking, and Elodie doesn't 'do space walks.' Besides, I'm not sure either of them would be much help in an ambush. And I don't hear you volunteering."

He swings around and opens a suit locker. "Because you told me I wasn't welcome."

I lift my gloved hand. "I didn't say that. I said we shouldn't leave the ship unattended."

"You strongly implied it. And it's not like the ship will be empty. Leo and Elodie can watch the shop." He puts the suit back into the locker and flicks his holo-ring. "Leo, Elodie, can you join us in the air lock?" Then he grabs the suit again.

I catch the helmet he tosses at me and watch as he pulls off his shoes. The pressure suits have built in foot gear as well as climate control and "plumbing." When Arun starts to shuck his pants, I turn my back. Not that nudity bothers me, but I don't know how he feels about it. And nobody likes to be stared at while they struggle into a pressure suit.

Besides, I need to keep a cool head, and watching Arun strip down isn't going to help with that.

"You can look now." Humor warms his deep tone.

I turn. The pressure suit hugs his legs and hips but is unzipped from the waist up, revealing his tan, washboard abs and broad chest. "Give me a hand with the sleeves, will you? I might have bulked up a bit."

He turns, and I help him pull the tight sleeves up his biceps and over his shoulders. Glad I'm behind him where he can't see my heated face, I suck in a deep breath and give myself a stern talking to. By the time he gets zipped, I've got my hormones under control. I hand over his helmet.

Elodie appears in the open hatch, Apawllo draped around her neck like an enormous scarf. "What's up, boss?"

"You been hanging around with Vlad?" I unfasten my helmet and pull it off. No point in wasting power if we're going to chat first.

"No, why?" Elodie gives me a puzzled frown.

"Never mind. Let's wait for Leo." I shuffle to the far side so she can join us inside the lock.

Leo arrives a second later and stops in the open doorway. "You're both going?"

"Come in and shut the hatch." I crook my fingers at him.

Leo steps over the lip and presses the button. The hatch slides closed behind him, and the lock clicks shut. The airlock is built for two people to gear up, so there's room, but it's tight with four.

I engage my scrambler and smirk when I catch Arun doing the same. Using a holo-ring through the suit gloves is awkward, but not impossible.

"What's with the secrecy?" Elodie drawls. "Don't you trust our new friends?"

"You're the one who identified Jones as a criminal," I say.

She smiles smugly but doesn't reply.

Leo glowers at us. "This is why I took that job on Sally Ride. I love traveling with you guys, but you collect some unsavory companions."

I jab a thumb at my chest, then swing it to include Arun and Elodie. "*We* collect—Grigori was *your* buddy, remember?"

Arun lifts both hands in a pacifying move. "Calm down. We all know Vanti's line of work—" At my grimace, he turns to Leo. "And Leo's background—might bring us into contact with unusual people. And no, we don't trust our new friends." He echoes Elodie's sarcastic tone of voice as he points at the external hatch. "But Vanti needs to enter the ship, and I don't want her going alone. So, we're leaving you two in charge. Jones is in his cabin, pretending to try to read the ship's files. We were able to get in fairly easily, so we know he's hedging. I suspect he's trying to find anything of value that he can skim. Vlad is on the bridge. He's watching for unexpected traffic and will alert you if he finds any."

"Do we trust him to do that?" When the chips are down, Elodie can be surprisingly business-like. The cat opens his golden eyes and gives me his soul-scarring glare.

"We do." I reach up to scratch Apawllo's ears. His accusing eyes close, and he purrs, rough and uneven, like a poorly balanced shuttle engine. "And we don't. Vlad is a CCIA agent. He could be a fake, like Jones, but we have no indication that might be the case, and part of this job is knowing when to trust. But Arun's got the system set to alert us too."

"Trust but verify." Arun's statement sounds like a quote, but I can't place it.

"Exactly. That's where you come in." I point at Elodie and Leo. "All three of our teammates are under our surveillance. If any of them attempts to do anything dangerous to the ship or you two, we'll know. You know where the arms locker is?"

Elodie and Leo exchange a look, then nod.

Arun flicks his holo-ring and swipes a couple of controls. "I've set the system to allow you access to it. It requires a DNA sample, then will require you to read a random passphrase to check your voice. It will examine your life signs for stress. And there's a duress code. I recommend you arm yourselves, just on the off-chance we've trusted the wrong people. There are stunners—easy to use and small enough to fit in a pocket. The good thing is, they don't trust each other either, so we've got a kind of checks-and-balances thing going on."

I touch Arun's arm. "Are you sure arming the civilians is a good idea?"

"It was your idea."

"I wasn't going to suggest they get weapons. I just meant they should know where they are. In case Jones or Zwani or Vlad try to break in."

"If my security is so easy for them to break through, we've definitely trusted the wrong people. And you've trained both Elodie and Leo to handle weapons. I say we put that training to good use."

Elodie giggles. "And heck, even if we stun each other, it's not like there are any long-term effects. We'd just be out for a few hours."

Leo holds up both hands. "I don't want to get stunned. I have brioche proofing in the engine room."

"No one is going to stun anyone. At least not anyone who doesn't deserve it." Arun gives Elodie a narrow-eyed glare. "And by 'deserve it,' I mean actively doing something to endanger the ship, not burning popcorn in the Autokich'n."

She smiles lazily and rocks her hand back and forth as if she'll think about it. Then she dusts her palms together and straightens up. "All kidding aside, Leo and I can handle this. And Vanti definitely needs a backup on this little jaunt. We got Jones in his cabin and Vlad on the bridge. Where's Zwani?"

Leo coughs. "She was helping me with the bread."

"Is that what you young people are calling it these days?"

Leo's face goes bright red. "Really! I was showing her how to make brioche!"

Elodie snickers. "Ha. You know she plays for the other team, right? Don't get your hopes up."

"She's not my type. And yes, I know she has a girlfriend." Leo glares at Elodie. "We were just making dough."

When Elodie snickers again, I put a hand on Leo's arm. "I'm not sure you're helping your case. Elodie can make anything sound like an innuendo."

Arun puts a hand over his eyes, slowly shaking his head from side to side. "We're doomed."

"Sorry, but when I get an easy target, I have to take the shot." Elodie points a finger gun at Leo. With a decisive nod, she lets her hand drop. "But seriously, we can keep an eye on the ship. We'll grab stunners and monitor the feeds you sent me. You two do your thing." As she turns to the hatch, the cat leaps from her shoulder to the deck and stalks to the external one. "Apawllo, this way."

The cat ignores her and sits facing the exit.

"You can't go with us." I pick him up and hand him to Elodie. "We don't know if the air is good, and you don't have a suit." The image of trying to stuff Apawllo into a cat-shaped pressure suit makes me both snicker and shudder.

Elodie hoists the huge animal, holding tight as he attempts to squirm away. Then he relaxes, drooping over her arm like a thick, furry blanket. She gives him a gentle squeeze, then follows Leo out of the airlock. It thuds shut behind her and locks, then the system lights blink to red.

Arun and I don our helmets, run diagnostics, and do a buddy check, then turn to face the external hatch.

CHAPTER TWELVE

THE *OSTELAH'S* HATCH OPENS, and I push off the deck, floating into the weightlessness of the FlexLock, the articulated transparent tube connecting the two ships. I want to send a drone inside the freighter, but the failsafes in *Fairwell's* system mean opening an emergency hatch from the outside requires a physical key. It's meant to prevent anyone from doing what we're attempting to do—access the ship without permission—except in a real emergency.

Vlad or Jones probably could have opened a cargo hatch remotely, but since I can't see inside the cargo hold, I don't want to risk blowing anything out of the airlock. And I'd prefer to do as much of this recon without their interference—or Zwani's explosives—as possible.

Grabbing a convenient bar beside the hatch, I swing my feet to the magnetic pad near the end of the FlexLock and lock my soles into place. I insert the key we printed from Aretha's many possible specifications. It's a standard Fenstron hull access key and will probably require some—nope, it slides in cleanly, and the hatch vibrates as the relays connect and the bolts respond.

"That was easy." I glance over my shoulder at Arun and raise a brow. "Too easy?"

He shrugs one shoulder. "Maybe. But if you're a legit cargo hauler, you'd want a rescue ship to be able to access your emergency passenger airlock."

"They aren't worried about pirates?" I open a panel and twist the wheel inside. The bolts holding the hatch shut groan and grind, but it turns. "Ready?"

"Ready." Arun has his stunner out and is crouched low just inside our airlock, using the ship for cover.

I hit the "explore" icon on my drone control, then push the hatch open a few centimeters. The insect-sized device flies through the gap. I shut the hatch and spin the locking wheel.

Arun crosses the FlexLock to my side, grasping my shoulder to stop his movement. He peers over my shoulder at the drone footage. The cam turns slowly, revealing a standard emergency airlock. It's narrow and about two meters long, with four lockers on each side, undoubtedly holding standard emergency suits. The dim lights make it hard to see, but it looks clear.

"No pirates hiding in the corners." I turn the drone again, slower, sending it toward the deck, then up to the overhead. "Nothing unusual. Can you pop the internal lock?"

Arun unspools a cable and plugs it into the receptacle inside the panel. His gentle push when he connects the cable bounces him away from the hatch, and I grab his arm to stop him. As he flicks through screens, he gives me a swift nod of thanks, then grunts. "Got it." A few more swipes and pokes, and the internal airlock opens. "Looks like it's running on emergency power."

"Not unexpected—it's been drifting for months." I guide the drone through the open hatch and send it down a passage. Specialized CCIA gear on the drone scans for explosives and booby traps—not that I'd trust it one hundred percent. "I'm sending the drone data to Vlad. Close up the internal hatch so we can go inside."

"We should wait until the drone can check the whole ship." Arun frowns at me. "Why are you in a rush?"

Gesturing at my body, I grimace. "We're all suited up. This is a cargo ship. Low risk." I reach for the controls.

Arun's hand closes around mine. "It *looks* like low risk. We don't know who's been on this thing. Remember—it was near Luna not long ago. The Leweians could have been aboard and left us any number of surprises."

I turn and flip my hand at his holo-ring. "If that's the case, the drone isn't going to find anything. These things are not infallible. It takes human eyes—" I break off as I notice movement behind Arun. Spinning, I shove him behind me, the lack of gravity making him easy to move.

"Hey!"

The FlexLock is empty, as is our ship's airlock. I frown. Nothing. With a shrug, I turn back to the hatch. "Do it."

I can feel Arun's frustration, but he does his thing, and the *Fairwell's* internal hatch closes, allowing me to open the external one. I push it open and detach my shoes from the magnetic pad. "You don't have to come."

"I'm not letting you go alone." He crowds in behind me. I give him a glare over my shoulder and catch movement again. This time, when I try to shove him out of the way, he doesn't move—there's gravity inside the airlock. "Get down!"

Obediently, Arun jerks aside and crouches, then lets out a laugh. "It's Noelle. How'd you get in the airlock, kitty?" He reaches a gloved hand toward the feline, and she moves closer to allow him to pet her.

I frown at the caat, then peer back the way we came. I'd swear the airlock was empty when we arrived, and I can't believe I didn't notice her. She must have snuck in when Elodie and Leo left and then crossed the FlexLock without us noticing. Felines are good in zero gravity, but not invisible. "You need to go back to the ship, Noelle."

The kitten stares up at me as Arun strokes her fur, her gaze regal. I get the distinct impression she's not going to comply. "Take her back to the ship, please."

Arun scoops up the kitten and rises. At the hatch, he turns to point at me. "You wait for me. No sneaking off into the derelict ship by yourself."

I consider his comment, then nod. "I'll wait for backup."

Arun pushes across the FlexLock and deposits the kitten in the *Ostelah's* airlock. "Stay here."

No.

"Did you say that?" I ask.

"I said 'stay here,' but I was talking to the caat." He flicks his holo-ring, and the *Ostelah's* hatch slides shut. Then he twists and pushes off against the closed surface and shoots across the FlexLock, grabbing the safety bar to stop. "Ow."

I push the hatch open. "Too much speed."

He grunts and rubs his wrist through the pressure suit but doesn't say anything else as he follows me into the *Fairwell's* emergency airlock. While it cycles, I look through my drone footage. Still nothing.

The internal hatch opens onto a long passageway, empty and dim in both directions. I pull a drone cloud from my pocket. Tossing the device into the air releases the ultra-tiny drones. They buzz in a cloud —hence the name—for a few seconds, getting their bearings, then shoot away, scattering in both directions.

"That's cool. I haven't seen those in action before." Arun watches the drones disappear, then frowns at me. "Why didn't you send those before we came in?"

"What's the fun in that?" I push the hatch wide and step into the passageway. "Boots on the deck is still the best way to do recon."

"Best? Maybe. Safest? No." Arun crosses his arms and glares down at me. It's almost intimidating.

"I didn't get into this line of work to be safe." I check my feed. The drone cloud doesn't have any cams, but it detects dangers like explosives, poison, low oxygen, and vibrations that might indicate humans. Our earlier, external scans should have found all of those things, but the cloud is more sensitive.

Despite my flippant comments, I take safety seriously.

Meanwhile, Arun has plugged into the ship's environmental system. "It's not actually running on emergency power." He extends his hand so I can read the holo in his palm. "This deck—all of the passenger decks—are on power-saver mode, but life-support is nominal. And the engine is running at a higher idle than necessary for that level of consumption."

"Something in the shielded cargo hold is drawing power?" I bounce on my toes to estimate the gravity. I'd guess the *Fairwell* is running at about seventy-five percent of standard. Arun's data screen confirms my guess.

Despite my training and expertise in space, I prefer planet-based assignments. I had a bad experience in an airlock early in my career, and that has given me a healthy dose of caution when it comes to stations and ships. Not a phobia, but an elevated stress level.

For some reason, I don't mind living on the *Ostelah*. She's top-of-the-line, and Arun keeps her in perfect condition. Besides, I've made sure I have access to all of the important features. Like the airlock controls. But being on the *Fairwell* is giving me a little case of the heebie-jeebies. I knew when Aretha gave me this assignment I wouldn't feel comfortable—which in many ways is a good thing. Keeps me on my toes. But *knowing* that doesn't make me *feel* any better.

Movement catches my eye again, but this time I spot the source. "Noelle! How did that caat get in here?"

Arun does a comic double-take, then scoops up the tiny kitten sitting at his feet. "You saw me put her back in the *Ostelah's* airlock. I shut the hatch."

I nod slowly, frowning at the caat. She stares back at me, her green eyes unblinking. "What are you doing?"

The caat says nothing.

I give myself a mental forehead slap. Of course the caat says nothing. The legends of Hadriana Caats using telepathy to speak with humans may be true, but Noelle has never spoken to me.

I take Noelle from Arun's hand and put her on my shoulder. She usually likes to ride there, but her little claws slide against the impenetrable fabric of my pressure suit. With a disgusted sniff, she leaps to the deck and stalks away.

"Good thing the life-support is functional." Arun starts after the caat. "But we should probably take her back to the ship. Or at least put her in the airlock."

"You tried that once, remember?" I hurry to catch up with the man and caat. "She wants to be here. She's never tried to leave the *Ostelah* before, and we know Hadriana Caats have a—" I break off.

We don't know much about them, except that they aren't normal cats. The species is native to Hadriana, a planet in the recently rediscovered Romara Federation. Caats look like—and occasionally interbreed with—Terran cats. According to the little information that leaks out of the federation, pure-bred caats are almost unheard-of.

Why do I have one? That's a story for another time.

Noelle stops in the passageway and throws a look back at me that makes me feel like she's privy to my thoughts and finds the idea that she *belongs* to me amusing. Then she stalks away.

I follow the kitten down the passageway, keeping one eye on the data streaming in from my drone cloud. Arun watches the feed from the larger drone, which has stopped at a closed hatch. "Bridge," he mutters.

The ship is old. We knew that but the idea is driven home by the flickering lights and the dingy bulkheads. The corridor kinks to the left, at an odd angle, and narrows.

"This isn't standard." Arun knocks his gloved knuckles against the wall, and it rings hollowly. "I'd guess they added additional crew accommodations here. Or possibly storage, but with that huge hold, I don't know why they'd need it."

We round another not quite ninety-degree turn and find Noelle sitting in front of a closed door. I wave my hand at the access panel, and it slides open jerkily, as if the mechanism has rusted. A faint grinding screech reinforces the supposition.

The room created by the flimsy bulkheads is empty. Cupboards run along both sides of the long, narrow space, with an empty countertop at waist height and additional cupboards above. It looks like a workroom. We open all of the cabinets but find nothing. Noelle bats a scrap of paper into the middle of the room.

I stoop and retrieve it. "Good job, Noelle."

"What did she find?" Arun crowds next to me to peer over my shoulder.

I extend the dingy fragment. "I'm not sure. Looks like the corner of one of Leo's ancient cooking books. It says something about temperature and time."

Arun takes the scrap, frowning at the smudged print. "Looks hand-written, not printed. Might be a family recipe. Or instructions for making a bomb. Or drugs. Or—"

I snort and point at a word right on the torn edge. "I'm pretty sure that says carrot. I don't know of any vegetable-based bombs or poisons."

"Who said anything about poison? Besides, this doesn't look like a kitchen. There's no sink or cookery thing."

"You mean a stove?"

"How do you even know what a stove is? You only eat protein bars."

"I've spent enough time with Leo. Did you know he's built an oven in the engine room? The thermal exhaust unit powers it. That's where he's been baking all of that bread." I take the scrap of paper and tuck it into a pocket, then dust my gloves together. "Let's keep looking. Where's Noelle?"

Arun frowns, then sticks his head through the open door. "She's headed that way."

As I follow him from the room, I give the empty space another once-over. Why did Noelle want us to look in there?

"I'm not sure I like the idea of eating bread that's been baked in a thermal exhaust. Who knows what chemicals and particles it might pick up." Arun strides down the passageway, his previous trepidation apparently wiped away by the normalcy of a kitchen. Or whatever that room was for.

"He's not baking it *in* the thermal exhaust. Kind of next to it."

"Heat transfer?" Arun looks impressed. "Clever. I wonder why ships aren't designed to use that for food prep?"

"Because most ships have an Autokich'n?" I stop in front of the bridge door. “The drones couldn’t get in here, so we’ll need to be careful.”

Arun points a finger at me. “Caution. I like it.” He waves at the access panel, but nothing happens. He taps it with his knuckles. “We might need to—”

My audio pings. “Vanti. Arun.” It’s Vlad. “We’ve got incoming.”

CHAPTER THIRTEEN

ON THE *OSTELAH'S* BRIDGE, Vlad stretches the holo wide. "See that ship?"

I squint at the tiny, blinking light. "That's a ship? I'll take your word for it."

In the pilot's seat, Arun opens his own holos. "Calculated trajectory shows it coming nowhere near us."

"I didn't say it was coming toward us."

"You said 'incoming.' Generally, that indicates a ship *coming in* toward you." Arun extends both hands toward the view screen, then moves them toward his chest.

Vlad stretches his arms wide, then pulls them across his body, sliding his hands past each other. "In-coming."

One of my alerts pings. "Where's Jones?" I leap out of the jump seat and lunge toward the hatch. "Why is he going aboard the *Fairwell*?" I swing around and glare at Vlad. "Did you bring us back so he could sneak over there?"

"What? No! I am not working with that—" Vlad breaks off and swipes another flashing icon. "Looks like someone else might be headed over too."

"Might be?" I hurl a file at his head as I exit, wishing it would hurt instead of passing right through. "Someone is definitely on their way. And Apawllo?" I stretch the cam feed from the FlexLock larger as I stride down the passageway to the airlock. A short figure in a puffy white suit steps into the FlexLock. The angle makes it impossible to see her face, but it's obviously Zwani. And two furry shapes follow her. "Great. Now we've got both cats on the ship."

"You left Noelle over there?" Arun jogs beside me, his helmet under one arm.

"Of course not. But she just went back with Zwani and Apawllo." I toss the vid to him, then snap my helmet back over my head.

"Huh." Arun glances at me, then weighs his helmet in his hands. "You really think that's necessary? The caat seemed fine without a suit."

"If I'm wearing this uncomfortable suit, I may as well make use of the full range of protection." I push off through the FlexLock and swing my feet beneath me as I sail through the *Fairwell's* open hatch, landing with a little run across the airlock. "As for the caat—who knows what kind of environments they can withstand. She might look like a cute little kitten, but she's a Hadriana Caat, which means technically she's an alien."

Arun stumbles a little when he lands. He might have more space time than me, but my background in gymnastics and martial arts gives me an edge. Not to mention the grav belt built into my pressure suit. But I won't mention that. A girl has to have her secrets.

"Any idea where they all went?" Arun pulls the stunner from his hip pocket and checks the charge.

I hide a smile of approval as I check my own. "Cargo. There's something on this ship that Sondre wants." I nod at the closed interior hatch.

"What about Zwani?" He counts down with his fingers then shoves the hatch open.

We dive through the gap, rolling across the passageway in opposite directions and both popping up to a crouch like a well-oiled machine. I check behind Arun. "Clear."

He does the same. "Clear."

The dramatic entry was unnecessary—my drone showed nothing —but it was fun.

"Shouldn't we check the bridge?" Arun asks as I head away from it.

"You set a deadman on it." At his raised brow, I go on. "You've set something that will notify us if anyone opens it. Like a hair across the edge of the hatch?"

"You saw me?"

"No, but I know you pretty well by now. And it's what I would have done. If I didn't have tech for that." I smile as I stride away.

"Then there are two deadmans. Deadmen?" He hurries to catch up.

"I left a drone perched across the passageway. It's a pretty neat piece of tech—it pulls power from the ship, so it can stay there indefinitely, transmitting data." I open the feed and show him my view of the hatch marked "Bridge." I don't bother showing him the second one watching both the door and the first drone—just in case.

He flings a file at me as we walk. His shows the same hatch from a different direction. "I'm not quite a caveman. Hair across the doorjamb is pretty basic. And it's called a vampire drone."

"Touché." I try zooming in, but my drone is too small to be spotted, even at Arun's surprisingly high resolution. "Nice work. Aretha might recruit you if you keep this up." I'm still not one hundred percent sure she didn't. He never explained his seemingly random call to Leo. Of course, I didn't ask.

Arun snorts a breath out his nose but doesn't reply.

As we walk, we've been checking the doors along the way. Most of them have opened with a simple handwave at the access panel to reveal empty crew cabins. Two were locked, so I marked them as 'check later' on the map my drones created. At this point, finding out what Jones/Sondre is up to is more important.

At the aft end of the ship, we take a ladder—this one an actual ladder, not a stairway named that—down. It ends on a small landing made of open metal grating, and another ladder continues lower. To my right, large double doors marked "Cargo" stand open.

Arun nods at the hatch. "Don't those things usually close on their own?"

I shrug. "I'm not a cargo ship expert."

"I'm not an expert, either, but I've never seen a live ship where the hatches didn't automatically shut. It's a safety thing. In case of a breach, you want to keep the oxygen inside. Humans like to breathe."

"Vlad said the ship is on low power mode. Maybe that has something to do with it?" I step closer and wave a hand through the opening. Nothing happens. "Onward?"

He gestures with his stunner. "Affirmative."

The cargo hold is vast and dark. The Fenstron was designed with a massive open hold that can be reconfigured into smaller sections using portable barriers. Ships like this can carry goods in easy-to-stack pods or loose stuff like ore or grain. I've heard of them being used to carry livestock, but shipping livestock between planets is an expensive and risky business. Usually, embryos are shipped in stasis pods to be gestated when they arrive instead.

I draw in a deep breath, but with my helmet on, I can't smell anything except sanitized air. My suit readout suggests the environment is breathable but stale, probably with a faint whiff of metal and solvent. With a tiny shrug, I step over the threshold.

Arun grabs my arm before my foot hits the deck. He tugs me through the opening and to the side of the hatch. With a quick squeeze of my arm, he jerks his head downward, then turns off the lights on his pressure suit.

I grunt in surprise. My suit is already dark—pretty much a standard for covert operations. Normally, civilians only use pressure suits in emergencies, and the lights ensure rescuers can find them floating around space. But Arun doused his illumination with a single gesture. Why would he need such a feature?

My suspicion that Aretha recruited him grows. Operatives require years of training. Arun was on Sally Ride for a few weeks—hardly time to scratch the surface. The idea that Aretha would send him on a mission without proper training reignites the ball of anger in my gut.

And then immediately douses it. Aretha would never send an untrained operative into danger. Especially without notifying me, since Arun's actions will impact my mission.

Below, lights move. Several small lights—equipment indicators—glow faintly, almost invisible beyond the glare of a headlamp. A person in a pressure suit. The mics on my own suit pick up movement—footsteps and a rough scraping. Another person comes into view. They're too far away to see faces, and even if they were closer, their headlamps would make it difficult.

But we know who's down there—Jones and Zwani. I toggle my audio to speak with Arun. "Why are we hiding?"

"Don't you want to see what they're up to before we let them know we're here?"

"Of course, but I was surprised you thought of that too." That came out wrong.

Arun's eyes narrow and his jaw tightens. "I'm not an idiot."

"No, of course not. I just— You're a trusting soul, so I—never mind." I look away to mask my confusion. "You're one hundred percent right, and definitely not an idiot. I expected you to trust the team, even though you know they aren't trustworthy. That's a civilian mistake, and you're suddenly not behaving like a civilian." My eyes dart back to his face. "Is there something you aren't telling me?"

CHAPTER FOURTEEN

ARUN TURNS his back on me and flicks his holo-ring. Light flares around him, then dies as he dials the illumination down to minimum. I grip the railing and peer down at the two people in the cargo hold. They lean toward each other like they're arguing, with heads jerking and arms gesturing in choppy motions, too preoccupied with each other to notice us.

Light from one of their headlamps catches movement, but the two figures don't notice. I squint into the dim corner of the hold, where I'm pretty sure Apawllo just slunk past. I wish, not for the first time, that he had more Hadriana caat in his genetic makeup. Those aliens are supposed to be able to speak telepathically with humans.

If they choose to do it. I met one once, and she deigned to speak to me. Even entrusted Noelle to my care. But the kitten has never said a word to me.

Didn't have anything to say.

I jerk away from the railing in surprise. The voice was warm and feminine. And inside my head. Like someone speaking through my audio implant, but more *real* feeling. Which makes no sense because audio implant voices sound like the person is speaking to you in a quiet room. But this voice felt—I can't describe how it's different, but once you've heard it, you know.

Hadriana caat.

"Noelle?" I whisper.

You don't have to yell.

"I didn't mean to," I subvocalize, like I would when using my audio implant. "Why are you talking to me now? I thought you were too young to speak."

A ghost of a laugh slides through my mind, soft and comforting, like a cashmere sweater but with a smug edge. *I am much older than I appear.*

I lean over the railing again, trying to spot the kitten. I can tell, somehow, that she's in this cargo hold with us, but I can't pinpoint her location. "Where are you?"

Down here. Two pinpoints of emerald-green glow near the suited figures below, close enough that they should have noticed, then vanish. Is she sitting there with her eyes closed?

No. Well, not completely closed. But they are too busy to notice me.

"What are they doing?" Arun asks through the audio implant.

I jerk upright. I'd forgotten he was with me for a moment. The difference between his voice and the caat's is startling. Arun, whose deep voice usually sends a little shiver of warmth through me, sounds watered down compared to Noelle.

I clear my throat and toggle the audio. "Looks like they've finished arguing. One of them—it's Zwani loading something onto a grav cart. I can't see Jones."

He's moved into the smaller cargo hold.

"I haven't been able to crack their comms, yet." Arun waves his gloved hand at me, the faint glow of his holo-ring visible through the fabric. "They must be using an encrypted short-distance point-to-point system. Like ours."

"He's in there." I point across the hold at a hatch outlined in faint glow-tape. "I'm not sure why." I try to project the words at Noelle as well as Arun.

He's looking through some human artifacts. The tone of Noelle's voice makes it clear they—like most "human artifacts"—are completely unimportant to her.

"Thanks."

Arun raises a brow at me.

I shrug and wave a hand, unsure why I feel reluctant to mention Noelle.

Because you're in the middle of an operation and the explanation will take too long.

I roll my eyes. "That's part of it."

"Part of what?" Arun asks.

Crap. I'm an expert at subvocalizing but maintaining two distinct conversations requires a bit more concentration—something I'm clearly lacking at the moment. "Let's go down."

I activate my grav belt and rise above the metal grating deck. No point in making noise climbing down the ladder. I turn to Arun to suggest he wait until I get to the bottom before following—so he doesn't alert the others to my presence—but he's already hovering a few centimeters above the deck.

"You didn't think I'd have a built-in grav belt?" His bland expression belies the smug question.

I toggle the audio again. "You buy the best equipment, so I should have expected it."

He nods once, and the corner of his mouth twitches up in a smirk. Then he taps his controls and slides out the open hatch, heading for the external ladder.

For a second, I consider simply dropping over the side and meeting him at the bottom—don't try to out-smooth a seasoned agent! But even with my suit lights off, I don't like the possibility of Zwani noticing me. I follow him to the ladder, then drop quickly to join him three stories below.

Where we realize our mistake. This hatch is closed. If we open it, Zwani will know we're here. Arun points up the ladder and raises his brows. I nod in agreement and shoot back to the top. Arun surges after me, his head even with my knees and gaining. He must have a really high-end grav belt. He jostles me as we rise, and I barely clear the opening in the upper deck as I pop out at the landing. These ladders were built for one person at a time, but there's no way I'd let Arun beat me to the top. He clearly felt the same.

He bumps me as we scoot through the cargo hatch again. I grab his arm and hit my direction controls before he can zip over the railing. He masses more than me, and the force of stopping him yanks my shoulder. When he swings around to look at me, I raise one finger and mouth, "Slowly."

Together, we rise over the railing, then slide down the wall at a snail's pace, hoping the darkness covers our movement.

I'll distract her.

"How?"

I get a quick impression of staticky fur and a hiss. Then the figure below us jumps in surprise, feet thudding loudly as they stumble back. A furry black creature streaks through the light of the headlamp, headed deeper into the cargo hold. Apawllo. The human puts her hands on her hips, head swinging as she tries to spotlight the black cat.

Arun touches down silently. My audio clicks. "That was fortuitous."

I try to keep the laughter out of my voice as I reply. "Definitely." I jerk my head to the right and slide away.

The faint scrape of Arun's boots as he lifts off to follow me sounds loud in my speakers, but the figure ahead of us doesn't seem to notice.

We slip through the darkness, staying close to the dark walls. I slow for a minute and activate the glow feature on my left glove. It provides enough light to see something close by, but when blocked by my body, it is virtually invisible to anyone more than a few meters away. I lift my hand to look at a seam—this cargo hold is lined with metal. "Why would they do this?" I trail a faintly glimmering finger across the surface.

Arun frowns. "Dunno. Metal is heavy and expensive. It's probably why we couldn't scan the cargo hold—there are certain amalgams that prevent readings. But lining your cargo hold with the stuff just screams, 'Hey, I'm carrying contraband! Come look.' No smuggler is going to do it."

"That's what I was thinking. It would prevent radiation leaks, though, right?"

"For the most part. If they were transporting radioactive materials, an impregnium-reinforced alutanium lining would make sense. But we got zero radiation."

"Maybe it originally carried—"

He shakes his head decisively. "No. There'd still be residual. This ship isn't *that* old. It could have been built for that purpose, but it was never *used* for it."

"I wonder—" Our quarry's headlamp swings wildly. I grab Arun's arm and yank him down, but the beam doesn't turn our direction. Apawllo streaks across the hold again, heading for the ladder. "Don't tease the cat, Noelle."

Arun throws a confused frown at me. I shrug and lift a finger in front of my face then jerk my head to the right. He nods.

We ghost around the edge of the vast room, but from this distance, we can't see what Zwani is loading on the grav cart. The boxes are small cubes, the size of loaves of bread. She lifts them one at a time, moving slowly.

"Are they heavy? Platinum? Gold?" Arun suggests. "Why isn't she using a grav lifter?"

"And why are they all over the hold?" I wave a hand at the floor. A random scattering of them litters the deck. I drift toward one, but Arun grabs my sleeve and pulls me back.

"Let's see what Jones is up to." He tips his head toward the faintly glowing door way ahead of us.

I nod and adjust my trajectory. We pause beside the door, backs to the wall. "Let me check—"

No need. Come in.

I glance at Arun, but he's watching me, waiting for my decision. I activate the cam on my right index finger, poke it around the edge of the open hatch, and open my holo-feed. My body blocks the dim image from Zwani.

Nothing moves inside the compartment.

"Where's Jones?"

The tiny caat's green eyes appear, like twin emeralds with an internal glow. She stalks toward me, then disappears behind a dark object on the decking. A second later, she jumps into sight, landing atop Jones's prone body.

CHAPTER FIFTEEN

"Is he dead?"

Arun jerks beside me. "Dead? Who? Jones?"

"Keep an eye on Zwani." After a quick look around the open cargo hold, I zip around the door frame and across the small compartment to the fallen man. Dialing up the glow on my glove, I squint and tap the external controls of Jones's pressure suit. Connecting my holo-ring gives me a vital signs readout. "He's alive. Unconscious but breathing."

"His suit should have reported a medical emergency to the *Ostelah*. Everyone was supposed to pair their equipment." Although he's across the room and facing away from me, the audio implant makes it sound like he's right beside me.

"I'm not surprised. He's not supposed to be in here, remember? My question is was this a freak medical thing or did someone do this to him?" I raise my brows at the caat.

She jumps off Jones's chest and sits with her back to me, lifting a paw to groom it. Giving me the silent treatment? Or maybe she doesn't know what happened and doesn't like to admit that. My one previous dealing with a Hadriana Caat gave me the impression they like to appear omniscient.

We don't pretend to be omniscient. But if I have nothing to add to a conversation, there's no point in saying that. My silence should be enough.

"Noted." I think the word at her, rather than saying it.

Arun glances over his shoulder from his vantage point at the doorway. "Who could have done it? Vlad is on the ship, and we were watching Zwani. I think he passed out or had a heart attack. Have you seen the way that guy drinks? Should I have Elodie turn on the med pod?"

I check over Jones's suit again, but he doesn't have a grav belt built in. "Probably. I guess this blows our operation. We need a way to transport him back to the ship. Go commandeer Zwani's grav lifter."

"On it."

I rise and turn on my headlamp to examine the hold. Jones came in here, and now he's unconscious on the deck. It could be natural causes—Arun was not wrong about his alcohol consumption. And despite his weightlifting, the guy was not what I'd term "healthy." But my natural tendency is to suspect foul play.

The *Fairwell* passed near enough to Lewei that it could have been detected by their sensors on Luna. We knew the Leweians might have already explored the ship. But those odd boxes Zwani was collecting made me think they hadn't noticed it. They wouldn't have left anything of value.

Unless it was a trap. It's possible they left it drifting in hopes of enticing someone from the Commonwealth to come investigate. Which would mean they watched us arrive and were waiting for us to wander in here and… what?

Did they leave agents on board to take out anyone who stumbled into the cargo hold? What a waste of resources. I can't imagine Aretha making such a decision. The idea is ludicrous.

Of course, the Leweians set a much lower value on human life, so it's remotely possible they dumped an agent or two here to wait indefinitely. The special shielding of the cargo hold would have hidden them from our scans. But why? It could have been weeks—or even years—before the Commonwealth sent a team.

Which brings up another question I hadn't considered: why did

Aretha send us *now*? The ship has been drifting around Shenzhou system for months according to the data we've recovered. Surely our government noticed it before it got this close to the planet.

I shine my light on the bulkheads, scan across the deck, peer up into the overhead. If I'd been left aboard a derelict ship, assigned to taking out any illicit visitors, I'd have set up camp in a place like this. It's small enough to be a cozy apartment. But there'd be signs of occupation. I check again. Nothing. Blank walls, empty decking—except for Jones. No hammock hidden in the rafters. No scraps of protein bar wrappers, no sanitation cubicle in the corner.

Of course, our mystery agents could be camping out in another section of the hold. But why make a move against Jones and not the rest of us?

Plus, physically knocking out one member of the team makes no sense. It would be so much easier to deliver a toxin via the ventilation system. I glance down at Jones. Except we're all wearing pressure suits.

"Zwani's not here." Arun appears in the open hatch, a grav cart behind him. "She must have heard us and cleared out."

"Maybe she finished whatever she was doing and left?" I step aside as he brings the cart closer. "She left the cart?"

"Yeah." He flicks the controls, and the grav cart settles to the deck beside Jones. "But the boxes are gone. At least the ones she had stacked on it. Did you call the ship?"

"Crap, no." I toggle my comm system and call Elodie. "We're going to need the med pod fired up. Jones is incapacitated. No visible signs of the cause."

"On it." Elodie can be surprisingly efficient when necessary. "Is Apawllo with you?"

I cast a quick look around the hold. "He's here somewhere. Vanti out."

Using the controls on Jones's suit, I set it to "transport" which aligns the nanotubes in the material. The flexible fabric stiffens, holding his body still and allowing us to lift him without disturbing any broken bones. I crouch at Jones's head while Arun moves to his feet. The guy is short but heavy. I strain with my arms and legs to lift him the few centimeters necessary to shift him to the grav cart. His head starts to sag. "Wait!" We put him back on the deck, and I tighten the buckles connecting his fishbowl helmet to his collar, then we try again.

The grav cart isn't long enough, so his legs stick off the end, but thanks to the stiffened suit, it will work. Arun presses the controls, and the cart rises to waist height. I step aside so he can maneuver it out the hatch. He gives it a gentle push, and it sails past me. Then Jones's extended foot bumps into the doorjamb, and the cart slides sideways. Arun lunges forward and straightens it.

"You coming?" Arun asks over his shoulder.

"No. I'm going to look around some more in here. See if I can figure out what Zwani did with those boxes."

He frowns, his brow furrowed. "Who's going to watch your back?"

I tip my head at the kitten still sitting on the deck. "Noelle's got it."

He looks from me to the caat and back again, eyes half-hooded. "The kitty cat is your lookout?"

"She's a Hadriana caat. They have skills."

Noelle's tail flicks back and forth, but she continues to ignore us.

"Besides, what's going to happen to me? Heart attacks aren't contagious."

Arun glances down at Jones's face, his headlamp bouncing off the curved plasglass surface of the prone man's helmet. "We don't know what caused this."

"True. But I think we can safely eliminate 'random enemy agent picking us off one-by-one' from the list of possible causes. What would be the point?" I pat Arun's shoulder. "Noelle will make sure no bogeymen sneak up on me. She doesn't like strangers."

"Smart kitten." He frowns darkly at me but doesn't argue.

I follow him into the main hold. Noelle pads along beside me. I gesture at the caat. "See, she's got my back."

He shakes his head in disbelief, then flicks his grav belt controls. "Not that I don't trust your feline friend, but drone surveillance might be useful."

As he and the grav cart bearing Jones's inert body rise slowly toward the overlook high above, I stare, my jaw slack. Drones. My drone cloud has been mapping the ship from top to bottom. Maybe one of them was in the hold when Jones collapsed.

I slink back into the smaller room to lean against a wall. Harder for someone to sneak up on me this way. Noelle prowls past me to survey the dark corners of the compartment. Or maybe to take a nap. I think the question at her, but she ignores it. Or maybe I don't think loud enough.

You're plenty loud enough.

With a grunt, I slide down the wall and sit on the metal decking. My pressure suit is top of the line, so I'm imagining the cold seeping into my rear end, but that doesn't make it feel less real. I flick my holo-ring and pull in the feed from my drone cloud.

Most of them are scattered throughout the ship. They're designed to work together to create a coherent map of any location. I got this upgraded version after our recent visit to Lewei, when my individual drones did a less than perfect job. According to the three-dimensional map growing in my data space, two of the drones were in the main cargo hold when we came down, but none of them were inside this compartment when Jones collapsed.

The mapping is only about thirty percent complete, so it's a wonder even two of them were here. I pull up the individual data feeds. These drones don't have cameras, and their other sensors report nothing of value in this case.

With a shrug, I push up from the floor. I don't know what happened to Jones and have no way to verify, so time to investigate something else. The larger room is still dark, so I connect to the ship's interface and turn on the lights. High in the overhead, lights flicker and brighten. A few appear to be non-functional, which is hardly surprising. Even lights require maintenance from time to time, and this ship was old and well-used before it was abandoned. As they slowly come to full brightness, most of the room becomes visible.

Although the center of the space has been cleared, a few of Zwani's boxes lay scattered around the compartment. I crouch over the nearest one and examine it with my multiple scanners. None of them identify it as anything dangerous, and this particular one appears to be empty. A faint bas relief scene depicting some farm animals covers the top. I tap it with my gloved finger, and it sounds hollow. Pushing against one side makes it slide across the deck until it catches on a rough joint in the floor panels and stops.

I look around the room. Should I open it? Zwani and Jones seemed to know what was inside—or at least suspected, since they were collecting the things. I slide the blade of my pocket knife into a seam-line and pry. The top pops off and clatters to the decking. The interior is empty. Just a small metal box with nothing inside.

Zwani didn't open the boxes she collected—she just put them on the cart. There could be any number of reasons for that. Maybe she knows what is inside.

Pushing off with my feet, I activate my grav belt and hop smoothly to the next box a few meters away. This one also scans "clean," but it doesn't move when I push it. I try lifting, but it's hard to get my gloved fingers between the box and floor, and when I try to lift from the sides, my fingers just slide off. I debate removing my gloves. Clearly the air in here is breathable—Noelle and Apawllo have exhibited no problems. Of course, Noelle is an alien. My friend Triana would tell me Apawllo is demon spawn, but I like the scruffy old guy. We have a lot in common. Not everyone can be cute and cuddly.

I use the knife again to open this box. The lid clatters away, even though I used less force. Some kind of pressurization? I peer into the small cube, but this one is also empty. When I tap the side, the box slides easily across the floor.

I thought it was heavy, but maybe suction held it to the floor. Or a magnet in the lid? I pick up the top, but it lifts easily. Lightweight, with a metal coating, or maybe thin metal sheeting. A tap of my knife against the lid makes it ring in a clear, bell-like tone.

"What do you think, kitten?"

After a long pause, she sighs. *I'm not a kitten.*

"You aren't?"

She doesn't reply.

I stand, my legs protesting after crouching so long. I grimace. I'm not old enough for that. Resolving to increase my squats, both number and weight, I walk to the next box. A quick nudge with my toe sends it skittering across the deck.

By the time Arun returns, I've covered half of the compartment, checked the boxes—all empty—and found three additional small compartments. One contained dusty, empty shelves. The other two held a few scraps of cardboard and one more of those confounded boxes.

I dust my hands together as Arun touches down. "Nothing of value here. Whatever was in those boxes, Zwani must have gotten all the full ones. Did she take them back to the *Ostelah*?"

He flicks a file at me as he shakes his head. "Nope. She returned a few minutes before I did, but she didn't take anything."

I stretch the vid he sent—a view of the *Ostelah's* airlock. Zwani strolls through, her hands behind her back. She stops to pop her helmet off, then tucks it under one arm and heads into the ship. I fast forward a few minutes to see Arun pushing Jones through the airlock.

"Hmm. She must have stashed the boxes between here and the exit." I tap my grav belt and surge into the air, aiming toward the small overlook near the upper hatch. "Time to expand the search."

CHAPTER SIXTEEN

ELODIE SETS a hot dish on the table. "You're just in time for dinner!" She crosses the lounge to the Autokich'n and pulls another dish from inside. "Did you wash your hands?"

"Yes, mother." I lift both hands and show her my palms. "I washed my whole body. That ship is dusty."

"If it's been circling Shenzhou for months, it would be." She pauses halfway to the table and frowns. "Or would it? Where would the dust come from? If life support is operating properly, the air handlers should remove any dirt from the environment during circulation, right? Normally crew would be responsible for most of the dust—fabric rubbing, skin shedding, hair, snot—"

"Ew." I take a stack of plates from the counter and set the table. "That's a pretty gross thing to talk about at dinner. Who is coming?"

"We aren't at dinner yet." She sets the casserole on a trivet, then grabs a handful of utensils. "Everyone but Jones should be here. He's still in the med pod."

"What was wrong with him?"

"Blow to the head. Well, neck actually." She lays a fork, knife, spoon, and chopsticks at each place, then returns to the cupboard for napkins.

"Someone hit him?" I set the last plate in place and cross my arms.

She pauses, a napkin in her hands. "Maybe he fell and hit it on something. Any low overhead beams?" With a few swift folds, she creates an origami bird and sets it on a plate.

While she finishes the table, folding more napkins into fanciful creatures, I visualize the room. Falling doesn't make sense. And I don't remember anything that would be easy to stumble into—especially for someone as short as Jones.

I imagine Noelle's fluffy gray face and green eyes, trying to *send* the thought to her. "Where are you?"

On the stuff hauler.

"The stuff hauler? You mean the *Fairwell*."

I can almost see the flick of her little tail, acknowledging my statement with a negligent flip. "Have you found anything… unusual?"

If I thought it was useful to you, I would have mentioned it.

"What does that mean? Did you find something you didn't think was useful? What was it?" Not that I don't trust the caat, but I like to look at all of the facts.

What did that little fluff ball do to me? Of course I don't trust her. She's an alien, and I don't trust anyone, especially aliens. Not that I've met many, but I'm sure they aren't more trustworthy than people. Most of whom are not at all worthy of trust.

As if in response to my thought, one of the few humans I do trust —mostly—wanders into the room. "What's that delicious smell?" Arun asks.

Elodie laughs. "Autokich'n menu forty-two."

He crosses the room and leans over the serving bowl to draw in a deep breath. "Forty-two never smells that good when I order it."

She nudges him out of the way with her hip and sticks a serving spoon into the cheesy dish. "I might have tweaked it a bit."

"I hope you used the auto-save."

"Like I'm going to share my culinary secrets with the rest of the world. It's my secret, never to be shared! Well, Kara knows it. And a few other family members. And I think I showed Leo. And maybe Hy-Mi—"

Arun's hand drops on her shoulder, cutting her off. "I'd rather have you here to serve it than learn the secret myself."

She beams, then whirls away to grab another dish.

Arun comes around the table to me. "You look pensive."

I raise a brow. "Really?"

"No. You look like you always do, with a perfect poker face. But I feel like you should be pensive after our little adventure."

I let the corner of my mouth twitch. He gets me surprisingly well. We've only traveled together a few months, and he seems to catch my moods faster than Griz ever did. And I've never been as close to anyone else.

Wow.

That's a lot to process. I shove it to the little room at the back of my mind labeled "later," stack a few mundane thoughts in front of it, and close the door. Then hang a "do not disturb" sign on the old-fashioned knob. And try to remember what we were talking about.

Oh, yeah, our recent adventure. "I'm wondering who took Jones out."

Arun steals a raw carrot stick from a dish on the table, earning a glare from Elodie, then turns back to me. "Too much beer. Fell and hit his head."

I frown. "Really? Did the med pod say that?"

He tips his free hand back and forth. "No, but it seems likely."

"Maybe it wasn't the beer. He seems to have a pretty high tolerance. Maybe he's allergic to cats."

The image of Noelle licking her nether regions appears in my mind—clearly the caat equivalent of a rude gesture. I choke back a laugh.

"What's so funny?"

I gaze at Arun, my face as blank as I can make it. "Nothing."

"Your lip twitched at the corner." He points, his index finger coming within centimeters of my mouth. "For you, that's like rolling on the floor."

"You'd better remove that finger if you want to keep it." Elodie appears beside Arun, grinning. "I've seen her bite people for less."

I turn my death glare on Elodie. “No, you haven’t. I don’t bite.” Under my breath, I add, “Unless they deserve it.”

“I heard that.” She claps her hands twice. “Come to the table. It’s dinner time.”

As we take our seats, Leo and Zwani appear. Leo carries a basket with a fabric-wrapped lump that steams gently. The intoxicating aroma of freshly baked bread wafts through the room, and my stomach growls. Loudly.

With a smirk, Leo puts the basket in front of me and peels back a corner of the checkered cloth, exposing the crusty loaf. “Carbs, Vanti?”

My stomach growls again. Lifting my chin, I reach for a knife. “Sure, why not?”

The rest of the room gasps in exaggerated disbelief.

“What? I eat carbs. Occasionally. When they’re really good.”

As I lean forward with my blade, Leo whisks the basket away from me. “Not with a knife! This loaf was made to be torn.”

“I thought you were making brioche?” Vlad asks as he strolls into the room. “That smells like sourdough.”

“I’m impressed.” Zwani sits next to Leo. “Most people don’t know the difference between *Viennoiseries* and naturally leavened breads.”

“Please. Everyone knows sourdough smells different from brioche. And no one knows what a *Veno-sary* is. Bread snob.” Vlad grabs the end of the oblong loaf and rips off a chunk.

Zwani smiles smugly as she passes the butter.

We eat for a while, the silence interrupted only by compliments to the chef and bakers. The hot sourdough complements Elodie’s casseroles perfectly, and the leafy green salad provides a crunchy, savory contrast to the heavy meal. I eat a little of everything, silently vowing to do an extra cycle in the FlexTrainer.

Arun sets his cutlery on his empty plate and pushes back from the table with a happy sigh. He sips his water, then sets the glass down with a thud that draws everyone’s attention. “I guess you’ve all heard about Jones.”

I watch Vlad and Zwani. Conveniently, they’re sitting at the same corner of the table. I hadn't gotten the impression they knew each other at all before this mission, but their casual banter at the beginning of the meal didn't feel awkward the way it might with new shipmates. Maybe they've worked together in the past. I'd have expected that information to be in the team dossiers Aretha sent, but perhaps she deemed it extraneous information. CCIA agents are expected to work with whatever team they're assigned to without complaint.

They both nod in agreement but say nothing.

Arun wipes his mouth, then sets his napkin beside his plate. "The med pod says blunt trauma to the skull. It didn't specify how. His reason for being on the ship was also unclear." Arun gives each of us a piercing stare. "No one should be boarding that ship without clearance from Vanti. And you definitely shouldn't be going alone."

Neither Vlad nor Zwani so much as twitch in response to Arun's implication Jones had gone aboard without backup. In fact, if I didn't know better, I'd swear Zwani knew nothing about Jones's foray onto the ship. The woman has a better poker face than I do. I file that nugget away.

Whatever Zwani and Jones are after, they don't want the rest of us to know. And she doesn't appear bothered by Jones's incapacity. She's a cold-blooded partner. I have to admire that kind of dedication to the mission.

"I've connected to the black box," Vlad says as he spears a piece of fruit with one of his chopsticks. He waves the chunk at us, splattering the table with fruit juice, then pops it into his mouth. He chews with his mouth open, then splatters the table again when he starts talking before he swallows. "The flight data is encrypted, of course, so it's gonna take a while to decipher. But I'm not sure this ship is actually the *Fairwell*." He stabs another wedge of melon and shoves it into his maw.

"Not the *Fairwell*?" I should have expected this simple mission to be complicated. Aretha wouldn't have sent a veteran agent like me if it was going to be easy—even for my first official team lead. "Someone tampered with the transponder?"

"Starting to look that way."

“How do you know?” Arun leans forward. “If you haven’t cracked the black box yet?”

“The flight recorder’s serial number is in plain text. And it’s not assigned to a ship named *Fairwell.* In fact, it’s not assigned to a ship at all.” Vlad chugs down his beer.

Arun’s gaze sharpens. “What is it assigned to? A donkey cart?”

Vlad laughs. “Good one, cap’n. Nope, it’s never been assigned. According to my database, that device was destroyed in the factory.” He shakes his single chopstick at Arun. “Defective.”

I exchange a thoughtful look with Arun. He knows way more about ships than I do, but even I know a “destroyed” black box means someone is hiding this ship’s origin and mission. I mentally page through the data Aretha sent. The report said the ship was a Commonwealth cargo hauler—that’s the reason we were sent here. Our job was to figure out why this ship was in Leweian space and to bring back any valuable data or cargo.

When did the name *Fairwell* first come up? Was it in Aretha’s briefing packet? “You’re saying someone made this ship look like the *Fairwell,* but it isn’t.”

He waves another skewered fruit at me. “’Zactly.”

CHAPTER SEVENTEEN

"Do we care?" Arun drops onto the SimuWeight bench and laces his fingers behind his neck. The rest of the team is still in the lounge, drinking beer and watching a movie. I excused myself to work out, but Arun joined me before I could get the FlexTrainer started.

I lean a shoulder against the bulkhead. "Do we care about what?"

"The name of the ship?"

"Objectively, no. They could call it *Serenity*. Or the *Flowered Bonnet* for all I care. But the fact is the ship's computer system said it was the *Fairwell,* but the black box says it isn't." I'd finally remembered where we got the name. "That means they're hiding something."

"Who's they?" With a flick of his holo-ring, he loads the machine, then rolls to his back to lift. "And what are they hiding?"

"If I knew that, the mission would be finished." I set my swim criteria and close the FlexTrainer around me. "If I didn't have all of these suspicious civilians along, I'd probably already have the answers."

With a grunt, Arun shoves the weight bar back onto its rack and sits up. "Suspicious civilians? You mean me and Elodie?"

I snort a little laugh. "You and Elodie are *annoying civilians,* not suspicious. Jones is suspicious." I hit go, and the system gravity lifts my body to horizontal. When the simulated current pushes against me, I start a front crawl.

"That's only one civilian in the suspicious column. Plural indicates more than one." Arun rises and leans against the bulkhead I'd used earlier. He points at me. "You don't suspect Leo, do you?"

I shake my head as well as I can without disrupting my stroke. "Nope. I was counting Zwani. Why did she go aboard the *Fairwell*? She deflected well when you brought it up."

"I thought so too." He pushes away from the wall and resets the SimuWeight for another exercise. "You wanna head back over there when we're done here?"

"I thought you'd never ask." Of course, I planned on going solo, but since he suggested it...

ARUN CHECKS the *Ostelah's* locator. Most of the crew are still watching a vid, and Jones has retired to his cabin after finishing his stint in the med pod. The system reports he's back to nominal health, although his cholesterol and blood pressure are still high. Probably too much beer and not enough aerobic exercise. The med pod is only a Band-Aid for poor health decisions.

I poke a finger at the medical stats. "You're not supposed to be able to see health data. It's protected."

Arun grimaces. "That's a Commonwealth law. We're in Leweian space."

I give him an admiring nod. "Look at you, following the letter of the law."

His shoulders twitch. "I'm not super comfortable with it, but I figured the more we know about our resident criminal element, the better."

"How'd you get the med pod to release that info? It doesn't care where we are." I pause, as the implications sink in. "They aren't geo-locked are they? Only constrained by local privacy laws?"

"No. It took me a while to hack in. That's why I was almost late for dinner."

I frown. He wasn't late for dinner. In fact, he arrived before Vlad, Zwani, and Leo. I know he's technically a genius, and I've seen him hack systems before, but if he was able to overcome a Commonwealth med pod's privacy settings in the brief time between our return from the *Fairwell* and dinner, that's a whole other level of smart.

We slink into the airlock and shimmy into our pressure suits. Once I get mine zipped up, I turn to face Arun. "Buddy check?"

He sets his helmet on the retractable bench by the lockers and waves a hand at my suit's connection sensor. He double checks my seals, then swipes a hand through the "verified" icon. "You're set. My turn." He pulls the helmet over his head and locks it into place.

I perform the check and verify the results. "I noticed you didn't suggest we skip the helmets this time."

"It doesn't take a genius to figure out Jones could have breathed in something dangerous on the *Fairwell*."

I almost choke at his use of the word "genius," but manage to hide it. Sometimes I think he can read my thoughts.

No, that's just me.

"Where are you, Noelle?"

Arun's brow furrows, then I can almost see the pieces click into place. "Is she talking to you?"

See what I mean? Who else would have put that together? Hadriana Caats are native to Hadriana, a planet in the newly rediscovered Romara Republic. Most citizens of the Republic don't believe they're real. And most Commonwealth citizens don't know the planet even exists.

Of course, Arun was there when I got Noelle. But I didn't expect him to remember her mythic origin. And immediately leap to this conclusion.

Genius.

I give a jerky nod.

"Cool. Where is she?"

I *listen* and get an impression of the corridor leading to the large cargo hold. "On the *Fairwell*. Still investigating."

You're getting good at this. I'm not surprised. You're more caat-like than most humans. A stealthy, smart predator.

"Thank you?" When Arun raises a brow, I shake my head.

We return to the *Fairwell's* cargo hold to find Noelle sitting in the center of the room. The overhead illumination is out again, but this time there are emergency lights casting a red glow over the whole space, creating weird shadows between the narrow overhead beams. Small boxes still lay in random locations around the room.

I stumble to a stop in the opening. I assumed they were random. Thrusting my arm across the entrance hatch, I stop Arun from entering. "What do you see, genius?"

A glimmer of a grin crosses his face, then it goes serious again. "An empty cargo hold?" He gives a tiny head shake. His hand lifts slowly, and his outstretched index finger traces a curve. "No, an almost empty cargo hold. And the remains of a pattern."

Frowning, I lean back and try to follow the line of his arm. With a frustrated grunt, I hit my grav belt and lift above the deck, staring down at a graceful Fibonacci curve. "How did we not notice this before?"

Arun rises to meet me. "Zwani was moving those things around. And we assumed the contents of the boxes were important. But this makes me think the positioning is also significant. But why?"

I drop to the deck beside the box I opened earlier. I don't remember its exact placement, but I don't have to. In the scarlet glow, lines are visible on the deck. Each of the boxes is set at an intersection of two fine lines. I push the empty one back into place, then glance up at Arun and lift my hands in question.

He shrugs in response as he descends. "Art? Ceremonial pattern? Religious? I don't know. Maybe if it was complete…"

"We need to figure out who was on this ship and why. And how they ended up marooned in Leweian space. I wish Vlad could crack that black box faster."

"Why is it encrypted?" Arun puts a hand on his neck, his fingers tapping against the back of his helmet. "Flight data shouldn't be secret. Black boxes are supposed to help investigators figure out exactly what we're trying to determine. They shouldn't be locked."

"If this ship was doing something clandestine, the owners might encrypt the flight data to hide their travel history. Even if they were marooned, they wouldn't want anyone to know they had been sailing into interdicted systems." I pace across the room and nudge a toe against another of the small boxes. It doesn't move. "Did you notice these boxes are stuck to the deck? At first I thought it was unintentional—maybe corrosion or something sticky got spilled—but the pattern makes me think they did it on purpose."

He grunts in agreement as he crouches beside one. "Might be glue. Or suction. Are the bottoms of the boxes curved or flat?" He tries to lift it, but his gloved fingers slide off. "Can't see the underside."

I lift the one nearest me, and it comes away from the deck easily. Turning it in my hands, I find no identifying marks except a set of parallel grooves near the corner. "Bottom is flat. But what's this?"

Arun takes the box and runs a gloved finger over the marks. They're all the same length, but different widths. He shrugs. "Do they all have it?" He tries again to lift the box by his foot, but it won't budge.

"Open it." I nod at his box, then bounce across the deck to the next closest one. It's also stuck. I flip the lid open to reveal nothing, but the box comes away from the floor easily. "This one has those marks too."

Still crouching beside his box, Arun nudges it with a finger. It stubbornly stays in place.

"Open it," I say again. "There's nothing inside."

"Remember the story of Pandora's box? Maybe you're letting whatever is inside out."

"I haven't seen any hordes of evil streaming away."

"Are you sure hordes of evil are visible to the human eye?" He taps the box again. "What does evil look like anyway?"

"Jones?"

He barks out a laugh. "Good one." With one more thoughtful tap to the top of the box, he rises, dusting his hands together. "I don't think we should mess with these things until we understand more about them."

"What do you think, Noelle?" I look around but can't spot the caat. "Where'd she go?"

Here. I get the image of another part of the ship—a smaller compartment with no distinguishing features. Somehow, the caat manages to transmit her relative location along with the image.

"Come on." I flick my grav belt and launch toward the platform overlooking the cargo hold. By the time I drop over the railing, Arun has caught up. His grav belt shouldn't be as fast as mine. I poke a finger at him. "Where'd you get that?"

"It came with the brain."

"What?" With a frown, I turn and head through the still-open hatch.

"You pointed at my stomach. I was saying the body came with the brain. It sounded funnier in my head."

"I meant the grav belt."

"I know. It's a new model. A friend of mine is experimenting with synchotronic propulsion, which provides faster, smoother movement. He's got a research contract with the CEC."

"CEC test equipment should be classified."

"I'm a certified beta tester." He grins as he flicks his holo ring, then puts on a burst of speed.

"But you don't know where you're going." I smirk as he turns to face me.

"Good point." He waits until I catch up, then spins again to fall in beside me. "Where *are* we going?"

"It looks like another storage area." I frown, recalling the image Noelle sent. She sends me another impression. "No, maybe a closet?" We fly down a passageway, then turn and ascend a ladder.

"You don't sound too sure. But you know where it is."

I stop beside a closed hatch and pat it. "Right here."

"How'd you know where to go? Did she send you coordinates? Or a map?"

I frown. "I'm not sure I can answer that. She made it clear how to get here, but I can't describe the mechanism." Tapping the access panel beside the hatch does nothing. "What she didn't make clear is how to get in."

"Let me try." Arun moves closer, his arm and leg pressed against mine. Even with the pressure suits, the contact feels intimate. "Budge over, will you?"

Maybe not so intimate as I was thinking. I suppress a frown and shift away. "Noelle, how'd you get in here?"

I have my ways.

"Great help, thanks."

Arun pulls a wire from a pocket and plugs it into a tiny port I didn't notice. He flicks through settings on his holo-ring, and the panel lights. Another swipe or two, and the hatch retracts. He gestures at the opening, then retracts his wire with a flourish. "Milady."

I glide past him and into a long, narrow compartment lined with empty shelves. "Another cargo hold? Without an external hatch?"

"Probably a storeroom for crew supplies." Arun taps one of the empty shelves. "This makes me think the crew had time to remove their belongings when they left. Why empty this compartment completely, but leave those random things in the hold?"

"This compartment is too big."

Arun frowns and stretches his arms, easily reaching the shelves on both sides. "Too big for what? She's in a space smaller than this?"

I drift to the side of the space and grab a shelf to stop. "Where are you?"

You're close.

Her mental voice is loud in my head, but I can't get a direction on it. Like a voice coming through an audio implant. I wonder if that's how she's talking to me? Did she hack into my implant?

Don't be silly. I don't need your ridiculous wires and metal.

"That's helpful, as always." I hope the caat understands sarcasm.

We invented sarcasm.

"There's a hatch here." While Noelle distracted me, Arun investigated the blank wall at the back of the storage room. He pokes the blade of a thin knife into a seam in the bulkhead and pries gently. The panel pops off, swinging easily on hidden hinges.

As we stare into the darkness, I swear I hear breathing.

CHAPTER EIGHTEEN

I SHOVE Arun away and fling myself to the side, so we aren't silhouetted in the opening. Noelle's emerald-green eyes glow within the dark, hidden compartment. Arun flicks his holo-ring, and the lights behind us go black.

The breathing ratchets up, faster and more ragged. My scanner picks up a racing heartbeat and a human heat signature.

"Who's with you?" I whisper.

Don't be alarmed. I'm not sure how I can tell, but the statement is aimed both at me and at whoever is breathing so quickly in the dark.

"Noelle?" I say aloud, willing my eyes to adjust to the darkness. "Who is with you?"

A beam of light leaps out from beside me, stabbing into the dark compartment. It flickers over Noelle's fur, then scans across the space, stopping on a huddle in the corner. Shaggy hair covers wide eyes in a dirty face.

A child.

I'm terrible with kids. If Griz were here, he'd be oozing his upper-lev charm all over this child, gaining its confidence, reassuring it, making friends. Learning what gender it is so he doesn't have to think of it as "it."

I stretch a hand forward, but the child flinches at the movement. Time to call in an expert.

I toggle my audio implant and call Elodie. "I'm going to need your help."

She yawns. "Where are you? That movie was so boring. I must have fallen asleep."

"I'm in the *Fairwell*. We've found a—" I pause. Who is this child? "—a survivor."

"I'll warm up the med pod. And have Leo make some soup."

"Okaaay."

Arun's headlamp dims to a less threatening brilliance, and he drops to the deck just inside the open hatch. Crouching, he reaches a hand across the small compartment. "Hi. I'm Arun."

The big eyes blink, then drop to Noelle. The caat—who looks a lot bigger in the child's lap—stretches up to put her front paws on the kid's shoulder and nudges her nose against the filthy cheek. The two seem to communicate. The shaggy head jerks up and down, then the child squints at Arun. "I'm Ris."

"Vanti? Did you hear me?" Elodie's voice through my implant startles me.

"Yes. No. What did you say?"

"I asked if we need clothing for the survivor. Blankets? Booze?"

I cough. "Blankets and clothes, yes. Booze, no. At least, not for the—it's a kid. Girl, I think."

"What?! Why didn't you say so? Is she okay? Let me—" She cuts out mid-sentence.

I call her back. "Don't come over here!"

You can't hear external noises through an implant call, but I can tell Elodie is running down the corridor. "I'm coming to help."

"Wait at the airlock. Do not enter the ship. We haven't cleared it for non-mission-essential personnel." I flick my holo-ring and pull up the ship's system to lock her out.

"Is she hurt?"

Arun has coaxed Ris out of her corner. She grips the edges of the hidden hatch as she steps through the opening. Her coverall is dirty and torn, but serviceable. Her greasy, knotted hair hangs over her face in a ragged fringe.

The lights behind me slowly brighten, giving all of us a chance to adjust easily. The girl—I'm not sure why we all assumed female, but the assumption feels right—lifts her chin and pushes her shoulders back, as if bracing for an attack. Arun takes her hand. "Are you hungry?"

The girl's head swings up and down violently.

Arun turns to me. "You got any food?"

"Who do you think I am, Triana?"

"I know you're prepared for anything." He raises a brow.

I pull a protein bar from a hidden pocket of my pressure suit. Keeping food in the external pockets of a sealed suit doesn't make a lot of sense—unless you also carry an emergency pressure shelter, which I normally do. I didn't bother for this trek, since the ship is space-worthy, but taking my emergency rations out of my pockets was more trouble than it was worth. "Do you need help opening—"

The little girl grabs the sealed packet and rips it open with her teeth.

I guess not.

The child crams half the bar in her mouth and bites it off, chewing furiously. She swallows, then breaks off a corner and crouches to offer the morsel to Noelle. The tiny caat sniffs the bit, then butts her head against the girl's hand, pushing it upward. Riz shoves the piece into her mouth and follows it with the rest of the bar.

Wordlessly, I offer another.

Arun waves me off. "Let her stomach adjust to that one. You aren't supposed to feed a starving person too fast."

The girl gives him a death glare, then her eyes drop. Noelle rubs against her legs, her little head barely reaching the girl's ankles. Why did she look so much larger a few minutes ago?

"Vanti!" Elodie's voice startles me. "Where are you? Bring her to me or I'm coming in!"

"No." I tap Arun's shoulder. "Elodie is waiting at the airlock with a blanket and… I think she said soup."

He nods, as if this makes perfect sense. "Right. Probably should get a med pod. Come on, Ris, climb aboard." He crouches again in front of the child and holds out both arms.

The little girl glances at the caat. With an infinitesimal shrug, she steps between Arun's arms and turns to face away from him. He scoops her up like a bride—one arm under her knees, the other behind her back—and lifts off the ground, straightening his legs as he rises.

I toggle my call to Elodie. "Did you bring the med pod to the airlock?"

"No. Do you need it? You said she wasn't hurt."

"I said I didn't *think* she was hurt. But she could be carrying something—virus, bacteria, genetically engineered death bomb."

"I thought you didn't watch that movie with us."

"What movie?" I wave my hand at the access panel and the compartment hatch opens.

"The one we were watching. After dinner. It was about an alien parasite that takes over an exploration ship and kills everyone. Or I think it kills everyone. I fell asleep."

"I haven't seen it, but you can understand my concern." I follow Arun and his charge down the corridor.

"No, I think your concern is fictional. Or based on a fictional situation."

"Elodie. Get the med pod. At a minimum, the child is malnourished and needs to be examined." I ignore Elodie's grumbling. We turn and take the ladder up, exiting the cargo area. Up here, the lights spring on as we approach—a standard low-power life-support setting.

We reach the ship's airlock. I wait until Noelle joins us inside, then cycle the hatches. Arun, still carrying the girl, pushes off from the threshold, sailing through the zero gravity and rotating his feet beneath him to land gracefully at the other end. His boots snap onto the magnetic mat, and he puts out a hand to keep from shoving Ris into the closed hatch.

We wait for the *Ostelah's* outer hatch to cycle, then enter the small airlock. Elodie waves through the plasglas window of the inner hatch. Despite her grumbling, the portable med pod fills the small room.

Ris clings to Arun when he tries to lay her in the open pod but doesn't say anything.

"We need to make sure you don't have anything broken." Arun gently sets his transparent helmet against the girl's forehead. "It won't hurt, I promise. It's warm and comfy. And we'll be right here when you wake up."

"Noelle too?" she whispers.

The caat meows loudly and scrambles up Arun's pressure suit to perch on his shoulder. She leans down, her front feet on Arun's bicep, her nose in the little girl's face. Ris rubs her cheek against Noelle's soft fur, then releases her tight grip on Arun's arm. He lowers her onto the bed and folds the lower half of the clamshell over her legs. Noelle leaps from his shoulder to the plastek cover and stretches out, belly low, nose and front paws at the edge of the lid. Ris touches the caat's nose, then lays back so Arun can close the top over her as well. Noelle creeps forward until she can see through the large window in the lid.

Arun activates the device, and the little girl's eyelids flutter shut. A red light illuminates on the side, and an androgynous voice says, "Examination begun. Please do not open the pod until the cycle is complete."

When he reaches for his helmet, I put a hand on Arun's arm. "We should run a flush."

"What about the caat?" He jerks his head at the med pod. "Where'd she go?"

The top of the pod is empty. We look around and under it, but there's nowhere for a caat—even a tiny one like Noelle—to hide. Unless she has developed the ability to open and close the lockers—which wouldn't surprise me, but we would have heard that—she's simply disappeared. The hatch to the FlexLock tube is closed.

"How'd she do that?" Arun stands beside the med pod, pointing at the place she has been lying.

I shrug. "She jumped down. It's not a bad leap, even for a small—

what the heck?" Through the clear window, Noelle blinks up at me. She snuggles into the little girl's arms and closes her green eyes.

"How did you get in there?" I tap on the window, but the caat ignores me.

Arun blows out a breath, ruffling the hair curling over his brow. "Impossible. But it makes this easy." He flicks his holo-ring and selects the "bio-flush" option.

Lights blink red, fans whir, and a loose scrap of paper flutters across the small compartment to the air handler. A yellow haze fills the space then dissipates, followed by a red light that slides from ceiling to deck. Then the red indicator flips to green and the internal hatch pops open.

Elodie rushes in, cramming herself into the space between the med pod and the suit lockers. "Is she okay?"

Arun puts a hand on Elodie's shoulder. "That's why she's in the med pod. I'm sure she'll be fine. Now, step back, so we can move her to the infirmary."

"That tiny closet is hardly an infirmary. But I guess it's better than this." With a dramatic, dismissive wave at the airlock, she squeezes back out and tromps down the hall.

Arun taps the controls on the med pod, and it rises from the deck. Another flick and swipe, and it eases through the hatch and around the corner. "We'll be there in a minute." He swipes the hatch closed and pulls his helmet off with a sigh. "I want to be there when she wakes. Too many strangers could scare her."

"She's got Noelle, so she's not alone. I wonder how that caat got into the med pod?" I remove my own helmet and set it on the bench beside me. Unzipping the front of my pressure suit, I let out my own sigh. I'm used to tight fitting clothing, but it's not usually as restrictive as the suit.

A towel hits my head, landing half over my face. I pull it from my hair and shoot a glare over my shoulder. "Thanks." The nubby towel cleans and dries in one swipe—or so the advertisements claim. I'll still take a sonic shower when I get back to my compartment. I wipe down my arms, legs, and torso as I peel out of the suit, then pull on my clothing, trying hard to ignore Arun doing the same behind me.

I might sneak a few looks, but I'm not telling.

CHAPTER NINETEEN

Once we're dressed, we put our pressure suits into the lockers, which will clean then store them, and head down the corridor.

Arun jerks his head at the hatch as it closes. "You left a protein bar in the suit. Doesn't the cleaning destroy it?"

I shake my head. "They're made for this kind of abuse. The wrappers are guaranteed for a dozen cycles. They even have an integrated counter—when the label turns red, you toss it."

We arrive at the infirmary, which is, as Elodie said, little more than a spacious closet for the med pod. She stands in the open doorway, watching the data stream across the screen as it works through the diagnose and treat cycle.

I point at the screen. "See that? Bacteria!"

Elodie taps the screen and rolls back through the log. "It says she's carrying a normal bacterial load. No treatment necessary." She glares at me, then swipes through the rest of the data. "And aside from minor nutritional deficiencies, she's remarkably healthy. She needs food and sleep."

"Which raises the question—where is she going to bunk?" I look from Arun to Elodie. "There's only one bunk in my cabin, but I could

—" I let the statement trail off. As I said, I'm not much of a kid person. She'd be much better off with Elodie.

"Don't be silly! I have plenty of room. She can stay with me." Elodie pats the top of the med pod. "The little couch in my compartment folds out into a bed. Easy peasy."

Arun puts a hand on Elodie's arm. "But she doesn't know you. She might be frightened."

Elodie taps her chin and gives Arun a narrow-eyed once over. "Since you two are so close, maybe she should stay with you. You know, because you've known her twenty minutes longer than I have. How about we let her decide when she wakes up. Which will be in six minutes and twenty-one seconds."

Arun lifts both hands, palms out. "I wasn't trying to—she can stay with whoever she wants."

While Elodie hovers over the med pod, Arun and I lean against the walls in the corridor. The minutes tick by slowly. After a long pause, we both speak at once.

"Who do you think—"

"How did she get—"

I point at Arun, then lift a palm, silently inviting him to go first.

"Why was she alone on that ship?" He scrubs his fingers through his hair.

"Are we sure she was?"

He blinks and his jaw drops. "Zark. I didn't think about that."

I nod slowly. "The shielding that kept us from scanning cargo could be hiding dozens of survivors. Or refugees. Or pirates."

"You think she's a pirate?" He peers over his shoulder into the infirmary as if he can discern her familial vocation by sight.

"No. But why was she on that ship? She's what, four, maybe five? She wouldn't have been alone."

He gives me a funny look. "She's at least eight."

"Whatever. I don't know kids." I shrug, then point at him. "But I do know an eight-year-old wouldn't have been alone on a cargo ship."

"No one is suggesting that. The real question is where did everyone else go?"

I nod. "And are they really gone?"

A muffled ping brings us around to face the infirmary. Elodie glances at Arun, then moves aside so he can open the pod. He taps the panel and swipes through the screens. With a flourish, he hits the green button. The indicators on the side of the device turn from red to green, and the lid pops ajar.

I always imagine vapor rolling out when a med pod opens, but that never happens.

The lid hinges up. Noelle meows once, then nuzzles Ris's cheek. The girl's eyes pop so wide the whites show all the way around. They dart from the ceiling to the caat to Arun smiling down at her. She goes still, like a rabbit in a wolf's gaze. The caat purrs and nudges Ris's chin with her nose and the girl relaxes. Her hand comes up to cradle the feline as she sits up.

"How do you feel, Ris?" Arun's deep voice is low and friendly.

Her gaze darts around the room again, stopping on me and Elodie in the doorway. It flits back to Arun and then drops to the caat. She mumbles.

"Are you hungry?" Arun holds out a hand to help her off the tall bed.

Ris eyes his hand suspiciously, then jumps down without touching him.

Elodie beams. "I'm Elodie. I've got soup, sandwiches, macaroni and cheese, cake, ice cream—"

"Elodie, she's just gone through a med pod cycle. She's probably more tired than hungry. It should have given her a nutrient boost."

"Him." Ris makes eye contact with me for a brief second, then looks away.

"Him? You're—a boy?"

He nods once.

"Oops, sorry." I glare at Noelle, still cuddling with the boy. "Someone said you were a girl."

I never said that.

Sure, caat.

Her head swivels slowly, and she turns her emerald-green glare on me.

Here's the thing with caats. Or at least this caat. That glare is soul-withering. Not many things scare me, but that creature can put the fear of God into anyone.

"Well, if you're a boy, you're definitely hungry. Come on, I'll take you to the grub." Elodie jerks her head toward the lounge and trots away. Ris looks at Arun, who shrugs, then follows Elodie, the caat still clutched in his arms.

I grab at Arun, but I must be tired because I miss. "We need to question him."

Arun gestures for me to follow them. "Let the kid eat first. Also, you might have lost your pet."

I snort. "I think you misunderstand the roles in my relationship with Noelle. But I get what you mean. I'm not too worried. She can keep an eye on the kid. And maybe snoop around in his head and find out what we need to know."

I get the impression of a narrow-eyed, emerald-green glare.

Oblivious to the fear-inducing mental glare, Arun pauses in the open doorway. Elodie introduces the boy to Leo, Vlad, and Zwani. Ris's gaze pauses on Zwani for a long moment, then flicks swiftly to the men one after the other. When Elodie hands him a loaded plate, Ris scoots his chair closer to the table and digs in.

Arun grunts softly and turns to me. "Looks like he's in good hands. Let's go see if there's a way to scan that cargo hold."

I follow him toward the bridge. "Wouldn't we have already done it?" Although now that he mentions it, how did Ris evade my mapping drones? The cloud of tiny cameras spread throughout the ship—it should have locked on to any movement and transmitted an alert. "How many secret compartments do you think that boat has?"

"Secret?"

"Yeah, like the one Ris was in. My drone cloud didn't find it, and it's not on the official specs for that model. If there's one, there's bound to be more. Smugglers don't do just one."

"Ah, so it's smugglers now, not pirates?" He chuckles as he opens his cabin door.

The captain's cabin sits opposite mine between the bridge and the "public" spaces. His office and living space mirrors the conference room, while his bedroom is the same size as my cabin. I assume, from the ship specs—I haven't actually been in his bedroom. In fact, I haven't spent much time in the office, either. We usually meet in the conference room or crew lounge. Or the gym.

A large desk fills one end of the room, with a comfortable couch and small foldaway table at the other. Arun gestures for me to take a seat on the couch, then opens a cupboard. He pulls out two round glasses and pours a generous measure of brown liquid into each. "Sarvarian brandy?"

I take the glass and sniff cautiously. "I thought we were going to scan the ship." I don't drink much because I like to be in control. But my tight shoulders could use something. A tiny sip sends a soothing wash of fruit and oak across my tongue. It goes down smooth, then a ball of warmth blossoms in my belly. "But I could get used to this."

"I guess the scan can wait until after we talk to Ris." Arun clinks his glass against mine with the satisfying ring of expensive crystal. I tend to forget Arun is the son of top-levs and wealthy in his own right. Most of the time, he comes across as a brilliant, independent pilot with a flair for business. Which he is.

"Smugglers." I try on the word for size as I set my glass on the table. "It makes sense. Shielded cargo hold. Encrypted black box. Family members on board."

"Do smugglers typically bring their underage children on a—what would you call it? A smuggle?"

I chuckle. "I think they call it a 'run.' And if you're living on your ship, yes, you bring the relatives. I know of a family in the Romara Republic with multiple generations aboard. Smuggling—unless you're carrying something dangerous like explosives or weapons—is relatively safe. You might get boarded by the Boundary Guards, but Commonwealth BeeGees ask politely for your papers. And if you don't run, they don't use lethal force."

"We aren't in the Commonwealth."

"Good point. Which is probably why Ris was hiding. I'm guessing the crew was bringing contraband—probably luxury goods—into Lewei and got boarded. Put the kid in hiding, then the rest of the crew gets hauled off to prison before they can mention the kid. Or maybe they thought he'd be safer on his own."

"But why was the ship still orbiting? Wouldn't the government impound it and sell it? They obviously took everything else that wasn't bolted down."

"Except those boxes."

"Except those." He swirls the liquor around his glass. "You don't like it?"

"No, it's good. But I'm on duty." I smile apologetically. "Gotta keep a clear head."

He nods thoughtfully. "Sometimes loosening up a bit helps you think outside of the box."

"I'm quite happy inside my box, thank you very much. You can do the outside parts." I snap my fingers. "Speaking of boxes, I'm still wondering..."

He laughs. "We can ask Ris in the morning. I'm sure he'll know."

CHAPTER TWENTY

THE NEXT MORNING, the entire crew meets for breakfast. Even Jones appears at the table, dressed in sweatpants and a white sleeveless shirt with a scoop neck. His hair is slicked back, and he wears a gold chain around his neck, like a stereotypical thug from old Earth vids. He grunts in response to queries about his health and ignores offers of food. Instead, he opens his holo-screen and retires to the couch on the far side of the room with a massive mug of coffee.

Elodie puts the egg casserole back on the table and focuses on her own plate. Leo glares at Jones, then sprinkles a little extra cheese on Ris's plate. Zwani stares at Ris, her gaze barely leaving the child's face as she eats. She's so distracted, she pokes her cheek with her fork. I watch them all with a superior smile.

Or at least a mentally superior smile. I wear a poker face as usual. Putting my fork down, I push back from the table. "Now that we've all had a chance to eat, can you answer a few questions, Ris?"

The boy looks up at me, eyes wide, mouth full.

Elodie waggles a spoon at me. "Let the boy finish his meal, Vanti." She smiles kindly at Ris. "Ignore her. Eat."

The kid crams another scoop of disgustingly bright stars and clovers into his mouth, then drops the spoon into the bowl, splashing pink milk on the table. He turns bright red, his eyes darting to Elodie. "Sorry." Milk drops from his chin.

She smiles kindly and tosses a napkin at him. "No problem."

Ris mops up his chin and the table, then carries his dishes to the counter. He stops, looking around the room. "Where's the disposal?"

Elodie bustles across the room. "These aren't disposable. We wash and reuse them." She takes the bowl and tips the milk into the sink. "Don't you do dishes on your ship?"

His shaggy hair swirls around his head as he shakes it.

"Those long-distance freighters use solar to power their printers." Zwani leans across the table. "If you use the right materials, it's more efficient to recycle and print new stuff than to clean it. Crazy but true."

"How do you know about long-distance freighters?" I play with my fork, feigning casual interest.

"Grew up on one myself. Long, slow crawls from the jump ring to the planet. Sell the cargo. Buy more. Long, slow crawl out." She shrugs. "So boring! Why do you think I joined the service?"

Her background must be one of the reasons Aretha assigned Zwani to this mission. My handler is known for her ability to choose the perfect tool for every job.

Speaking of tools, Jones lets out a loud belch and looks up from his holo-screen. "Lovely story. Who locked me out of my data stream?"

Arun lifts his gaze from his own holo-screen, a tiny smirk playing around the corners of his mouth. "What are you locked out of?"

"My data stream. I was reviewing cargo manifests from the *Fairwell*."

"Last I heard, you still hadn't cracked the passwords." Arun's eyes narrow.

"Well, you haven't heard the latest, then. I got in, but now I'm locked out. Did you do that?" He rises on his spindly legs and flexes his ridiculously large pecs.

Arun raises one brow, not intimidated. Knowledge of their financial superiority gives top-levs a disdain for threats. Most people won't take on a top-lev for fear of legal retribution. But Jones isn't a normal person. Based on the information we've collected, he's used to taking what he wants and using lethal force if necessary. I slowly slide toward the front edge of my chair, ready to take Jones down if it comes to a physical altercation.

"I did." Arun sips his coffee. "You were injured—incapacitated. We had no way of knowing what your mental state might be, so I locked you out of the *Fairwell* to safeguard the data there. Brain injury can cause impulsive behavior, and I didn't want you to... accidentally... destroy evidence."

Jones's hand clenches around the handle of his mug, his nostrils flare, and his jaw tightens. He sucks in a deep breath and holds it for a long moment, then lets it out. "I did not experience any—the med pod cleared me, so I need to get back in."

Arun sits forward. "I'll see what I can do. But first, who hit you?"

Jones's gaze darts to Ris, still standing by the sink. The boy stares back, eyes wide. Elodie moves to his side, putting a motherly hand on his shoulder.

With a tiny jerk, Jones snaps his attention back to Arun. "I don't know who hit me. They snuck up from behind. But we know who was on that ship."

Arun doesn't even look Ris's direction. He points at me. "Vanti. Me. You. Zwani." He smiles a little at Zwani's immediate denial. "You were there. We saw you." He turns back to Jones. "Lots of people on that ship. People who shouldn't have been there. Let's talk it through. It had to be someone large enough to swack you on the head, which eliminates Ris and probably Vanti." He mimes hitting someone.

I bite my tongue on my instinctive protest. I could *easily* take Jones out from behind with both hands tied behind my back. In fact, a roundhouse kick is my preferred method. But Jones doesn't need to know that.

Jones doesn't argue. Even though he should. Agents all get the same training, and my name is on a lot of plaques and trophies around the academy. If we hadn't already known he was an imposter, that lapse would have alerted me. But it also shows his intel on me and this mission is less than complete.

"Elodie and Leo were both on the *Ostelah*," Arun continues, speaking in a conversational tone. "I have vid of the FlexLock, and they never left the ship. Same for Vlad—he was on the bridge. That means the only possible attacker would have been Zwani. But we saw you walk into that inner room alone."

Jones glares at Arun. "Or you."

Arun sets his mug on the table and spreads his hands wide, palms up. "Or me. But why would I do that? Oh, and I was with Vanti, so she'd have to be in on it too. Which makes no sense. She brought you here. Why would she take you out?"

Leo slaps both hands on the table and rises. "What I'm hearing is there's someone else on that ship." Without waiting to see how this bombshell is received, he snatches up both serving dishes and carries them away.

"Hey!" Vlad waves the serving spoon he'd just taken from the dish. We ignore him.

Arun nods in unsurprised agreement. "I agree." He swivels in his chair to face Ris. "Who's with you?"

The boy's eyes grow wider. His lower lip trembles and he stutters. "I don't—just—there's—" He blinks and tears run down his cheeks. "I was alone!" he wails.

Elodie flings her arms around him, pulling him into a fierce, protective hug. "Don't badger the boy! He's obviously traumatized." She turns the child toward the door. "Come on. You don't have to listen to those mean people." As they disappear, Ris flips a quick look back at us.

Was that triumph?

"Noelle?" I whisper under my breath. "Can you read him?"

The caat doesn't respond.

Arun rises, walking past the still posturing Jones without another look. "Time to crack the cargo hold shielding."

Lifting a brow at Leo, I get to my feet. I flick a glance at my plate. Leo rolls his eyes, but nods. I leave the dishes on the table and follow Arun.

I catch up to him as he hovers near his cabin door. "What's your plan?"

He starts, then sighs. "I don't know. I've already tried everything I know of. There's no known way to read through an impregnium-reinforced alutanium hull. It was created to contain everything."

"You said we'd see if there was anything radioactive inside."

"Sure. You can't load a ship without leaving residual emissions behind—we'd have seen particles around the hatches. But people—any residual data is impossible to differentiate from that of perfectly legitimate activities. Unless we have a comprehensive database of all known members of the crew, and any and all visitors, we have no way of correlating the—"

"We can't tell who's inside. If anyone." I rub the bridge of my nose. "Your technobabble was giving me a headache."

"I'm just trying to approach this from a logical direction."

"Well, my gut says we need to do a physical sweep." I point at the deck. "In person. By hand."

"I concur with that assessment. I wish we had more boots to put on the ground." He grins. "I know that's not right, but you know what I mean."

I smile back. "Boots on the deck? We should be able to use my drone cloud's map to identify any unmapped areas within the ship's footprint."

"Already on it." He pivots smartly on his heel and heads for the bridge. "I started the data run last night."

I hurry to catch up to his long stride and follow him into the small compartment. Someone—undoubtedly Vlad—has hung a hammock from the overhead and left clothing strewn around. I flick a sock off the co-pilot's chair and sit. Apawllo, draped across the back rest, opens his eyes and yawns. "Where's Noelle?"

He blinks twice, then leaps to the deck and stalks away.

Arun slides into the pilot's seat and opens a holo view. He throws data links into it, and they coalesce into an image of the *Fairwell*. With a couple more swipes and flicks, the image turns into a three-dimensional line drawing, showing the location of interior decks and bulkheads. A few locations glow red.

"This is the layout of the ship, based on the data collected by your drone cloud. The red areas—" He stretches the view to zoom into one red block. "That's where we found Ris. The others are anomalies—places where the measurements taken by the drones reveal a larger than expected space between bulkheads. Hidden compartments."

I give him a dark look at the last two words. "Yeah, I got that." I reach past him and pull the image closer to me, turning and stretching it. "I suggest we set drones to watch all of these red sections, then investigate each in person, starting with this one."

He frowns at the red block I poked. "Why start there? Because it's the biggest?"

I turn the image and zoom out a little. "No. Because it's connected to that compartment where Jones got knocked out."

CHAPTER TWENTY-ONE

"VANTI, can I speak with you a moment?" Leo hovers outside the bridge, pacing nervously.

"Sure." I open the door to the conference room. "You want Arun too?"

"I—no." He smiles apologetically at our pilot and host. "No offense, but—"

Arun frowns a little. "No problem. I'll go ahead and set those monitors we talked about, Vanti. Meet you in the cargo hold."

"I'm not sure you should go aboard alone." I bite my lip. "Maybe take Vlad? Or Zwani?"

"I'll be fine." He taps the insignia on his designer sportswear. "I've got software to help."

Pressing my lips together, I frown. "What software?"

"It's this new tech I'm testing for—I can't tell you who I'm testing for. But it watches the space around you and reports… intruders."

"Intruders into your space?" I take a large step across the corridor, stopping a couple of handspans from him. "Like this? Or do you mean your personal space?" I move closer, our chests nearly touching.

"You're too close. It wouldn't be much good if it didn't alert you until the enemy was within smelling distance."

I take a surprised step back. "Do I smell?" I turn my head to sniff my shirt.

"Gardenia." I jerk in surprise. I'd almost forgotten Leo was standing here. He draws in a deep breath through his nose. "Cinnamon. Coffee. Probably from your breakfast."

Arun's jaw tightens as he tries to hide a grin. "Exactly."

I will my face not to heat. "Did your fancy system tell you Leo was out here waiting for us?"

"No, I had it turned off." He flicks his holo-ring and manipulates a couple of icons. One flashes green. "See—it's telling me he's here now. Green for friendly."

I peer at the data. Leo's name blinks in tiny green letters. "Why is there only one? Shouldn't I show up on that thing too?"

"I don't need an app to know when you're around." Arun's face goes red, and he hurries away.

"That was… enlightening." Leo walks into the conference room.

I play clueless. "Really? How so?"

"Clearly he has a thing for you." He chuckles. "Not that I didn't already know that. It was obvious before I left the ship. But the dynamic has… changed. It's more—"

I hold up a hand. "I don't need your analysis of my relationship with Arun, thanks."

"You asked."

"Forget I did. What's up with you?" I close the door and drop into a chair.

"I got a message."

I sit up straighter. "From whom? None of us should be receiving messages. We're in covert mode."

He nods wildly. "That's why I'm freaked out!" He flicks his holo-ring and throws a file to the table. Text appears, spelling out gibberish. The letters change, sliding back and forth.

I reach forward and freeze the vid, turning the image this way and that. "Old school. I like it. Text only message gives us less chance to identify them, and they did a good job of scrubbing the meta data."

Leo throws me a disgusted look. "You *like* it?"

I wave him off. "Let's say I appreciate the spycraft." A flick of my finger restarts the message. The letters slide around, then form a message: "We see you. We're coming."

I pause it again. "And you think this was aimed specifically at you? Why?"

Leo points at the message. "It came to me! He's clearly talking to me! He says he sees me!"

"Leo!" I snap the word out like a slap. When he stops babbling, I go on. "That message is very generic. He doesn't mention his name, your name, where we are, or what he thinks we might be doing. It could easily be an automated message that plays on continuous loop in hopes it will reach *someone* and freak them out. Part of the perpetual Leweian psyops campaign against outsiders. Or even a prank."

"Did you get one last time you were here?"

"No, but that's been a couple of years. We can ask Vlad—he said he was here two weeks ago."

"No! I don't want him to know I got it."

"Leo." This time I lean forward and grab his hand. It's icy. "He's already seen it. He monitors all incoming data." Leo pulls his hand away, and suspicion settles in my belly. "Unless this didn't come in through the ship's message system. How did you receive it?"

He flushes and looks away.

I slap a hand on the wood table with a crack. "Leo! Did you break our cover? How'd you get the message?"

Leo cringes at the slap, then darts a look at me. "I might have logged into my Leweian messaging account."

My eyes widen and my nostrils flare. Shoving back from the table, I surge to my feet and lean over, slapping both hands on the wood again. I lower my voice to a whisper. "You did what?"

Leo's shoulders slump as he bites his lip and looks away. "I logged in—"

"I heard you! Are you insane?! Do you *want* to be captured and taken back to Lewei?" I need space. Flinging myself away from the table, I scatter the chairs on my side as I stomp across the small room.

When I reach the wall, I spin and stomp back. "We're all going to end up in Xinjianestan prison. When did you do it?"

He shrugs. "Maybe five minutes ago."

I lean over the table again and get in his face. "Check the time stamp. I want to know exactly—to the second—when you hit that login icon."

Leo cringes deeper into his chair but pulls up his comm app. "Twenty-four minutes and thirty-seven, no eight. Nine—"

I hit an icon on my holo-ring and wave to cut him off. "Got it. Assuming your login *immediately* set off an alarm, and that the nearest Leweian vessel is at Luna, we have twenty-three hours and seventeen minutes before they can possibly reach us. With any luck, no one is monitoring that account in real time. You've been gone over a decade... When's the last time you checked that message box?" With a flick of my wrist, I fling a count-down clock onto the table projector.

His face flushes even redder. "Last time we were at Gagarin." The words come out in a tiny whisper.

I'm so furious I'm not even angry anymore. Ice cold settles in my bones. "You checked it when we went to Gagarin. That's how Grigori found us."

Although it isn't a question, he nods.

I need space to think. Pointing at him, I straighten. "Do not do *anything*. Don't mention this to anyone. And definitely don't check your messages again!"

"Can I bake bread?" I barely catch the question as the door slides open.

I take a deep breath and swing around. "Yes. That's a great idea. Just don't mention this to anyone."

"Got it, boss."

I grit my teeth. I wish they'd stop calling me that.

I consider checking in with Vlad, but if he saw this message, he should have alerted me or Arun immediately. The fact that he didn't dismays me a little. Either his surveillance isn't as complete as he claimed, or he neglected to mention receiving it. I initiate a call, but it goes to his message system. That's odd, but hardly cause for alarm. He's probably still eating breakfast. I'll check with him later.

When I reach the airlock, it's empty. I'd hoped to catch up to Arun, but I guess I'll find him in the cargo hold. I debate wearing my pressure suit—obviously the ship was safe enough for Ris and the caats, and the life-support systems read green. But training wins over comfort, and I squirm my way into it. The helmet locks into place, and I run diagnostics, wishing for a second set of eyes to double check. I have worked alone for a lot of years, but I still like to have a partner for this kind of thing.

Or maybe I have gotten used to having a particular partner again. Pushing that thought to the back of my mind, I cycle the hatch and sail through the FlexLock.

My footsteps echo loudly on the metal deck, so I hit my grav belt and lift off. Ris claimed to be alone, but the tears felt forced to me. And although I'm one hundred percent capable of dealing a blow to the back of Jones's head, I have my doubts about Ris's ability to do it. Which means he has an accomplice.

"Noelle, are you on the *Fairwell*?" The words sound loud inside my helmet, but with my external speaker off, no one else will hear them and just thinking them didn't get her attention.

She still doesn't reply. Which, like Vlad, is not alarming on its own. But with neither of them responding, a ball of trepidation lodges in my stomach. I toggle my audio and call Arun. "Status report."

"I'm in the cargo hold. Waiting, as I promised." His deep voice sends a soothing wave through my body. "Nothing happening here. La da da."

I roll my eyes as I speed through the corridors. Arun gives up on the singing before I reach the cargo hold. As before, the upper hatch is wide open, but now all of the lights are on, bathing the large, empty space with a harsh brilliance. With a quick glance, my nearly photographic memory tells me more of the boxes have been removed. Has Zwani been down here again? When? And why did my surveillance feeds not alert me?

"Arun?" I pop over the railing and plummet toward the deck.

Arresting my speed before I smash into the deck, I settle to the dusty floor like a leaf on the wind.

"Arun? Not funny. Where are you?" I flick my holo and bring up my locator. Arun's location shows on a three-dimensional map of the ship. He's in the same small chamber where we found Jones. A faint tremor shivers through me, and I pull out my stunner as I ease to the open hatch.

This room is dark, but light from the hold behind me glints on the plasglass dome of Arun's helmet, sitting beside a puddle of blood.

CHAPTER TWENTY-TWO

Heart pounding, I lurch to a stop beside Arun's helmet. The round plasglass fishbowl rocks gently, as if it was dropped recently. Arun spoke to me just minutes ago, so whatever happened occurred between then and now. I try to remember if it was moving when I first peered into the room, but my memory fails. I have a crystal-clear impression, but it's a still image. The helmet in the middle of the small room, the dried blood from Jones's head wound, the dusty footprints.

Footprints. And a couple of blurry tracks, as if something heavy was dragged. I turn on my helmet's lamp and trace the thick, wavy lines across the floor. They end at a blank wall. A quick flick of my holo-ring confirms what I remembered—that one of the red, unscanned areas lies beyond this bulkhead. And clearly, there's a way *through* right here.

"Got you." I whisper the words under my breath as I trace a seam. The walls are covered in meter-square panels, each one butting tightly against the rest. The opening could be a single square or a larger section. There are no marks in the dusty floor—beyond the marks from Arun's heels—so the door must open inward. I press my gloved palms against the lower square, but nothing happens. Working my way across the panels above and on either side nets me nothing.

I lift off the ground and go to work on the top row of panels. Still nothing happens. Methodically, I work my way around the room, starting with the bottom square, then the middle, then the top. Drop to the deck and repeat. Still, nothing happens… until it does.

With a click, the four-panel section where the path dead-ended jiggles. I launch across the deck and press my shoulder against the crossed seams where the four sections meet. The panel slides away from me, then stops, recessed only a few centimeters. I cram my fingers into the gap and pull sideways, then up, then down.

The section drops into a slot in the deck, the upper row of squares sliding behind the lower. The space beyond is dark. I turn so my headlamp illuminates the long, dusty recess. The marks—clearly caused by Arun's heels dragging through the fine powder—lead through a narrower opening at the left. I double check my stunner and head into the abyss.

Why is there so much dust?

The recess is narrow enough that I wonder how they got Arun's broad shoulders through here. I slow down to check the sides. No obvious marks on the walls, but the dust is mostly on the ground, so unless they snagged his suit, there'd be nothing visible.

Why didn't they use his grav belt? The newest models make transporting an unconscious person easy. Maybe they don't know he's got one. Or maybe his fancy new one doesn't allow anyone but him to access it. He said it was part of a beta test.

Yeah, I might be a bit envious of his advanced tech.

Ahead, light glows, revealing another turn to the left, around the end of the cargo hold. Using my own belt, I lift above eye level and drift closer to the turn. Then, with a mental head slap, I pull a drone from one of my many pockets and launch it. With the holo on its dimmest setting, I watch the drone reach the turn. It rotates, revealing a solid wall. I try to visualize the ship's map and realize this is a dead-end.

Where could they have taken him?

I follow the drone around the corner, then stop with a gasp, grateful I'm still airborne. The passageway continues, but with a ladder straight down.

I can't believe I missed that. I forgo another mental head slap and instead pull up the schematic on my holo-ring. Clearly my "almost photographic" memory is on the fritz today. I push my fear for Arun's safety as deep into my mind as it will go and slam the hatch on it. Knowing he's incapacitated means I have to make additional contingency plans, but dwelling on it will only cloud my judgment. I take in a deep breath. I'm a professional. A stone-cold agent who doesn't let emotional attachments interfere with her mission.

I run another analysis on the ship's schematic. Stretching the graphic larger, I trace a continuous line of narrow spaces that could link the larger red sections. Spots where the bulkheads are wider than absolutely necessary for the life support and electrical run between them. A network of passages could link the entire ship through multiple tunnels.

And the chute dropping below me leads to a large, open chamber. A place likely to house hostages. With a decisive nod, I drop through the opening, weapons hot, headfirst.

Halfway to the lower deck, I flip to put my feet beneath me, weapon still out. The big, empty space mocks me. As does the drone hovering above me. I am really off my game today. I should have sent it first. I take another deep breath and try to center myself.

An odd sound reaches my helmet mic. A faint, angry hiss. Using my suit's built-in triangulation system, I trace the noise to a dark corner at the end of the compartment, tucked behind the shaft I just descended.

"Apawllo?" The cat is trapped in a caged space that protects a blocky, unrecognizable piece of equipment. His fur stands on end, and his eyes glare daggers. I find the opening—wedged shut with one of those blasted boxes—and let him out. With an ungrateful shriek, he streaks past me and up the ladder leading back to the cargo hold.

I heft the box thoughtfully. The placement of the box was intentional. Someone trapped him in there. Why anyone would bother is a mystery. "Noelle?"

The caat still doesn't answer. I've been operating under the assumption she was ignoring me, but maybe she's trapped too. Surely that wouldn't keep her from responding to me, though.

Leaving the empty box on top of the cat trap, I cross the compartment to another passage. There are three ways in and out of this space, so I look for tracks through the dust. Unfortunately, the deck here has been cleaned. Or maybe the air handlers do a better job of filtering the dust in these larger areas.

At the far end of the compartment, a narrow walkway leads forward. At ninety degrees, another, tighter passageway hung with ducts and wires heads off to the starboard side. I pull up the map. Both routes eventually lead to the large space near the engines, but the narrower shaft is shorter.

Of course.

Using my grav belt, I lift off and turn sideways. Leading with my right shoulder, I slide into the narrow space. My helmet rubs against an overhead cable, so I go horizontal. I'm not claustrophobic, but slithering sideways between the pipes, cables, and ducts requires a few deep breaths and a mental pep talk.

The narrow cleft ends in another small, irregular opening. This one looks occupied, although not at the moment. Several hammocks hang overhead, and a neat row of bags and boxes line a wall. If I weren't worried about Arun, I'd stop to investigate. Contenting my curiosity with a three-sixty vid as I rush through, I exit on the other side.

This passage is wider, and I'm able to face forward again. It twists and turns at seemingly random places as it winds through the bulkheads. Ahead, the passage lightens, and I slow to a halt. Voices reach my mics.

"—not telling you." A deep, male voice cracks and pops into a higher register on the last word. A teenaged boy.

I send my drone into the room. The lights are low, leaving two people in shadow. They're arguing over a third person lying on the deck between them. A quick look reveals no other people in the compartment, so I shove my feet against a convenient outcropping and launch myself into the small space.

"Freeze!" With an acrobatic flip, I land two meters from the combatants, covering both of them with my stunner. They jerk with surprise and turn to face me. My helmet lamp glares into their faces.

"Arun?"

He puts a hand up to block the light. "Vanti, is that you?"

I glance from him to the adolescent standing on the other side, then focus on the body. "Jones? Again?"

That startles a laugh out of Arun. "He does seem to get hit on the head a lot. D'ya mind not pointing that stunner at me?"

I glance down at my hand, almost surprised to see the weapon still there, then shift my aim to the boy. "Who's he?"

Arun takes a couple of steps to my side, then puts his hand on top of the stunner and pushes the muzzle toward the floor. "That's Yivan. Ris's brother."

CHAPTER TWENTY-THREE

I STARE in surprise at the teen. Then revise my estimate of his age down a few years. He's probably thirteen or so—he has that stretched-out, gawky look of a boy in a growth spurt. His sleeves don't quite reach his wrists, and his pants are too short for his legs, even though they hang low and loose on his hips. His curly dark hair looks very much like Ris's.

I gesture at Jones. "What's going on with him? Why did the boy conk him on the head again? Does he need a med pod?" I glare at Arun while still keeping my weapon between me and the kid. "And why did you leave your helmet in the cargo hold? I couldn't track you!"

Arun jerks his head at the boy. "Yivan wouldn't let me come with him with the tracker on."

"You need to get yours out of here too." Yivan points at my head, which is a good thing because his accent makes his words almost incomprehensible. "We can't let them know where we are!"

"Relax." I reach up to my helmet and press my holo-ring to a hidden sensor. "I can turn my tracker off. But who are 'they'? And why are you hiding?"

Yivan glances at Jones. "How long will he be out?"

Arun wrinkles his nose. "I hit him with the minimum charge, so maybe ten more minutes?"

"Why'd you stun him? And what are you planning on doing with him?" I'm not the most patient of people, and I want to know what's going on. Besides, if Leo's message was real, we've got a ticking clock with bad guys on their way.

Arun grunts and leans down to run a scanner of some sort over Jones's body. "This estimates nine point three minutes. We need to secure him. Then we can talk." He turns to me. "You got slip ties?"

I finger the hidden pocket on my right thigh seam, but don't open it. "What's your long-term plan? Keeping hostages is not an easy business. Even if you have a brig, you have to feed them, provide sanitation, keep them quiet..."

Arun gives me a quick, narrow-eyed look. "I don't want to know how you know that."

That surprises a dry chuckle out of me. "SERE training. Survival, evasion, resistance, and escape. If you don't care about your captive's human dignity, keeping prisoners is a lot easier. But we're civilized people, right?"

The kid spits on Jones. "My family is in Xinjianestan thanks to him. I don't care about his dignity."

"How about we lock him in his cabin on the *Ostelah*?" Arun suggests.

"You would let him live in luxury while I must survive here, like a *shoo-ahg*?"

I frown at the boy and turn on my translator. He's speaking Standard, but that last word sounded Leweian. "What's a *shoo-ahg*?"

"Rat." Arun rocks his hand back and forth. "Or more accurately, a rat-like creature from Szu-ahn, which is where Yivan and Ris's parents were from."

This triggers a flash of comprehension, and I whistle in surprise. "They defected from Szu-ahn, and now they've been captured by the Leweian authorities?" I raise a brow at the boy, and he nods. "Why in the galaxy did they fly to Leweian space? Could they not think of a more dangerous place to take their children?"

Yivan's face darkens. "We didn't fly here willingly. This man is responsible for all the ill that has befallen us!"

As if in response to the angry declaration, Jones moans a little.

"We need to secure him." Arun finds a piece of rope—maybe part of a damaged hammock—and kneels beside Jones. "Hold this." He hands the cord to Yivan, then rolls Jones over with negligent ease. Taking the tie back, he secures the prisoner's hands behind his back, then grabs another scrap and threads it through the man's boots.

"Again, what's your end goal?" I put a hand on Arun's shoulder. "He can only stay in that suit for forty-eight hours. Assuming he hooked up the plumbing."

His brows come down as he looks up at me. "Vanti is worried about the health of a prisoner? He wouldn't hesitate to do this to you."

"I don't stoop to their level. I'm one of the good guys. It's kind of my brand, you know?"

Arun heaves out a sigh and stands. "You're right. And even though I don't feel it in this moment, I agree."

"Look. We don't know how long we'll need to restrain him, and we might not want to keep him on the *Ostelah*. In fact, we might want to leave. Soon." Before the boy can spit on Jones again, I swing around to face him. "You got crew cabins on this boat, right?"

He rolls his eyes. "Of course. Where do you think we lived?"

I gesture at a stack of crates against the wall. One holds bottles of water, another blocks of protein that would be used by an Autokich'n. "It kind of looks like you live here."

"We *hide* here. When there are infiltrators aboard our ship." He throws an angry glare at Jones again, then glares at me and Arun.

"I propose we move Jones to the sanitation module. I assume there's a shared one?" When Yivan nods, I continue. "He has access to those basic human needs I mentioned. We can throw a mattress and blanket in and a couple ration packs. And there's no computer access from there if you take his holo-ring."

Arun pats his pocket. "Already got it." He leans down and lifts Jones's shoulders. "Point the way."

I hide an eye roll as I remove my grav belt. "Let's do this the easy way, shall we? Why didn't you use yours?"

Arun takes the belt. "It's integrated with the suit."

"I think you should submit a bug report on that."

"Right. Because you never know when you might need to transport an unconscious captive." He lays the belt on the ground and rolls Jones onto it.

I chuckle. "Well, if they're designing for the military, then, yeah. But if it's a CEC contract, they might need to transport injured teammates."

Arun brings the loose ends of the belt over Jones's body, then stops when they don't reach around. "We might have a problem."

With a reproving head shake, I crouch beside him. My belt was custom built to fit me, but for the reasons I just mentioned, it has an emergency extension. I pull the thin, webbed strip across the gap and link the two ends. Then I activate the belt and raise Jones from the deck. "Lead on, Yivan."

The boy moves to the side of the compartment and releases a latch, allowing the bulkhead to slide into the floor like the one in the cargo hold. This opening is smaller, and we have to crouch to get through. As we emerge, emergency lighting flickers and brighter lights come on.

I point at the overhead illumination. "This is why you've been living in the walls? If the lights come on when you come out here, it's easy to find you."

Yivan nods but doesn't reply. He turns and stomps down the narrow corridor to a ladder. "We go up."

"Okay." I nod for him to precede me, then use my holo-ring to send Jones toward the opening in the ceiling. "After you."

Arun hesitates. "I can watch your rear." He goes bright red. "I mean, the rear."

I hide a laugh. "Usually, we use the term 'six,' which means six o'clock. Like looking down on a clock face: twelve is in front of you, three is to the right, nine to the left. But you go ahead. I prefer to watch our six myself."

He presses his lips together but activates his integrated grav belt and rises after Jones. I set my drone to alert status and climb the ladder behind them. Not that I'm terribly worried about anyone sneaking up on me—but the last time I assumed this ship was empty, Jones ended up with a blow to the head. Then we found Ris. And now Yivan. Who knows who else might be hiding in here?

When I catch up to the others at the top of the ladder, Arun looks fresh as a daisy, of course, since his grav belt required zero effort from him. Yivan's respiration is a little faster than normal, but that's the only indication he just climbed four levels. I suck in a deep breath to slow my heartrate. My arms are burning. I've obviously come to rely too much on my grav belt. I make a mental note to add ladder climbing to my workout routine. You'd think swimming would cover it, but ladders must use different muscles.

We're in the same short hallway that leads to the bridge, but Yivan turns the other direction. "This way." He leads us past four closed doors to one at the stern which slides open at his approach. "Sanitation. I don't see how this will work. It locks from the inside."

I slip past him and look around. There are two sinks in the outer room, then another door to a small space which houses the toilet and a sonic shower. Like on most cargo ships, this module was pre-fabricated and installed during construction. They're built to make it easy to add as many as a ship needs depending on the crew size, but the single-piece construction makes them ideal for restraining prisoners.

"I'll grab a mattress." Arun waves a hand at one of the crew cabins and disappears inside. He returns with a ten-centimeter-thick pad and a thin blanket which he tosses to the floor beneath the sink.

"Grab some food." I jerk my head at Yivan, then crouch beside Jones to unhook my grav belt and pull it free. While I wait for Yivan to return, I buckle the belt around my waist, then cut the cords holding Jones's arms and legs. "We might have incoming."

Arun's eyes widen with alarm. "Incoming? Like more of those Leweians who took Yivan's family?"

I lift my shoulders. "No idea if they're the same people. Leo got a message." I tell him about Leo's security blunder. "It has to be automated—triggered by his login. It's been months since he last used the account, so chances they've got anyone actively monitoring it… I'm sure it's connected to a surveillance system, and an alert went to someone. Whether that someone cares to act on it—"

"He's the runaway son of a deposed dictator. Why would they bother?"

I shrug. "Personal grudge? Maybe Grigori set it up? We don't know what happened to him after we left. He could have made friends with the government again. Or—" I break off as Yivan reappears carrying a crate full of individually wrapped rectangles.

"Survival rations." He drops the crate outside the door to the sanitation module. "They taste terrible but will keep you alive. He doesn't deserve them."

I nod absently as I take one and scan the wrapper with my holo-ring. My translator converts the Leweian script to Standard. "Each bar is a day's rations? No wonder they taste terrible. How many should we give him?"

Arun picks up two bars. "If what you just told me is true—I say we give him a week's worth." He takes four more and tosses them onto the mattress beside Jones's still body.

"I could sell those—or trade them to get my family back." Yivan glares at Jones again. "Since it is his fault they have been captured, he can starve."

Arun puts a hand on the boy's shoulder. "You heard what Vanti said. But a little hunger won't hurt him." He leans forward to snag one of the bars.

Jones's legs snap up and lock around Arun's waist, pulling him down. Arun easily breaks free, but Jones gets one of his massive arms around Arun's neck.

I have my weapon out, but Arun is between me and my target. "Let him go."

Jones struggles to his feet, using Arun as both a shield and a support. "Not a chance. He's my ticket out of here. Drop your weapon."

CHAPTER TWENTY-FOUR

JONES'S ARM tightens around Arun's neck, and Arun's face goes red as the blood flow is restricted.

"I don't have time for this." I raise my stunner and fire it at Jones's face. His eyes go wide, then he slumps to the ground, his arms sliding from Arun's neck. Arun lands on top of him with a thud.

"Nice shooting!" Yivan offers me a high five.

I half-heartedly slap his palm with my own. "It was hardly difficult. Three meters to the target, and with a stunner, collateral damage is not a lethal problem. His head is plenty big enough." I lean over to offer Arun a hand up.

His fingers close around my hand, and I lean back to give him the leverage to rise. "That was not fun." When he regains his feet, he rubs his head. "My brains hurts."

"Sorry. Stunner flashback is a bear. And getting choked out is no picnic, either." I lean into the sanitation module long enough to take all but three of the ration bars back, then straighten and drop them back into the crate. "Shut the door."

Yivan taps the panel next to the hatch and the door slides shut. "How will you disable it?"

"That part is easy." I pry the access panel open and twist the door indicator to "lock." After the bolt snicks into place, I disconnect two wires. "These things are built to be replaced easily. After hundreds of years of space travel, plumbing is still one of the most unreliable parts of a spaceship. So, manufacturers build them to be swapped easily. Just lock it closed, disconnect the leads, and pull the module. Can't be done out here in space, of course. Too much risk of depressurization. But it makes them an excellent prison."

The boy's jaw drops. "Really? It's that easy?"

I point at him. "It is not to be used on younger siblings."

A sly smile skips across Yivan's face and disappears. He rolls his eyes. "Of course not. Space is not a joke." I can almost hear his parents saying this to him, much like my parents used to warn us about the swamps of Grissom.

"Let's get back to the *Ostelah*." Arun rubs his head again, as if it's still hurting. I feel bad about the stunner flashback. I could have taken Jones out without the weapon, but it would have taken longer. And might have resulted in injury to Arun or Yivan, so I don't regret my choice.

"Before we go, I want to know what's going on." I point at Yivan, still standing beside the locked sanitation door. I'm not sure I trust the boy—in fact, I'm quite sure I don't trust him. I don't know him. And while I'm not worried about him releasing Jones, there's a high probability he will come back and try to hurt the criminal. And probably accidentally let him go. Or try to jettison the entire module, which despite what I told him, is easier than it should be.

Don't ask me how I know.

Yivan gives me a dark look, then appeals to Arun. To my satisfaction, Arun makes a rolling motion with his hand. "Tell the lady what she wants to know."

Yivan sighs. "Fine." He leans against the bulkhead beside the sanitation module and slides to the floor. "My family runs this ship. It belongs to—or used to belong to a consortium of exporters on Szuahn. There were some lean years when I was a kid, and Jones Interstellar bought out over half of the families." He throws a dark glare at the locked door. "Then Jones showed up and demanded we transport his cargo to Lewei. My parents refused—if they get caught on Lewei, they'll go to Xinjianestan for the rest of their lives. But Jones insisted. And he took my sister to force our cooperation."

"Your sister!" Arun looks up in surprise. "You didn't tell me this part."

Yivan waves a hand. "I didn't want to deter you from helping us."

"Why would—huh?"

"My sister—older sister Hashima—is now married to Jones." Yivan makes a sour face as he says it.

This time both Arun and I turn stunned faces on the boy.

He makes a spluttering noise of disdain. "Jones kidnapped her. Hashima was about my age when he took her. By the time she turned eighteen, he'd convinced her he was the hero, and she married him. I think she's his fifth wife or something like that." He spits on the deck again.

I cringe internally and make a mental note not to touch the deck.

"How long has this been going on?" Arun asks.

"Five years? No, Hashima has been married for two, so maybe eight? Almost as long as I can remember."

"So, for the better part of the past decade, you've been sneaking into Leweian space to deliver contraband for Jones?" Arun looks appalled.

The boy nods. "It's what we do. We're smugglers. But this time, things went strange. We must have made a mistake when we jumped in. We enter a system far outside the normal jump bands to avoid detection, which means we have long transit times."

"It also means if your calculations are off, you miss the mark by a long way." I look under my lashes at Arun. He looks terrible, so I need to wrap this up and get him back to the ship. And possibly a date with the med pod. "I take it you jumped in way off course."

The boy nods. "And we had an engine go out. Jones doesn't care about our ships, and we haven't been able to afford a decent overhaul in years. My dad and I keep things running, but—"

"Even long haul cargo ships need a full dry dock rework once in a while." Arun leans his head against the bulkhead, eyes closed. "Overrun that by too much, and catastrophic damage could occur."

"Exactly." The boy nods. "We couldn't jump back out—we were too far from the exit beacons. And with the in-system drive down to one, we were crawling. We've been in system for ten months!"

"That explains a lot." I open my mission log and make a note.

"Finally, we passed near Luna, and Mom reached out to distant family there. But someone must have turned on us because we were boarded."

I blow out a sigh. "It was more likely that the Leweians saw you—your ship isn't exactly stealthy."

"We were running dark. No one noticed us. Then we call Luna, and BAM! The Leweian Border Patrol shows up."

"You might have been running dark, but even the Commonwealth knew you were here." Although that might be due to spies in the LBP rather than our technical prowess. "We had no trouble locating you once we got in-system."

"I think Mims might have sent a message back to—"

"Mims?"

Arun's eyes open. "That's Szu-ahnian for 'mom.' Mims and Pipo, right?"

Yivan nods. "Exactly."

I watch the boy carefully. "Who did your mims send a message to?"

"I dunno." He goes a little pink, as if he does know, and he doesn't want to tell me.

I decide to let that lie for now. "So, you were boarded. By the LPB?"

"That's who they said they were. Mims sent me and Ris to the bolt-hole. They took Mims, Pipo, Hingan, Delasa, and Lomas."

"Who?"

"Hingan is my father's brother, and Delasa is his wife."

"What about Lomas?"

"She's the dog."

"You had a dog on the ship?"

Arun perks up. "What kind of dog?"

I raise a hand to cut off that line of conversation. "It's not important right now. After they took your family, you waited, then we showed up. Why did the Leweians leave the ship? Why not take it away for scrap?"

"They left it for Jones to retrieve."

I gape at him for a moment, then close my mouth with a snap. "Did they actually use his name?"

The boy nods. "Everyone knows 'Sondre Jones.' It's such an unusual name, but easy to remember."

"I want to hear more about the dog," Arun says.

"Not helpful." I punch his shoulder. Hard.

"Ow." He rubs his bicep.

"You punched him." Yivan stares hard at me, then looks at Arun. "And you let her."

Arun rubs his arm again. "I didn't *let* her. She just did it."

"But you didn't slap her for her insolence."

I push away from the bulkhead I've been leaning against. "Because I'm a woman? What kind of backward place is this Szu-ahn?"

Yivan's jaw drops. "Because you are a woman? That's stupid. No, because he is the captain, and you are the underling. This behavior would not fly in my family. If Pipo behaved so, Mims would throw him in the—"

"Throw him in the what?" Arun darts a look at the sanitation module. "Do you have an actual brig on this ship?"

"Brig?"

"Prison? Cell. Jail. Lockup. Hoosgow—"

"No. There is no place to lock up. She would throw him in the airlock. Then if he did not repent, she would drop him on the next planet to fend for himself."

Arun and I exchange a look. "The airlock," he says. "Why didn't we think of that?"

"Maybe because it's in use?"

"There's a bigger one in the cargo hold. But the sanitation module is more humane." He turns to the boy. "Has she actually done this or just threatened it?"

"Oh, no. She's done it. Pipo is my third father. We left Da on Tereshkova. And Padre left us on Luna City." He shivers. "That was a scary time. We don't talk about it."

"Luna City? You're going to have to talk about it. When were you in Luna City?"

Pounding from the sanitation module door interrupts his answer. Jones hollers, but the ceramic and metal skin of the module blocks sound surprisingly well, rendering his shouts indistinct.

I jerk my head toward the ladder near the bridge entrance. "You can tell me on the way. Let's get back to the *Ostelah*." I reach a hand to Yivan, but he leaps to his feet as if on springs, making me feel old and creaky.

I'm only thirty-one, but that's past the age many top-levs get their first rejuv treatment. Not that I can afford those. Yet. If I stay with the CCIA, they're part of the health care package starting at forty.

"I don't know much about it. I was little—maybe five. Mims decided to make a trip to Leweian space—this was before Sondre Jones took over. I think there was a family member in Luna City, but I really don't remember. Just that everyone was scared, and Padre didn't come back with the rest of the crew. He was mean to me, so I was okay with it."

"Was Padre your birth father?" Arun's warm voice hints at sympathy without expressing pity.

Yivan throws up his arms in a big shrug. "Who knows?" He jumps onto the ladder, his feet on the outside of the vertical bars, and slides away.

Arun sweeps his hand toward the ladder with a dramatic bow. "I know you don't want me watching your six, so you'd better go first."

I narrow my eyes at him and cross my arms. "I'm watching *our* six, and I'd better not catch you watching mine."

With a smirk, he follows Yivan down the ladder, doing a credible job of imitating the boy's effortless slide. I wait until he's cleared the landing zone, cast one last look over my shoulder at the now silent sanitation module, then dive headfirst down the ladder shaft, giving Arun no opportunity to get a peek at my six.

CHAPTER TWENTY-FIVE

WHEN YIVAN FOLLOWS me and Arun into the crew lounge, there's silence. Then Ris cries "Yivi!" and launches himself across the room into his brother's arms. We leave the two boys whispering together and meet with the rest of the team in the conference room.

I gave Elodie a heads up, so she left snacks for the boys and set us up with some food and beverages too. I pop the top on a beer pack and pour it into my glass. "You didn't leave any of this where they could get it, did you?"

Elodie rolls her eyes. "This is not my first rodeo. I raised two kids, remember?"

Leo grins. "There's enough cake, pie, and candy to put them into sugar comas. No alcohol necessary."

"You made cake?" Arun looks around the room and under the table. "Did you—"

Leo points at a covered container on the table. "Cupcakes. Chocolate and strawberry."

Arun lunges across the table to grab the container and pull it to his place. "I'm so glad you're back, Leo."

The Leweian smiles, but it's strained. And he's about to get a lot more stressed. I set my beer down with a thud and flick my holo-ring, throwing an image of a planet onto the table projector. Leo's smile drops like a rock in double gravity. "Xinjianestan," he whispers.

I nod.

Leo swallows hard, staring at Lewei's infamous "reeducation center." "Why?"

"We need to rescue Yivan and Ris's family."

Arun's eyes light up. "Really? I thought you were just supposed to find out whose ship this is and why they're here. We've done that. I figured you'd say anything else was outside the parameters of your mission."

"I would never say 'outside the parameters of my mission.' I might say it's beyond the *scope,* but my missions rarely have firm parameters."

"You say Teresh-KOE-vah, I say Ta-RESH-kah-vah."

"No one says Ta-RESH-kah-vah."

Leo raises a hand. "Ta-RESH-kah-vah is the correct Leweian pronunciation."

I glare at him. "No one *from the Commonwealth* says it that way. But my point is, I have a great deal of flexibility in my mission. And I say we need to get Yivan's family before we leave the system."

Leo's gaze returns to the planet spinning benignly above the table. Xinjianestan Reeducation Center is known throughout the inhabited galaxy as the most inhumane prison in existence. His face goes pale, and a sheen of perspiration appears above his pencil-thin moustache. "Do I have to go?"

I frown. "Your options are kind of limited. I suppose you could stay here with Jones. But we're expecting visitors, aren't we?"

He shrugs, flicking a quick look at Elodie.

"Leo, what did you do?" Elodie chides.

His dark head drops to the table, his forehead impacting with a soft thud. "Something stupid. It's my trademark."

She puts a hand on his shoulder. "Is it possible that deep-down, part of you *wants* to go back to Lewei?"

"What? No!" Leo's forehead thuds a few times. "Maybe?" More thudding. "I think I'm homesick."

"They aren't going to welcome you back to the premier's palace, so I'm not sure why your subconscious thinks going back would be a good idea." She rubs his back.

Thud. "That makes four of us." He lifts his head long enough to make eye contact with me. "I'm sure Vanti and Arun agree."

We nod silently.

"I wouldn't wish a *shoo-ahg* to Xinjianestan," Arun says.

"Speaking of rats, has anyone seen the cats?" Elodie asks.

Elodie knows Szu-ahnian? I tell her about finding Apawllo in the ship. "But I haven't heard from—I mean, I haven't seen Noelle since yesterday." My stomach drops. "You don't think she's trapped on the *Fairwell*?"

"She's too smart for that." Arun flicks his holo-ring. "I'll check the cams I set." But Noelle doesn't show up on any of the vids. Arun sets a filter on the video library, but the only feline that appears is Apawllo. "How is that possible? We have zero vid of Noelle?"

I frown and lean across the table to pull the holo toward me. "It's not possible. Is that yesterday?" I point at an image of me sitting in the lounge, petting... nothing? "That's Noelle. She was in my lap last night. Is she invisible on cam?"

We all stare at each other in disbelief, then look at the vid again. I sit there stroking an invisible cat, like a mime in training for a supervillain role.

Arun points at the vid. "Is that one of the Hadriana caat's *interesting abilities*? I seem to remember talk of strange visual interactions when you got her."

The beginnings of a headache tiptoe out of the back of my mind and take up residence in the front. "I guess it must be." I rub my forehead and think the caat's name as loudly as I can.

What. The impression of a yawning kitten accompanies the petulant thought.

"Have you been sleeping all this time?" I can tell she's in my cabin. "Thanks for the added stress."

You're welcome.

"Does she talk?" Elodie asks.

I nod sheepishly.

"That's so cool. I wish Apawllo could talk!"

She doesn't really. He only thinks about tuna and naps.

I relay the message to Elodie, and we all laugh. Then Leo points at the planet still spinning idly over the table. "What's the plan?"

I sigh again. "I wish I knew."

WHEN WE RETURN to the lounge, the boys are playing a game on one of Arun's many virtual systems. He uses his holo-ring to display an image of what they see, and we wait until they finish a level to interrupt.

"Can we talk to you for a few minutes, Yivan?" Arun's gaze flicks to Ris and away. "Without your brother?"

Yivan's brows come down for a moment, then his frown turns to laughter. "My brother? Did that actually work?" He turns to Ris. "I can't believe you tried it."

Ris shrugs. "Mims insisted. Some people are so backwards."

"What?" Arun looks from one boy to the other.

Ris smirks again, and I snap my fingers. "Ris is a girl."

"But you said—"

I cut Arun off. "She said she's a boy to protect herself. Good idea. Some people *are* backwards. But you're safe with us. Is your name really Ris?"

She nods. "Yeah. Short for Risandra. But no one calls me that. Not even Mims. And I figured with a badass like you in charge, I'd be safe, but then I saw Sondre Jones."

I push aside the flood of warmth her approval washes over me and nod. "He's no longer a problem. But we have a new one. How do we get your family out of Xinjianestan?"

Yivan gulps. "You're asking us? No one knows how to get out of there."

"It's not a closed system. People do leave. Do you know anyone who's been there?" I look at the others. One by one, they shake their heads. I sigh. "I wonder if Vlad knows anything? He said he was on Lewei two weeks ago."

"Vlad can't help you with that, but I can."

CHAPTER TWENTY-SIX

VLAD and Zwani stand in the doorway. When the short woman moves forward, Vlad slides around her and makes a beeline to the counter and the remains of the snacks Elodie prepared.

Zwani ignores the food, instead focusing on the children. "Yivan. Risandra."

The kids exchange a look, and the boy steps closer to his sister.

"I am Zwanilda, your mother's sister."

The kids exchange another look. Yivan moves a little ahead of Ris, putting himself between the woman and the girl. "So?"

Zwani rocks back on her heels in surprise, then gives herself a shake. "I should have expected that. Coppelia and I were not always on the best of terms."

"Is that what you call it?" Vlad laughs. "Not on the best of terms? You two hated each other."

"Wait a minute." I leap out of my seat, arms outstretched. "What is going on here? Are you all related to these kids? How the heck did that happen?" Aretha is going to get an earful when I get back.

Vlad laughs again. "Yeah, you need to do a better job of vetting credentials."

"It's not her fault. We're legit." Zwani gives me a pitying look. "Vlad was assigned to your team. He's been in and out of Lewei on behalf of the CCIA more times than any other agent. And I'm an agent too. But when Vlad found out you were coming here, he might have pulled a few strings to bring me along."

"A few strings? I called in every favor I had and promised a few future favors to get you on this team. And it turns out we could have just slid you in like Jones. He eliminated the agent he is impersonating." Vlad shakes his head in mock dismay and points at me. "And you didn't catch the switch."

Zwani smacks Vlad's arm. "You didn't either. Not until I clued you in."

"Hey, don't share all my secrets, Nilda."

"Don't call me that!"

I raise my voice. "Would you two stop?!" They break off their bickering with a glare at each other but no obvious remorse. "Let me get this straight. Jones killed the agent assigned to this mission and took his place. He must have swapped biometric information too."

Vlad nods in agreement. "He has an extensive support organization with good tech skills. Zwani recognized him almost immediately when we arrived, of course, but we didn't want the mission scrapped. She came to rescue her sister's family." He juts his thumb at the two kids, then shoves half a bagel into his mouth.

I gesture at Zwanilda. "We have a CCIA agent who wrangled her way onto my team for personal reasons. And a second agent who helped her do it." I flick a finger at Vlad. "And neither of you bothered to let me know an enemy agent had infiltrated my mission team, even though you knew he was dangerous."

Vlad nods and speaks through a mouthful of food. "Sounds about right."

"I have one question." I look from one to the other, then pin my gaze on Zwani. "What's up with the boxes?"

The two kids snicker. Zwani throws them a disapproving look, then turns to me. "Nothing. Those boxes are completely immaterial to any of the other matters at hand."

"They're toys," Ris says. "Pipo made them for us. I was bored, so I made patterns in the cargo hold."

"She likes to pretend she's signaling aliens." Yivan makes a swirling motion by his temple in the ancient sign for crazy.

"But what makes them stick to the floor?" Arun asks.

"Suction. You don't want stuff floating around if you lose gravity." Ris lifts her hands and wiggles her fingers. "'Specially if you have anything fragile in your cargo. So, Pipo builds things to stick to the floor."

"And there's nothing inside?" I bring up a vid of the hold with Zwani collecting the boxes. "Why do they open?"

"That's how you break the seal," Ris says, as if it's obvious. "I dunno why *she* was taking them."

"They're all carved. Each one is different. I wanted them as keepsakes of my sister, in case we didn't find her."

Vlad laughs, spewing crumbs across the table. "Isn't that sweet? She loves her sister. She also loves the credits she can get from selling handmade crafts. Those things will bring in a pretty penny on the arts and crafts market."

"I love my sister!" Zwani's dark face flushes darker, and she refuses to meet anyone's gaze. Then she rolls her eyes. "And the boxes will sell well."

"Fine. The boxes were a red herring. Once we found Ris, why didn't you come clean?" I ask Zwani.

She finally meets my eyes. "I was hoping I wouldn't have to. But if Coppelia has been taken to Xinjianestan, I need your help to get her back."

ZWANI'S PLAN is simple but extremely dangerous. One of us will allow ourselves to be captured, so we have inside intel from inside Xinjianestan, then the rest of us will break that person out. Obviously, the children are out, as are the civilians. That leaves me, Vlad, and

Zwani. I don't trust either of them, but I don't want to volunteer. I'm intrepid, not reckless.

"There's got to be a better way to get them out." Arun surges to his feet, shoving his chair away from the table so hard it slams into the wall and dents the faux wood wainscoting. "For one thing—how do we know our… tribute will get taken to Xinjianestan? We're all foreigners. They might send us back to the Commonwealth."

"If it were you, I'm sure that's what would happen." I point at Arun, then swing my finger at Elodie. "Or you. They'd ransom you to your family or the government. And who knows where they'd send Leo."

Leo flings up both hands. "I am one hundred—no, a *million* percent *not* volunteering."

Arun frowns at Leo's ridiculous math but lets it pass. "We aren't asking you, Leo. Like I said, there's no way to guarantee you'd go to Xinjianestan. Speaking of which—" He turns to look at Yivan and Ris as he drops back into his chair. "How do you know that's where they went?"

Yivan taps the rectangular device strapped to his wrist. "Mims has a tracker. My Ncuff tells me she is there." He stabs a finger at the hologram planet still spinning lazily above the table.

Arun crooks his fingers, and the boy unstraps the wide band encircling his wrist. A thin screen curves along one side with physical buttons along the outer edge. "Why do you have one of these instead of a holo-ring? You live in the Commonwealth, right? You said you're from Szu-ahn but that you've been living on the ship in our space. You should have holo-rings."

The boy snorts. "Holo-rings are for the wealthy. They are custom fitted to your hand. My Ncuff has been passed down through the family and anyone can wear it. And they do the same things." He reaches for the wrist strap.

Arun holds it out of Yivan's reach. "They aren't quite the same. I need to get your mother's tracking data." He taps the screen and pages through a few screens, reading the Leweian easily. He scrolls and taps some more, then the device beeps. "Got it." A pinpoint of green appears on the holographic globe. He hands the device back to the boy.

"My Ncuff allows me access to the ship's network, which means it can do anything your ring can." Yivan wraps the strap around his arm and pats the bulky device lovingly.

"Sure. Okay, we know Coppelia—or at least her wrist device—is here." I poke a finger into the hologram, stopping the planet's spin, then stretch it larger. Without looking at Yivan, I use my holo-ring to zoom in farther and shrink the window to a manageable size. *Try that with your arm band, kid.*

Don't blame the child for his faith in his familial artifacts.

I glare at Noelle who strolled into the conference room as we started planning. *You're the queen of sarcasm and snark. I'm just... venting. At least I didn't say it aloud.*

Noelle doesn't respond.

Why didn't you tell us about Ris and Yivan? You were in the Fairwell, *and you have these omniscient powers that allow you to read people. In fact, now that I think about it, why didn't you warn us about Jones?*

Noelle stretches, then stalks across the floor to my chair. With a negligent flick of her tail, she leaps to my lap—a distance at least ten times her height. *Jones, you already suspected. With your healthy sense of suspicion, I had nothing to contribute. The kittens—* An accompanying image of the siblings makes her meaning clear, but her tone turns disgruntled. Almost... embarrassed? *Something in the structure of the ship blocks me. That's why I didn't hear Apawllo in the cage. Or the kittens in hiding.*

"Vanti, are you listening?" Arun pokes my arm.

"Sorry, I was thinking. What did I miss?" I run a hand over the kitten's head and try to squash the ridiculous memory of what petting an invisible caat looks like on vid.

"We're thinking Zwani might be the best—what did you call it, Arun?" Vlad cocks a brow at the captain. "Victim? No, that's not quite right."

"Tribute."

Vlad grabs a handful of cookies from a plate half-hidden beneath the holo-map. "That's it. Tribute. Like that *Ancient TēVē* vid. Do you volunteer as tribute to save your sister, Zwani?"

Zwani opens her mouth, but I speak before she and Vlad can get started again. "What is between you two? You clearly know each other, but your relationship is quite touchy. You said Vlad pulled strings to get you on the mission, so that makes me think he owes you—"

"He's my brother."

I rub my head, where the headache has ramped up from a dull pulse to a throb. "Seriously?"

Vlad grabs another cookie. "Step-brother. Her mother and my father had a long-term relationship when we were kids. Zwani lived with us part of the time. I'm not directly related to any of them." He swirls his hand at the woman and two children sitting at the far end of the table. "But I kind of owe her for taking care of my dad when I couldn't be there."

"Before you ask, Coppelia and I have different mothers, so she never lived with Vlad's family. Our mothers weren't particularly close, so we didn't spend much time together as kids. And grew further apart as adults. But when her daughter was kidnapped by Sondre Jones, she asked for my help. I tried to extract her, but the girl refused to leave. Life at Jones's compound was much more luxurious than in a broken-down space ship." She waves vaguely in obvious indication of the *Fairwell*. "After that, Coppelia and I stayed in touch. Then she went missing."

That explains the weird combination of friendship and animosity between Vlad and Zwani and the lack of connection between Zwani and the kids. Not to mention Vlad's disinterest in the rescue mission.

Zwani takes a deep breath. "I will go to Xinjianestan." She waves a finger around the table. "And, stars, I can't believe I'm saying this, but I'm trusting you to save me."

CHAPTER TWENTY-SEVEN

Two days later, we're still waiting. We've sent an anonymous message to a base on Luna, moved the kids into Zwani's compartment on the *Ostelah,* and set her up in the captain's cabin on the *Fairwell.* It's the only one with a private sanitation module, since Sondre Jones occupies the shared one. Then we disconnected the FlexLock and pulled away from the big cargo ship.

The *Ostelah* has been hovering at the edge of the Leweian asteroid belt, monitoring the situation. Communications with Zwani have been kept to a minimum. While we want her to be discovered and retrieved, we don't want the Leweians to find us in the process.

"I wonder if Jones is still alive." Leo kneads his latest batch of dough on the counter in the lounge. He's used the waiting time to perfect his engine room bakery. The smell of baking bread fills the ship, constantly tempting me to abandon my healthy eating.

Arun looks up from whatever he's studying on his holo-ring. "Those three emergency ration bars should be more than enough to keep him alive if he's careful. Each one has enough calories for two to three days. And he has easy access to clean water and air."

"And you think Zwani is just letting him chill in the sanitation module? That dude kidnapped her niece and has held her family on the edge of financial ruin for years. And is now responsible for more of the family being thrown in the most notorious prison in the galaxy. You think she's okay with that?" Leo grabs a thin metal scraper and chops a chunk of dough off the blob with a forceful smack.

Arun stares at him, mouth open. He turns to gape at me, his jaw working like a fish out of water. Then he snaps it shut, giving me a reproving look.

"Good question." I close my reader and rise. "I guess leaving him to her mercy might not have been the smartest choice." I poke a finger at the chunk of dough he just cut. "What is that, sourdough?"

"Does it smell like sourdough?" He rolls his eyes at me. "And don't tell me you didn't think about this before we did it. You're too wily to have missed the probable outcome."

I sneak a look at Arun—he stares at us like we're monsters. Abandoning the play at innocence, I lean my butt against the counter and face Arun. "What else could we have done? There's no place to put him on the *Ostelah*. We could have, I don't know, sedated him in the med pod, but that means it's not available if anyone gets hurt. Which, let's face it, is highly likely in a rescue operation. He had to stay on the *Fairwell*. The only way to ensure his safety would have been to *not* put Zwani on the same ship. Which means one of us would have been the… tribute."

Arun crosses his arms, still staring at me. He clearly disagrees but can't come up with a better solution.

"I talked to Zwani before we left. She agreed to leave him there for the LBP to find. Remember at the beginning of the mission—he was ready to jump ship if we were going to Lewei. He's definitely persona non grata there."

Arun rubs his chin. "You don't think that was part of his cover?"

I shake my head. "Nope. In fact, I thought it was very odd that Aretha assigned an agent who would refuse to go to Lewei, given the location of the ship. That wasn't an act. He's terrified. I suspect he's double-crossed the wrong Leweian at some point in his long and despicable career. Which is what I told Zwani. She liked the idea of him being taken back to the planet."

Arun grunts. Noelle jumps into his lap and curls up, and his face softens as he strokes the little caat. She's definitely good at defusing tension.

I'm good at a lot of things.

Touchy.

I heard that.

I meant you to. With a smirk, I push away from the counter and head for the door. "Time to work off some stress."

"That'll be your third trip to the gym today." Leo puts a towel over his newly shaped dough, then pushes past me to the door. "Outta the way! Delicate bread coming through!"

"Better to work out than bake more carbs," I mutter.

The ping of the intercom brings us all up short. "Hey, guys, we finally got a ship coming to investigate." Vlad's voice rings through the room at top volume. "Oops, sorry." The decibels decrease as he speaks. "Looks like a Leweian cruiser."

I dart out the door, Arun hot on my heels. We clatter into the bridge, even though we could have easily viewed a holo in the lounge. Vlad has the forward screen magnified, with a ship arrowing toward us, its path from the planet highlighted by a red, dashed line. I tap the ship, and it unfolds into a data display pulled from its transponder.

"Leweian Cruiser *Houjian*. Small patrol vessel. Carries a crew of twenty." I swipe upward to reveal more information pulled from my CCIA files. "Based out of Luna Dark Outpost. I'm not sure if that's good or bad. They send the troublemakers to Luna Dark. The ones who aren't troublesome enough to be sent to Xinjianestan."

"A patrol vessel full of slackers and hotheads?" Arun rubs his chin.

"Or free-thinkers who are smart enough to keep their mouths shut." Vlad's fingers dance through the data, and more info populates the holo. "Current trajectory shows they'll arrive in seven hours. That's a fast little boat to be assigned to a loser base."

"They have long distances to cover, so fast is smart. It's hard to catch pirates and illegal emigrants if your ship is slow." I open my mission dossier—it said something about Luna Dark. Ah, here. "Oops.

Good thing we have a med pod. We're going to need it. These guys are not known for being kind to prisoners."

"We can't leave Zwani over there by herself!" Arun buckles his seat restraints and reaches for the ship intercom icon.

I grab his wrist. "We have civilians—children—aboard. And Zwani knew what she was getting into. She had access to the same data I have."

He shakes me off. "Maybe."

"Relax." I give his shoulder a firm slap. "We have a good plan."

WITH A QUICK APPLICATION of positioning thrusters, Elodie adjusts the *Ostelah's* slow spin, then cuts the tiny engines. We drift along the interior edge of the asteroid belt, comms dead, power plant cold, transponder off. From a distance, we should register as one of many oddly-shaped chunks of ice and rock. But instead of idly drifting, we're heading to a specific destination.

"We'll be in the shadow of the *Fairwell* in three. Two. One. Now."

At Arun's barked command, Elodie hits the positioners again, stopping our spin. Arun slaps a hand through the big red virtual button in the middle of his holo-screen, and the distant thrum of the powerplant coming back online hums through the ship. I don't normally notice it, but the deep vibration is extremely conspicuous after it's absent a while.

The ship blasts forward, rocketing toward the *Fairwell* now that the Leweian patrol boat can't see us from the far side. "Tell me again why we didn't leave a crew aboard? Like a Trojan horse," Arun grumbles for the millionth time.

I grit my teeth, but I can't take it this time. "Because I'm an idiot."

"No, that's not—"

"This is my mission, Kinduja. Stop questioning my plans. Yes, we could have left a team aboard, hiding in the smuggling spaces. But that team would have been me, and I had preparations to make. The first thing that Leweian boarding team is going to find is Jones. And chances are good he's going to lead them straight to any hidden spaces, now that he knows they exist." I shove myself out of my seat and head for the hatch. "I'm going to prep for the boarding party."

Ignoring his mumbled apologies, I stomp to the ladder and climb up to the shuttle bay. I could have taken the lift panel, but that thing is slow and noisy. And stomping up the steep steps is more cathartic.

I reach the top, sad to see the dumb shuttle in Helva's place. Not that it looks much different from the AI driven ship, but we all know it isn't her. Who knew you could have feelings for an AI? I shove that thought away and finish my prep. I could have stayed aboard the *Fairwell* with Zwani. The shielded cargo hold and hidden compartments would have provided excellent cover for a classic Trojan horse maneuver, and I know I could have outsmarted any Leweian search party—especially one from a low-end base. But I have a different plan.

Pulling my fishbowl over my head, I move to the maintenance hatch, a human-sized opening in the landing bay's doors. I double check my pressure suit, personal propulsion unit, and tool kits strapped to each leg. Then I toggle my audio implant. "I'm ready."

Elodie's voice comes through in response. "We're matching vectors with the *Fairwell* now. Hang on… one more puff… aaaaaaand, matched! You're go for exit."

"Thanks, Elodie." I open the maintenance hatch and step onto the narrow ledge. The cosmos stretches out before me, with the bulk of the *Fairwell* on my right, blocking the sun, and the asteroid belt on my left. The vastness of space reaches into my soul and grips it with a momentary gasp of awe. I give myself a second to marvel, but nothing more. Our little ship is hidden from the Leweian cruiser by the bulk of the *Fairwell*, and I can't risk the civilians aboard. She'll slip away as soon as I give the command.

I tap the PPU's start button, then use my holo-ring to set the course. As soon as my feet leave the narrow deck, I send a signal to the *Ostelah*.

"Roger, Dark Quasar, you're away. We'll give you two minutes, then go." Elodie's tone softens from the crisp, professional pilot to loving friend. "Be safe, Vanti!"

"Acknowledge ship departure in two. I am en route." I speed away from the *Ostelah,* curving toward the end of the *Fairwell.* I'll be vulnerable for a few seconds as I clear the nose. Hopefully, no one is looking too closely when I round the end and hit the burn.

"Burn" is not the right word, of course—there's no fire involved. My PPU uses the same technology as our grav belts to move me parallel to the surface of the larger ship. For longer distances across open space, it has tiny engines, but I'm not planning on using those today.

Getting as close as I can to the skin of the ship, I skim around the nose and across the side. I'm banking on our visitors being busy searching the *Fairwell* and not paying attention to their external scans. I've got a scrambler running which should help hide me from those scans, but it's not one hundred percent reliable. As I dodge between protruding equipment, I review my ingress plan.

Leweian cruisers have two personnel airlocks and a small bay for the tiny skiffs that transport crew and equipment to and from the base. Their port side airlock is currently attached to the *Fairwell's* using the Leweian version of a FlexLock. Like most Leweian tech, it's a clumsy, less capable version of a Commonwealth design.

The starboard airlock is closed and in full view of the planet—if Leweian tech could see that far, which is doubtful. But my destination is the skiff bay. According to our intel, a typical LBP boarding mission includes an external review of the ship in addition to the internal search. Which is why the timing of my mission was critical—we needed to make sure the *Ostelah* escaped before the skiffs could get to the far side of the *Fairwell.*

I pause outside the skiff bay. The main door—about five meters by three, is open but protected by a visible blue force shield. The two skiffs are gone—a quick check of my holo scan shows them skimming over the far end of the *Fairwell.* Fortunately for me, Leweians don't like to deviate from their plans, and the scan protocol starts at the airlock and moves toward the stern. Clearly, surprise and innovation are not their strong suits.

Using a thin cable pulled from one of my many hidden pockets, I plug into an external data port beside the bay door. It's intended for maintenance personnel—naval ships don't expect to be taken down by a single bad actor in the depths of space. A feral grin spreads across my face as I connect to their system and insert a video loop in their oversight cams.

Rather than turning the shield off, I install a glitch code Arun created. It introduces a seemingly random flicker that looks like a malfunction. The second five-second burst lowers the density of the shield enough for me to slip inside.

It also allows a great deal of the atmosphere out, so I hope they've got their internal hatches closed.

My counter pings, and I slip through the flickering blue field, trusting Arun to have done his work. If I miss the window, or he didn't get the intensity right, it could fry my nervous system, leaving me incapacitated for an unknown length of time. But Arun is a genius, and I trust him.

That doesn't stop me from holding my breath as I zip through.

CHAPTER TWENTY-EIGHT

A FRISSON FLICKERS through my body as I transit, but by the time I reach the far end of the bay, I feel even more alert than usual.

Step two of the plan—at least version A of the plan—requires the remaining crew member aboard to come investigate the glitch. I hover near the hatch, waiting for them to exit. The wait feels interminable. Finally, the green lights above the hatch flash, and it rotates inward.

I press myself closer to the wall outside the hatch, my pressure suit shifting to match the dirty gray walls. A bulky space helmet appears, followed by the rest of the maintenance worker in his cumbersome suit. I tense, ready to launch myself at him the moment the hatch closes, when another helmet appears.

Blast! They've deviated from the standard plan. So much for Leweian consistency. I ease back into the shadows as they head toward the visibly flickering force shield and set my audio scanner to find their voice channel.

Incomprehensible words roll through my audio implant. With a subvocal swear, I flick the connections and reroute the audio to my translator.

"—can see, the modulators are not compensating for the magnetic field generated by the—"

I let the technical jargon roll over me—my maintenance tech must have a trainee with him.

A trainee who left the hatch open. With their attention trained on the "malfunctioning" module, I slip through the hatch and close it behind me. As I cycle through, I imagine the confused discussion between that maintenance tech and his trainee once they've "fixed" the glitch.

But my grin fades as I contemplate the ruins of my plan. Typically, a cruiser this size would have a crew of twenty. Seventeen of them should have conducted the search and seizure, leaving behind a pilot to monitor the ship and its surroundings, the supply chief, and a maintenance tech—because poor maintenance schedules and low budgets mean Leweian ships fall apart constantly. The intern makes me wonder how many other personnel might still be aboard.

As soon as the internal hatch opens, I send my drone cloud into the cruiser. The tiny flying cams disperse to map the ship and identify any humans. I get three pings before they've had time to canvas more than the top deck. Two people on the bridge and one asleep in the—is that the brig? More pings. What is this, take your intern to work day?

The only upside to this mess is no one should notice an extra random spacer. I hope.

Leaving a stationary drone to watch the hatch to the skiff bay, I make my way through the corridor toward supply. When I reach the second hatch, my translator scans the words printed on the gray metal and confirms I'm in the right place. The hatch is closed, so my drones couldn't get inside. They can infiltrate any place that isn't airtight, but the supply compartment is traditionally well-protected.

Supply on a ship this size isn't a warehouse but a printer with a wide variety of materials to create virtually anything from scrubber filters to silverware to uniforms. Because they can make almost anything, Leweians protect the supply closet like a gold depository. Which explains why most crew members don't have access and makes it the perfect place to hide.

I use one of Arun's apps to open the hatch. Before I get it more than ten degrees open, a querulous voice barks out a question. The infinitesimal delay feels like forever, then my translator kicks in. "What do you want?"

They say the plan never survives first contact with the enemy.

I push the heavy hatch the rest of the way open and stun the occupant squarely in the chest before I even have time to look at them. The ancient woman's eyes open in surprise, then she topples forward off her stool. Great, I've just stunned the oldest Leweian spacer in history.

I roll the woman over, so she's not laying on her face, then step over her prone body to the console beside the stool. Leweian tech uses old-school interfaces, like wired input devices and physical screens. Our analysts claim the defense budget is spent mainly on perks for the ruling generals, which means the soldiers on the line must make do with equipment handed down from their great-grandparents. It also explains why supply is guarded like a deposit of gold.

A quick look confirms the make and model of this console—exactly the one detailed in my database of Leweian naval ships. I pat down Grandma and find her access card, removing several weapons in the process. Sliding the card into the reader gives me access to the system. My visual translator helps me locate the correct files, and I print a Leweian space force uniform built to my measurements, complete with rank and insignia. I have it print Grandma's name—Ji Shinwa—on the chest. While I wait, I scan the supply chief's face with my personal video disrupter so I can hide in plain sight. When the printer is done, I slip the uniform over my form-fitting pressure suit.

Feeling functionally invisible, I relax a fraction and get to work on the ship's command and control. Before leaving the *Ostelah,* I loaded a suite of hacking apps on my holo-ring. Some are CCIA standard, a couple are specialty systems Triana built for me, and two are new programs Arun came up with while we waited for the Leweians to investigate our ship.

The commander of this ship is a Kaptan Liu Rober. His second in command is Leftenant Zharo Lotus. The ship currently carries a complement of twenty, as expected, but they're supplemented by five cadets from the Zhang-Kuznetsov Academy. I have nothing about that school in the limited data set downloaded to my ring, but a bunch of students could allow for mayhem that will not be traceable to me.

The individual in the brig is one of those students—Cadet Andreeva Rosalia. Her record lists disorderly conduct and insubordination as the charge. That could be anything from getting drunk to being accused of insulting a senior spacer's dog.

Do Leweians even have dogs? I'm pretty sure they're rare on Luna and probably not allowed on Dark Base.

I briefly consider taking over Andreeva's identity instead of Grandma Ji's—a wildcard cadet would be easier to impersonate than an elderly supply chief. But that would require me detouring to the brig, and I don't have time for that. Or rather, I'm going to make sure I don't have time for that. I connect my audio to the ship's transmitter, send an encoded signal to Arun, and shut it down again. If an overzealous communications officer is watching carefully, they'll spot the transmission, but keeping it short should prevent them from tracking it back to me—or to the *Ostelah*.

Stashing my fishbowl helmet beneath the console, I drape a fold of fabric over it. That won't fool anyone who's looking, but I'm planning on being well away from this ship by the time anyone realizes I've been here. I use Arun's stun scanner—a useful device he invented that evaluates the victim's nervous and cardiovascular systems to estimate their time to revival—then hit Grandma with another dose of my stunner. I tuck her into a corner behind the shelf of fabric bricks and let myself out of supply, locking the hatch behind me.

I carefully set the required security and leave one of my drones behind for extra measure. If anyone gets inside before this mission is over, I will have to improvise a lot more. I'm counting on no one knowing Grandma's exact schedule.

Fingers crossed, I stride down the hall to investigate the rest of the ship. As I round a corner, I come face to face with the first hurdle. A young female with leftenant's rank stops in front of me and barks out a question.

Hoping Grandma Ji's age gives me an excuse for slow processing speed, I hold my breath while the translator's nearly unnoticeable pause seems to stretch for hours. Finally, the question rings through my implant.

"Ji! What are you doing out here?"

Busted.

CHAPTER TWENTY-NINE

I stare at Leftenant Zharo, certain she can see through my PVD even though the model I use is guaranteed effective unless the viewer physically touches the wearer. I've just reminded myself of this specification when Zharo grabs my arm. Her eyes meet mine, and she jerks in surprise. "Who are you?"

Blowing out an exasperated sigh, I pull my stunner and hit Zharo at point blank range. She goes down like a drone with a dead power cell. Stowing my weapon, I grab her under the arms and drag her back to supply. If it were farther, I'd use my grav belt, but I feel more secure keeping it on. The seconds required to unlock the hatch make my skin crawl, but I get her inside with no one the wiser.

Depositing the officer next to the supply chief, I consider my options. Arun's scanner shows I've got a good two hours before Zharo wakes and three for Ji. I wrestle Zharo out of her uniform jacket, then secure the prisoners with slip ties—in case I can't get back here before they rouse. A piece of fix-all tape from my left thigh tool kit will keep them from talking. Leweians aren't supposed to have audio implants, but I take a few minutes to run a scan—just in case. Nope, nothing.

I pat the lieutenant down and remove her sidearm. Killing them would be easier, but I don't like to do that if I don't have to. Karma is a—

Pounding on the hatch interrupts that thought. Making sure my captives are hidden, I unlatch the door and let it swing open a few degrees. "What?"

The young man outside looks terrified. A single, red slash on his collar indicates he's the lowest ranking spacer on the ship. He snaps to attention. "Kaptan Liu has found two prisoners on the derelict, and we're taking them to Xinjianestan. Orders from Luna Dark."

I hide a grin. Arun's part in this game was to hurry the mission along. Liu must have reported capturing Jones and Zwani to Luna Dark. Arun intercepted the call and gave them orders for transport. "Why are you telling me?" I growl.

The kid's eyes go wide, and his stiff body goes completely rigid. "The kaptan said to notify the staff. You are always the first to be notified, Chief Ji."

"Acknowledged." I slam the hatch shut, hoping Ji is as terrifying as the kid thinks she is. I also reevaluate my plan to impersonate her. Maybe I should have grabbed that kid. The lower the rank, the easier to fake. Except everyone is going to know, and likely haze, the kid with the red stripe.

Leftenant Zharo's identity will give me much more flexibility. I slide on her officer's vest in place of the enlisted jacket I printed. It's tight through the bust, but I don't want to take the time to print a new one. Another scan with the PVD, and my new identity is in place. I check the mirror on the back of the hatch and straighten my collar, staring at the unfamiliar face. With another tug on the vest, I step through the hatch, make sure it's locked behind me, and make my way toward the bridge.

Following my memorized ship schematic, I make my way deep into the ship. Leweian cruisers bury their bridge in the center of the ship, relying on external cams and sensors to relay data. It's smarter than the Commonwealth ship design—we put the bridge out where there can be actual windows—but less sexy for the pilots.

A short, dark-haired man—Kaptan Liu based on the uniform—

glances at me as the hatch slides closed and frowns. "Where have you been?"

My nervous system seems to have decided the translator's delay is not as long as previously thought. The words feel almost instantaneous. "Supply."

His eyes narrow, but he doesn't ask any questions. "Then you know we've been sent directly to Xinjianestan. Command has decided our new prisoners are high risk and must be deposited there immediately." His tone sours. "They think *we* can't contain them."

I hide a smirk and slide into the empty seat I assume must be Zharo's. I think command is right about Liu's ability to contain prisoners, although in this case, Zwani isn't going to cause any problems. Jones could be a wild card.

Screens—actual, physical displays like in supply—stretch above a two-meter-wide desk. They show multiple views of space, including the *Fairwell* growing smaller as we depart. I tap a control panel and scan across the ship, end to end. The *Ostelah* is nowhere to be seen. They should be following soon, but I don't want to draw attention to them, so I flip the display back to its previous setting.

"What are you looking for?"

I jerk in surprise and glance over my shoulder. The kaptan moves as stealthily as I do, the stained carpet muffling his steps. I shake my head a little. "Nothing, sir. Just monitoring the situation."

"Why? That's not your job. Get out of Specialist Pederson's way." He shifts to reveal a nervous-looking young man wearing three silver slashes on his collar.

I rise and vacate the station.

Liu stares at me for another long moment. His gaze goes down to my toes and up my body in a way that makes me squirm internally, but I keep still. When he finally meets my eyes, he glares until I lower mine. "How many times do I have to tell you to get a new uniform? That one is too tight. Go see Ji again, and tell her I demand she print you a new one. I don't want to see you again until you're appropriately attired." Is there a slight tremor in his voice?

Everyone seems to be afraid of Grandma Ji. Shoulda stuck with her.

"Yes, sir." I turn on my heel and march to the door, feeling his stare between my shoulder blades until the hatch shuts behind me.

Taking refuge in the supply compartment, I push Ji and Zharo into the corner and drape a piece of fabric over them. Leaving them lying there uncovered feels disrespectful.

How long can I hide here? The transit to Xinjianestan will take two days. The original plan had been to hide in supply—usually no one is allowed inside. I prowl through the long, narrow compartment, peering between the tall shelves. At the back, I find a hammock hanging across the corner formed by two shelves. Beyond it is an autocook, a single recliner with a side table, and a portable sanitation module with a curtain.

Does Ji *live* here?

That would be highly irregular. But it would explain Zharo's surprise at seeing me in the passageway. And based on the little information we have about the Leweian military, not unprecedented. Senior enlisted personnel with the right connections can get away with virtually anything.

Which brings up another potential problem—Ji's connections. But we won't be in Leweian space long enough for that to be an issue.

That sounds like famous last words.

AFTER THE USUAL ANNOUNCEMENTS, the ship jumps to the Saffron system, where Xinjianestan orbits. I listen to the reports of other departments and bark a gruff, "Supply, clear," when the comms ping. The XO acknowledges and moves on to Life Support without comment. Then I start a thorough search of the space.

In addition to the usual raw materials, Ji has amassed a vast supply of luxury fabric, a surprising stash of Commonwealth products that are not usually available in Lewei, and a small cache of contraband weapons. I close the hidden cabinet, use a tiny plasma welder to seal the latch shut, and stack a bale of protein bricks over the recessed compartment.

My prisoners should be out for at least another hour. I don't want to visit the bridge again and draw attention to myself—and no one appears to have missed Zharo. I've dug into the databases a bit more. Her responsibilities are largely ceremonial and nonexistent during transit. Her messages include only gossip and discussions about clothing with her mother, but those communications ended months ago. I don't see anything to indicate why they stopped talking. Another search on the ship's system nets me additional information: Zharo's parents are high-ranking members of the government. Their apparent falling out seems to coincide with Zharo's assignment to this ship.

Ji, on the other hand, is the former spouse of another party member. And a thorough search of her illicit living space nets me images, vids, and even paper letters that indicate she once had intimate relationships with not one but *two* previous premiers. According to the CCIA's research—and Leo's actual experience—when a premier loses power, he and his supporters are purged. The fact that Ji is still alive and has retained a high enlisted rank in their navy indicates a level of political power that boggles my mind.

Zharo and Ji appear to be the only women on the ship, and both of them have political connections. I stare at their fabric-draped bodies, wondering if there's a way to use that information.

What the heck. I'm bored to tears.

I drag the drapery away from Zharo's head and shoulders and hit her with a stimulant from the med pack I found in Ji's quarters. Then I settle back, stunner drawn, and wait.

Revival doesn't take long. After a few moments, Zharo's eyelids flutter, and she sucks in a deep breath. Her gaze wanders aimlessly across the overhead, then drifts down and around the room, skidding past me without a hitch. Then it snaps back to my face.

"Who are you?" The words come out breathy and strained. "Why do you look like me?"

I give her a blank stare. "Maybe I am you."

"Zharo Lotus. Leftenant. Identification number 948-395-93855." She presses her lips together, as if she fears I'll pry more information out of her.

I nod. "Daughter of Senior Defense Minister Zharo Ternin and Education Minister Zharo Vedalia. I'm shocked they allowed their only daughter to join the Leweian Navy."

Her lips press together again in a sneer, but she doesn't reply.

I shrug. "Whatever. How do you feel? Do you need some water?" I point at a glass I placed near her prone body.

"How do I know you didn't drug it?"

I shrug again and wave my stunner at her. "Why would I bother?"

She eyes my stunner, then slowly sits up and takes the glass. After a long look, she sips daintily. "What do you want? How did you get aboard the ship? Are you a CCIA agent?"

I hide a jerk of surprise at that last question. How did she know? Although, who else would infiltrate a Leweian Navy ship? Probably just a good guess. "Thanks, I'll ask the questions."

"You're definitely Commonwealth." She glares, then gulps down the water and sets the empty glass aside. "Gagarians would have killed me. They know they'll get no information from me. And they wouldn't have thanked me."

"I wasn't expressing gratitude."

"No, but the habit of speech gives you away." With another careful look around, she scoots back to lean against the wall.

I snap my fingers in mock concern. "Ya got me."

"What do you want? You wouldn't have woken me if you didn't have questions."

I can't help admiring her cool attitude. "I was bored. I was hoping you'd be interested in a game of quon lo."

"*You* play quon lo?" She laughs, a single harsh bark. "A Commonwealth agent can't possibly expect to compete against a Leweian officer in quon lo. We start learning as children. It's easy to learn but takes decades to acquire real skill."

I wave my free hand sharply. "We don't have to play if you're worried I'll win. That would be embarrassing."

She draws in a sharp breath and sits up straighter. “I am not afraid of your abilities. Bring it on.”

CHAPTER THIRTY

I PUT the quon lo board I found among Ji's belongings on the deck between us, keeping my stunner pointed at Zharo. "You go first."

"Rookie mistake." She picks up three of the stones and places them on the board.

We take turns, placing our stones, then she raises a hand. "This would be more interesting with a third player. We should invite Ji to join us."

"I think I'll stick with a one-on-one. Trying to watch two adversaries might mess with my concentration. And as you said, I'm already at a disadvantage."

She frowns. "I could give you my word that I won't attempt to escape or alert anyone."

I raise my brow. "Your word? What's that worth?"

She puts a hand to her chest in what should be a melodramatic gesture but somehow looks natural. "I am a member of the house of Zharo! My word is my bond!"

"Well, I'm a member of the house of skeptical, so I'm not buying." I put my last three stones on the board.

"It is as I thought—Commonwealth agents have no honor."

I roll my eyes. "I wouldn't say we have no honor, but we aren't stupid. No way I'm reviving both of you unless you're secured. And it's hard to play quon lo with your hands behind your back."

She flutters her hands in a graceful, complicated gesture that seems to say she's disappointed with my decision but respects my reasoning, then moves two stones.

I move three in response. She nods and moves two more. We go back and forth for a while in silence, each watching the other closely. Then she moves only one. "Sit check."

I blink in feigned surprise and frown at the board. "Already?"

Her complacent smile would make me furious if I hadn't purposely thrown the game. She points at the piece in danger. "You shouldn't have made that move."

I grunt and nod, then push the stone to her. "Your point. You're very good at this. Who taught you?"

"As I said, I've been playing since I was young. My father's father was a master of the game." She gives me a sly glance from under lowered lids. "Even in the Commonwealth, you must have heard of Master Zharo Tenpai."

I frown, as if trying to remember the name, then shake my head. "Nope."

"How can you learn quon lo without knowing of the masters?"

"Uncultured, I guess." I point at one of her stones. "Hey, why'd you do that?" I let her explanation wash over me as I consider this new information. She's the granddaughter of Zharo Tenpai. The famous quon lo master defected to the Commonwealth twenty odd years ago. He left behind his grown children—this woman's father and her father's sister. According to Leweian custom, he should have been deleted from the family tree and never spoken of again. Why would a Leweian naval officer admit to the connection?

"What do you plan to do with me?" she asks after a while.

"Well, that depends on you. I don't like killing people if I don't have to. If you behave yourself, I'll let you live."

"I'd rather go with you."

I do a double take. "You what?"

"You're going back to the Commonwealth, aren't you? I'd like to go too."

I stare at her. "You're a leftenant in the Leweian navy and you want to defect?"

She nods. "Being a woman in the Navy—" She huffs out a bitter laugh. "I thought I could defend my country. Make a difference. But the level of misogyny in the military—my mother was right. I shouldn't have joined. They treat me like a—like an ornamental trophy. I'm not allowed to *do* anything."

I raise a hand. "I'm not buying it. Why would the daughter of two high-ranking ministers defect? Why not resign your commission?"

She stares at me, her jaw dropping. "How do you not know?"

"Not know what?"

"My parents are in Xinjianestan."

It's my turn to stare. "Your parents are—why are you on this ship? Why would they let you anywhere near Xinjianestan if your parents are imprisoned there?" Keeping an eye on her, I holster my stunner and wiggle my fingers. "If you try anything, you'll be dead in seconds. These are lethal weapons."

She raises both hands to shoulder height in surrender. "I will not attempt anything. You have my word."

"About that." I flick my holo ring and lift my hand so I can watch her through the data stream as I work. "Your grandfather defected. Your parents must have done something to lose the trust of the government. I'm thinking your word is really not all that you'd like to imply." I pull out my databases and run a search on her parents' names.

Her eyes narrow. "My grandfather defected because it was the right thing to do. My parents were arrested because they stood up to Premier Shento. They behaved with honor. Shento did not." She almost spits out the last phrase.

"Whoa, girl, chill. I'm with you on that one. I've got no love for the Leweian government." I flick through my information. "I also have nothing to back your claim about your parents."

"Why do you think I'm here? After my parents were arrested, they threatened to incarcerate me as well. I swore allegiance to the Navy, so they let me stay but shipped me off to Luna Dark. It's where all of the potential troublemakers end up. They don't trust me, but I haven't given them reason to dump me in Xinjianestan myself. I managed to get myself assigned to this ship in hopes I could—"

Under the draped fabric, Ji stirs.

I swipe the data away and wave Arun's app at Ji. We've been playing long enough for the stun to wear off. I pull my weapon out and aim it at the still covered supply chief.

"Wait!" Zharo lurches forward.

I swing my stunner at her.

She lifts both hands again as she jerks away. "No! Ji can help us. She's the one who got me assigned to this ship."

Ji moves again, forcing me to make a decision. "Hands." I point at Zharo.

She extends her arms. I snap a slip tie around them and pull it tight, then hand her a second one. "Restrain Ji."

Zharo pulls the fabric away from Ji. The older woman is still unconscious—or pretending to be. She mutters under her breath as Zharo pulls her arms in front of her body and slides the restraints on. I watch carefully, then have Zharo move aside so I can test her work. Satisfied, I move across the room, leaving the other two women beside the quon lo board.

Ji scrunches her face, then blinks rapidly. She says something which my translator identifies as profanity. Then she squints up at Zharo. "I hate waking up from a stun. You got any water?"

Zharo glances at me and I nod. She rises and refills the glass from the water pack I left nearby, then takes it to Ji. The old woman pushes herself to a seated position and takes the cup, drinking slowly. As she does, she looks around the room, her gaze coming to land on me. When she's finished, she sets the glass on the floor beside her. "Who's your twin?"

"I don't know her name, but she's a Commonwealth spy." Zharo slides down the wall to sit just out of arm's reach of Ji.

Ji looks me up and down. "And she'll help us?"
"Us?" I ask. "Help you do what?"
"Prison break."

CHAPTER THIRTY-ONE

I BLINK at the two women, then shake my head in denial. "You're trying to tell me you want to break Zharo's parents out of Xinjianestan. That I just *happened* on two defectors who have the exact same—" I ignore Zharo's instinctive jerk of denial at the word defector. "I'm sorry, but I don't believe in that level of coincidence."

"Who says it's a coincidence?" Ji groans as she shifts position. "I am getting way too old for this."

"Silly me. If it's not a coincidence, then what? *You* planned for *me* to sneak aboard your ship so I could help you break into—and out of — Xinjianestan."

"How would we have engineered that?" Ji shifts again.

Zharo lifts her hands, still bound together. "May I get Chief Ji a cushion? The floor is hard on old bones."

Ji glares at the younger woman. "Who you callin' old?"

"You called yourself old." I swipe the pillow off the chair at the nearby console, run a quick scan for weapons, then toss it to Ji. "Now, if you want my help, explain yourselves."

She scoots the cushion under her rear end. "What is there to explain? The adversary of my opposition is my temporary collaborator. We have a common goal we can work together to achieve. I propose a provisional cessation of our enmity."

"You want to call a truce? And I should trust you… why?"

She waves her bound hands at the ceiling. "You have a recording of us admitting to treason. There is no better guarantee for our cooperation. We cannot double cross you. Even if we claimed we were lying to gain your trust, you know the Leweian government would rather throw all three of us into prison than risk pardoning the wrong person."

"Good point." I frown at the two women. "I could keep one of you stunned to guarantee the good behavior of the other."

The two scoff at this, in almost identical fashion, then turn on each other. "You wouldn't—"

"You would leave me to rot?"

"You would do the same to me."

I lift a hand. "Obviously, neither of you would risk yourself for the other, so you're useless as collateral. I have to either trust you or keep you contained." My personal inclination is to stun them both for the duration, but our plan is flimsy. Get into Xinjianestan—easy enough—then break out in some undefined manner. These two could be the key to making that second part work. And my gut tells me they're on the level—to a point. "Right. I will trust you—to a degree."

Ji lifts her hands and pulls them apart. "That's good. Otherwise, I would have had to remove you from the equation."

I snap my jaw shut, determined to not show how surprised I am by her ability to extricate herself from the slip tie. I could do it of course, but I shouldn't underestimate my adversary. She has survived for decades under an extremely volatile and hostile government. I nod once and extend a fist. "You can call me Linds."

Ji gravely bumps her knuckles against mine. I offer her a hand and pull her to her feet. She pops up easily, belying her ancient appearance. Leweians don't provide rejuv treatments to anyone below the ruling class. I can't let Ji's wrinkled face put me off guard. She'll be a strong ally and potentially a dangerous foe.

Ji snaps her fingers at Zharo, then holds out a hand to me. "May I borrow your knife?"

I return her own. "You can use this one. But you obviously don't need it."

She smirks. "It's easier on my old hands." She flips the blade open and cuts the slip tie from Zharo's wrists. Then she offers the knife to me.

"Keep it. If we're going to work together, I want you to be adequately armed. Which reminds me..." I pull out the other weapons I removed from her earlier—a stunner, another knife, and a mini blaster. "Where'd you get that one? They aren't usually issued to supply chiefs, are they?"

She hefts the tiny but deadly gun in her palm. "This is a family heirloom. I'm very happy to have it back." She turns to Zharo. "You know where the rest are?"

The younger woman nods jerkily and heads into the warren of shelves. Ji turns back to me. "We have been preparing for this for a while. Let me explain the plan."

TWO DAYS LATER, we arrive at Xinjianestan. The planet orbits the weak star Saffron at a distance that renders it cold and gloomy year-round. A small station orbits the planet, but it's completely automated. Ji, Zharo, and I listen in as the ship's comm officer announces our arrival.

Zharo fiddles with the controls, turning down the volume on the long-winded announcement. "It's a required formality—follows a script. The video is stored in the database as 'proof' of arrival. I'm not sure anyone ever looks at it again."

"They're scanning for potential duress signals," Ji says. "The system is measuring his vital signs and comparing his speech against a previous recording to make sure he's not being coerced. It's a prison—they don't want to let in any terrorists or subversives." She cackles.

"Makes sense." I check my suit's diagnostics again. "How much time do we have?"

"This first announcement indicates we've achieved hailing distance. It will take a couple of hours to reach our parking orbit, then the shuttles will descend. How long can you stay outside?" Ji taps a finger against my helmet, still tucked under my arm.

"We've been over this so many times!" Zharo throws her hands up and stomps across the compartment. "Let's get on with it."

Ji narrows her eyes in a glare so cold Zharo stumbles to a halt and cowers. The older woman points at the officer. "You have nothing to complain of. Linds and I have been trapped inside this compartment for two days while you have had the run of the ship."

Zharo mutters something incomprehensible. Her juvenile behavior has become increasingly difficult to endure, and I'm stunned she's survived in the military this long. Of course, as the pampered daughter of high-ranking officials, she probably had it easy until they fell from power. We've encouraged her to continue her usual activities during the voyage, so she doesn't bring unwanted scrutiny to Ji.

I didn't tell either of them I assigned a surveillance drone to monitor her, but Ji was not surprised to find me watching the young officer.

I pull my helmet over my head and secure it with a twist and snap. Ji double checks the connections physically while I run yet another scan with my holo-ring. Then I swipe through the cams on the corridors between here and the shuttle dock. I shouldn't encounter anyone on the short trip.

Ji checks my drones and gives me an awkward thumbs up. I suppress a grin and return the gesture, then exit the compartment. Walking swiftly, I reach the shuttle bay without encountering any other crew members. I connect my holo-ring to the access panel and use one of Arun's apps to prevent it from reporting my exit to the bridge. Holding my breath, I open the hatch and cycle out of the ship. I turn on the clumsy comm system we patched into my system that allows me to speak with Ji on an antiquated receiver. "I'm out."

"All green—your egress was not detected." Zharo's clipped voice comes through loud and clear. When occupied, she has excellent focus. I don't envy Ji's job of keeping her on task. "I'll inform you when the crew escorts the prisoners to the shuttle."

"Affirmative. Linds out." I switch off my PVD—no point in using power. If anyone discovers me out here, pretending to be Zharo won't do me any good. Trusting my suit's stealth mode to hide me from the *Houjian's* cams, I make my way to the larger shuttle. The landing bay is outside the ship's artificial gravity, so a quick push of my feet sends me to the top of the little transport. I grab a convenient handle on the way by and adjust my direction.

At the top of the ship, I snap a hook-latch around an antenna support, so I don't float away, and erect the small camouflaged shelter Ji printed. It's barely big enough for me to crawl into—like a tiny tent attached to the top of the ship. It's supposed to protect me as we enter the atmosphere. The shuttle's external shields should be enough, but when we're talking about burning up on reentry, a little extra protection seems like a good idea. I shimmy inside, set my alerts to audio, and close my eyes for a short nap.

A single buzz brings me back to reality, followed by Ji's voice in my ear. "The kaptan is escorting the prisoners himself. Four soldiers as security detail, plus the copilot. Cadet Andreeva Rosalia is with them."

"Is she the one who was in the brig?" I tighten my straps to ensure I'm tight against the hull. "What was she in for?"

"For being female." Zharo's angry tone comes through clearly. "She dared to contradict a male cadet's assessment—correctly, I might add —and was punished for inappropriate behavior."

"Are all Leweian officers this sexist, or is Liu a special case?"

"They are all pigs."

I recall Kaptan Liu pushing Zharo away from the comm system.

"There is a strong bias toward male officers," Ji says. "Enlisted women are tolerated. One reason I never tried for a commission. Besides, supply officers get stuck dirtside, and I wanted to be out in the black."

I snort. Ji had wanted to come with me on the outside, but I convinced her we needed her expertise inside. "Are you en route?"

"Affirmative. Zharo, you're up." Ji told the kaptan she'd accompany him to the surface. He had argued, but her status apparently made him unwilling to refuse. Likewise, her obscure political connections ensured he didn't question her reasons for joining the party.

One of my drone cams follows Ji as she exits supply and joins the small team assembling outside the shuttle bay. The kaptan, a pilot, and four uniformed men surround the small group of prisoners: Zwani, Jones, and a young woman who must be Andreeva. All three bear bruises on every centimeter of exposed flesh. Their clothing is tattered and dirty, their hair matted. Liu doesn't treat prisoners well, but since he's transporting them to the most notorious prison in the galaxy, that's no surprise.

The team moves across the shuttle bay and into the transport. Beneath my body, the ship shakes with their footsteps as they enter the vehicle. My drone follows them inside, revealing a cramped space with a dozen hard chairs. Everyone straps in, the kaptan taking the left seat, leaving the co-pilot's chair for the other officer. The airlock retracts, and the shuttle comes away from the deck with a tiny jerk.

I take a deep breath and grip my restraining straps tightly, closing my eyes. If I'm going to burn up during reentry, I don't want to see it. I try to drop into a meditative state, but the vibrations from the shuttle's engines rumble through my body, disrupting my concentration.

External warmth radiates from the makeshift shelter covering me. I open my eyes to see the bright orange glare coming through the protective sheeting. Ji warned me I'd get warm up here but promised I'd stay alive—if everything went right.

The twenty-minute descent feels like hours. My suit works overtime trying to keep me cool, but by the time we land, I feel like a fish poached in foil. But I'm alive.

Now for the fun part.

CHAPTER THIRTY-TWO

WHEN THE SHUTTLE TOUCHES DOWN. I hastily shimmy out of my ragged shelter and collapse the fabric against the ship's hull. We've landed in a small courtyard formed by a long stone wall and a low building. The vehicle vibrates beneath me as the hatch opens. Rough, empty land stretches away for kilometers in every direction. Far to the west, a low mountain range sticks up like broken teeth, but the flat shale disappears over the horizon on the north and south. As I watch, a blue force shield extends from the top of the wall, enclosing the shuttle in a shimmering dome.

Kaptan Liu strolls down the short ramp, then turns back toward the ship and waits. I lie still—if he looks up, he might notice me, but he's focused on the open shuttle hatch. Ji wanders up beside him, looking around like a tourist at a new destination. She speaks, pointing toward the south, but he ignores her and turns to face the building.

The four soldiers and their cowed prisoners stumble down the ramp, following Liu toward the featureless wall. As they approach, a portion slides away, leaving a three-meter-wide opening. The soldiers march stiffly behind the kaptan, pushing their prisoners between them, with Ji ambling along in their wake.

Once the gate closes, I use my grav belt to drop to the ground beside the shuttle. This is the riskiest part. If my suit's camouflage malfunctions—or is overridden by the installation's surveillance—I'll be clearly visible. Holding my breath, I hurry up the ramp and into the cramped ship.

The co-pilot lazes in his seat, feet up on the console, chair tilted back, eyes closed. Silently, I zip over the seats and hit him with a stunner before he knows I'm there. He collapses and slides off the chair into a heap on the floor.

I drag him away from the chair, taking a moment to secure his arms and legs, then deposit him beside the still-open shuttle door. Then I settle into the copilot's seat. Zharo assured us her parents are both skilled pilots, but I've learned to leave nothing to chance. I might not have my credentials yet—and might be substandard by Arun's criteria—but I can get us off this rock if necessary.

Except I can't get the ship to turn on. Growling, I stalk across the shuttle and wrench the pilot's bulky wrist device from his arm. Ji said it might be necessary to fly the ship, and it appears she is right. I snap it around my wrist and tap the screen.

Then have to pry the pilot's eyelid open to respond to the request for a retina scan.

Once the device activates, I use my holo-ring's translator to decipher the screens. A few taps and pushes find the shuttle's connections, and I get into the system. I won't start the engines until Ji calls, but I want to make sure I've got everything figured out.

My oc-cam allows me to run my holo-ring's translation software directly on the script as I look at it. The system translates it, then displays it on my holo in Standard. I've heard the CCIA research lab is working on a direct connect to the ocular nerves, but while I have no problem using an audio implant, the idea of beaming visual data directly to my brain is not something I'm keen to test any time soon.

I work through the shuttle's startup checklist, taking us to a depressed idle. If it works like the Commonwealth counterpart, this should allow us to launch within thirty to forty seconds, but based on my experience with Leweian tech, I mentally double that estimate.

Taking a deep breath, I turn my seat to face the open hatch. I've done my part—now it's Ji's turn.

My surveillance drone pings softly, indicating someone approaching the shuttle. I jump up to crouch behind the seat, pulling my stunner out.

Ji stomps up the ramp, hands raised. "Just me."

I flip on my PVD and rise from behind the chair, stunner still out. "What's going on?"

"We might have a problem. The package is not here." Ji looks uncharacteristically flustered.

"What do you mean, 'not here'? Where are they?"

"Intel on this facility is almost non-existent. Apparently, this fortress isn't the prison." She turns to wave out the open airlock. "The planet is the prison. The fortress is where the 'guards' live. Their primary responsibility is security for shuttles dropping new prisoners. Otherwise, they leave the inmates to their own devices."

"Like Botany Bay?"

"I don't recognize that reference."

I wave a vague hand. "I don't know much about it, either. But apparently on Ancient Earth, they made a whole island into a prison—they dumped people there to survive. Or not. But I'm pretty sure it was more hospitable than this place." I glance out the forward screen to the barren landscape.

"There is arable land beyond the mountain range." Ji crosses her arms. "Prisoners are given food and water for three days and told to walk."

"Why bother?" I stare at her in disgust. "Why not just kill them? It would save a lot of agony. Not to mention transport costs."

She snorts a laugh. "True. And sometimes they do. But the government can hardly claim to be benevolent if they're shooting everyone who causes problems. Xinjianestan is known as a reeducation center."

"No one believes that." I frown at her. "How did you not know about the internal workings of this place? Surely former guards talk."

She shrugs. "I think they pay a substantial non-disclosure fee to retired guards. And the threat of being returned here—for a long tour, as they say—probably keeps them quiet. But I'm surprised there have been no rumors. Maybe this is a new system. Either way, we're going to have to go find Zharo's parents. And complete my mission."

"*Your* mission? You didn't mention anything except rescuing Ternin and Vedalia. What are you planning?"

She lifts her nose. "That's none of your concern. Our best bet will be to take out the garrison, then broadcast a message to the survivors."

I point at her. "You want to take over the entire garrison? How many people are we talking about?

"Chief Ji!"

She looks over her shoulder and stiffens. "You need to hide. And take him with you." She points at the pilot lying beside the hatch. "I'll try to stall this guy."

I flick on my drone cam still hovering outside the shuttle. A uniformed junior officer marches across the space between the shuttle and the wall. Ji strolls down the ramp, stopping him before he reaches the ship. They talk for a few minutes, then she turns toward the garrison. When the officer continues toward the shuttle, she swings around and speaks sharply to him. He waves her off, coming closer to the ship.

"Show time." I hurry to the side of the open hatch and watch him approach in my drone feed. He strides up the ramp and nearly trips over the prone pilot. He stops, does a double take, then looks up. I hit him with my stunner. "That's two."

Ji stops at the bottom of the ramp. "Is that your plan? We pick them off one-by-one?"

"I didn't have a plan for taking down the whole prison! I was going to rescue a few people. And a dog. Not the entire planet!"

"I guess we'd better start improvising." Ji pulls the mini blaster from her pocket and a larger weapon from the leg of her coverall.

CHAPTER THIRTY-THREE

Ji holds my arm, dragging me across the dusty slate toward the opening in the stone wall. She's hidden her weapons again, hoping to get as close to the enemy as possible before they realize what we're doing. We pass through the building to an internal courtyard. I kick up as much dust as I can, struggling against her grip, but the walled yard remains empty.

"I guess they aren't worried about anyone showing up unannounced." Ji glares at the building in disgust. "They trust their systems implicitly. Fools."

"Our lucky day."

We approach a door, and a young soldier smacks right into Ji. She shoves him away with her free hand. "What are you doing, you clumsy idiot?" Her speech is peppered with words my translator refuses to acknowledge, much less convert to Standard.

The kid stares at her, his mouth hanging open, then he snaps to attention. "Sir, yes, sir!"

"Don't call me sir! I work for a living!" Ji steps forward and pushes him again. "Call out the garrison. I have a gift for your commander."

The boy gives me a wild-eyed look, then bolts for the door.

"I still think stealth would have been a better option." I pull my arm free from Ji's tight grip and rub it where her nails bit into my flesh, grateful for the thick pressure suit.

"Perhaps. I detest sneaking around." She wraps her bony fingers around my bicep again and drags me a few meters farther into the courtyard.

"If we don't get them all at once, this will turn into a firefight. And this place is made to repel prisoners, so I don't like our chances of breaking in if they close the door."

"My plan will work. You might have noticed that boy recognized me."

"Why is that, exactly? The supply chief on a small cruiser posted to the most detested station in the system doesn't seem like the kind of person who'd collect a following."

She snorts. "Hardly. But the former mistress of two different premiers might have a bit of notoriety." She wrinkles her nose in thought. "And my Our Space page probably doesn't hurt. I have two point three million followers."

I choke. "You have a social media presence?" I try to imagine what a supply chief might post and come up blank.

"It's frowned upon—and therefore ignored—by the naval ministry."

"Why haven't they thrown you in here?" I gesture at the still empty courtyard and the building.

A tiny smirk crosses her lips. "I am rumored to have a vast trove of information... and a deadman switch to disseminate it if anything happens to me."

"You're blackmailing the entire ministry of the navy?"

"No, only the important people." She jerks her head toward the door. "Here they come. Look dejected."

"As if," I mutter, but I force my shoulders to slump.

Kaptan Liu exits the building accompanied by a rotund man with a similar uniform and an additional gold slash on his collar—the garrison commander. Behind them, twenty men in plain black garrison overalls march in lockstep, turning crisply and halting in a tidy four-by-five formation. I don't see the *Houjian* guards who came with us. The two officers stomp across the slate as if trying to break it with their steps.

"Chief Ji." The garrison commander stops a few centimeters out of arm's reach. "To what do I owe this honor? What have you brought me?" He glares at me with disdain, then his eyes widen as he takes in my unmarked, top-of-the-line suit and helmet.

"I didn't bring you anything. I saved you from the top ranked agent in the CCIA."

I try to pull away, but she grips my arm tighter. Our plan had been to start firing as soon as they assembled. What is she doing?

"Saved me? Are you telling me she infiltrated the most secure prison in Leweian history?" He draws himself up, trying and failing to suck in his beer belly.

"She's here and she was free. Now she isn't." Ji's other hand comes up, pointing her massive gun at my helmet.

An icy spike of fear rams through my core, and I stare at her in disbelief. She's double crossing me! How did I let myself get taken in by this woman? Usually my instincts are dead on, but she's an enemy combatant, and I believed her when she said she'd commit treason. How could I have fallen for her story? I shake my head in disgust. Anyone this stupid *deserves* to end up in Xinjianestan.

The garrison commander takes my other arm and pulls me from Ji's grip. He turns to face his men and starts yammering on about the might of the Leweian people and the inability of the Commonwealth to stand against them. I let the words flow over me as I contemplate my future.

Although it looks bleak, I have no intention of spending the rest of my life in the most notorious prison in the galaxy. I have the skills and perseverance to escape. Plus, I'm confident Arun and Elodie will extract me. They know exactly where I am. But I'll never live down the embarrassment. The great Vanti taken in by an old Leweian woman.

The bloviating commander flings me forward. I let the momentum take me away from him and slide on my knees across the dirty stone, pulling my nearly forgotten stunner from the secret pocket of my pressure suit. I might have been stupid to trust Ji, but she didn't think to search me.

As I yank the tiny gun free, blasts ring out, echoing against the featureless stone walls. Thick red beams sizzle over my head, taking down most of the first row of soldiers. Behind me, something thuds to the ground and the commander's head rolls past, bouncing a little. Ji cackles madly and the blaster fires again and again.

Time to jump into the fray—figuratively. I'm staying low because of the crazy crone with the laser blaster behind me. I stun the few soldiers she missed before she can swing back and cut down the rest. It's over in seconds. Swallowing my trepidation, I turn slowly, still crouched in the dust between Ji and the field of dead. "Thanks?"

She laughs again, sounding like the knell of death. "You thought I double crossed you, didn't you?"

"It certainly crossed my mind." I rise slowly, keeping my weapon out and my eyes on Ji. I hate to turn my back on the enemy before ascertaining they're all dead, but I'm more concerned with the supply chief's intentions. "That was… unsettling."

She jerks her chin at the smoking remains of the garrison. "You have no taste for death?"

"If I did, you wouldn't be here," I remind her.

She gives me a once-over, then drops the muzzle of her huge gun toward the dirt. "Fair point. Let's make sure there aren't any stragglers." She strides to the four men I stunned and fires once into each prone body.

"You didn't have to do that. We'll be long gone before they would have come around."

"Keeping captives is hard work." She tilts the gun up and rests it against her shoulder. "Besides, it was an act of mercy. They wouldn't want to be taken alive by their former prisoners. Who will be coming over that ridge soon. Another reason to get moving." Nodding at the mountain peaks barely visible beyond the wall, she pats the stock of her gun, then heads inside.

We find Zwani, Jones, and Andreeva in a set of glass-walled cells inside the blocky building. The four soldiers from the *Houjian* snap to attention, and the senior salutes Ji. She returns the gesture and sends them to clear the building. I follow along—I don't trust anyone to do the job as thoroughly as I would. Amazingly, the entire compliment of the garrison turned out for Ji's "gift." Much as I hate to admit it, her strategy worked. Crazy risky, but efficient.

"There's no one else." I return to the main room where Ji stares in at the prisoners. "You gonna let them out?"

She points at Zwani. "Let her out. Those two can stay."

I grimace as I open the door to Zwani's cell. "Jones I get, but the cadet?"

Zwani stumbles out of her cell. "What's going on?"

"Call me Linds," I whisper. "I don't need the old lady to know who I am."

Zwani's brow creases as she looks from me to Ji and back. "What happened? Everyone left, and we heard shooting!"

With a flourish, I indicate Ji. "She cleaned house."

Zwani's gaze returns to Ji, and her eyes widen with recognition. "Is that—that's the Shade of Lewei."

The name tickles the back of my brain like a feather. I've heard it before, but I'm not sure where. "Chief Ji, of the *Houjian*. She was planning her own liberation run, so we combined forces."

Zwani leans close. "You can't trust her."

I snort and give a tiny nod. "Noted. But we got the job done." I turn to Ji. "This is Zwanilda Serevdoba. We came to get her family."

Jones and Andreeva watch us, clearly poised to escape. When Ji and her entourage head for the inner offices, they start pounding on their cell walls. The muffled thuds and shouts barely reach our ears. I hurry to catch up to Ji. "Jones is a cretin, but why are you leaving Andreeva in there?"

Ji looks back at the girl. "Do you know who her parents are?"

"No. And I don't care. I don't usually judge people's worth by their family members. We've all got at least one relative we wouldn't want to be stranded on a desert island with. Or a desert prison planet."

"Don't worry—I have plans for her." She turns and sweeps out of the room like royalty. With that graceful movement, the stories of her dalliances with two different premiers make perfect sense.

"I agree with Ji on that one." Zwani hurries to catch up with me. "That girl is poison."

"Good enough for me." I raise my voice. "Ji! Where are you going?"

The old woman slaps a hand on a heavy metal console with a greenish window in the front above a flat surface covered in small buttons. I recognize it as one of the ancient computer systems they use in this part of the galaxy. "There's data to be mined." Ji plugs a small square into the machine and taps a key. The screen lights.

I tilt my head. "I thought you had prisoners to liberate."

"I said I had a mission." She pats the console. "I'm trusting you to find Zharo's parents. Either way, I'm not passing up an opportunity to mine more dirt."

"Huh. I guess that's how you stay out of trouble in Lewei?"

She smiles, her eyes glinting. "Exactly. Go get your friends. I'll be a while. Oh, and don't try leaving the atmosphere. You won't make it."

CHAPTER THIRTY-FOUR

As Zwani and I head out into the courtyard, I send a pulse message to Arun on his encrypted comm system. There's a small risk the *Houjian* will intercept it, but without their kaptan, they're unlikely to take any risks. They'll undoubtedly report it to Luna Dark, but by the time another ship arrives, we'll be long gone. I hope.

I stop beside the shuttle. "Ji's done something to this ship—she says we can't leave the atmosphere."

"Do you believe her?"

I shrug. "Doesn't matter. I promised to bring Zharo's parents back here, and I'm not going to renege on that. But how are we going to find your family? Coppelia's Ncuff signal showed her here, but they take them away from prisoners. We found a pile of them inside."

Zwani pats the ship. "We'll fly out over the mountains and send a signal."

"If you could signal them, why didn't you tell me? We could have done it before we dropped and had them waiting."

She shakes her head. "For one thing, we didn't know they have the run of the planet. And for another, the signal isn't—" She waves her hands in the air.

"Isn't what?"

"Not a radio signal. I need some paint." She looks around, as if she'll spot an open can and brush lying in the dirt.

"Okay." I head back inside. Ji, still cackling randomly, sits at the computer console poking buttons with her index fingers. "Ji, where would I find paint?"

"Probably in the shed out back." She points without raising her gaze from the screen. "This is so good!"

"Right." I head down the hall she indicated past a training room and a small barracks. Stairs on the right lead to the commander's suite —a tiny two-room apartment I checked before. At the end of the hall, I exit the building and to another dusty courtyard. High walls enclose a small space that looks—and smells—like it might be used for smoking the pungent tobacco popular in Lewei. A rough shed in the corner is locked from the outside.

Using my plasma knife, I cut the lock and pull open the door, stunner ready. I wouldn't put it past these Leweians to hold prisoners here for extra special punishment, but the small building holds only typical maintenance supplies. Toolboxes, rakes and shovels, and a few cannisters of paint. I grab one splashed with red and another with black.

When I return to the courtyard, Zwani grabs the red paint and crawls under the shuttle.

"What are you doing?" I crouch to peer underneath.

She lays on her back and gestures at the belly of the shuttle. "Painting my signal." Frowning in concentration, she grabs the flexible nozzle of the paint canister and points it at the ship. A thin stream of red shoots from the end of the hose which she wields with a flourish. "We're going to fly low over the main camps. Coppelia will recognize this symbol—crap!" A splotch of red paint drips down the side of her face.

Smothering a snicker, I rise. "I'll leave you to your art."

By the time Zwani declares her masterpiece done, Ji has moved on to looting the dead. I'd bet she's already gone through the barracks and the commander's apartment. Fighting off a shudder of revulsion, I approach the old woman. "You done inside?"

She looks up from her work as I draw close. "Don't be silly. It will take hours to download all that data. But I don't need to be here. It'll run on its own." She rises with a groan. "You can't have that shuttle."

I grimace, unsurprised. "I don't want to keep it. Can *you* fly it?"

A shadow of doubt crosses her features for the first time, then disappears. "No. Never bothered learning. The auto return should take me back to the *Houjian*."

"I thought it can't leave the atmosphere?"

She sniffs. "Not right now. I know how to turn that off."

"So you can fly it if you can figure out how to make it work. That will take time too. Maybe you'll find a flight manual in all that data you're liberating." I casually slide my hand into my pocket and close it around the smooth, comforting stock of my stunner.

Ji's eyes drop to my pocket and the corner of her lips twitches up. "Don't worry, I won't leave you stranded. I told you—prisoners are of no use to me. What's your plan?"

I explain Zwani's intention, and Ji nods. "Better than nothing. The garrison tracks movements of prisoners, though, so I can give you a general direction and distance."

"Thanks." I take a small step back as she rises. "What do you want in return?"

The old woman throws back her head and laughs. "I like you, Linds! Smart woman. Once you've found your friends—and Zharo's parents—you're going to get me back to the *Houjian*. Now that Liu is gone, Zharo and I will liberate the ship."

I frown at her. "You're defecting?"

She laughs again. "With an armed ship and the information I've acquired, I have no reason to defect. I'm launching a coup."

Aretha is going to kill me. I was assigned a covert operation—check out the *Fairwell* and find out why it's here. Helping to overthrow the government was not part of the plan.

I take another step back, and Ji smirks. "Don't worry, I'm not dragging you into this. You have been a useful tool but are not part of my master plan. Although, if you're interested, we might come to an arrangement after I take power. I'll need to establish communications with the Commonwealth, and having a respected CCIA agent on my side could help."

"No offense, but I'm not 'on your side.' We are not partners or collaborators or accomplices—not outside this one small mission. Our ways part here." I cross my arms.

"Relax. I'm not trying to turn you. But I might give you a call later." She lifts her fist with the thumb extended toward her ear and her pinky near her lips. "Keep an open mind." She dusts her hands together and turns to survey the carnage in the courtyard. "Remind me to have someone clean this up."

"Again, not your employee." I poke my thumb at my chest.

"Not you." She rolls her eyes and taps the earpiece she must have *liberated* from one of the soldiers. "I'm making notes for my new assistant."

"Zharo?"

"No. She's useless. Andreeva, in the lockup. I got more dirt on her, and she's going to be very useful to me." She strolls away, still laughing.

ZWANI AND I fly the shuttle across the barren landscape. Despite Arun's lack of confidence in my skills, I am a credible pilot—better than Zwani, at least. She nearly crashed on takeoff, which is an impressive feat given the automatic safety protocols on this boat. I set the altitude to a safe distance above the ground and lean back in my seat.

The pilot and the young lieutenant I stunned earlier are tied up in the passenger area, still incapacitated. Given Ji's treatment of the kaptan, his security detail, and the garrison personnel, I declined to remind her of their existence. I don't need any more blood on my hands, and they might become useful.

We skim above the desolate plain, then pop up when we reach the mountains. Winds buffet us near the tops of the low peaks, but the autopilot compensates well. This ship really is easy to fly.

A klaxon rings out and the ship jinks hard to the left.

"Is someone firing at us?" I scrabble at the antiquated interface, finally pulling up the external cams. A puff of smoke rises in our wake. "That's a projectile weapon." I increase the magnification. "From a trebuchet!"

Zwani's face goes pale. "The prisoners are trying to eliminate the guards!"

"Probably. I'm surprised, though. That stuff you painted on the underside should make it obvious we aren't from the garrison."

"They probably don't care. We obviously came from there—"

Another alert blares and the ship jerks aside.

I slap the auto pilot and increase our altitude by a thousand meters. As we watch, two more huge fireballs rise and fall short. "It's a good thing Ji gave us these prisoner tag codes." Lights blink on the navigation screen, two red and four green.

Zwani taps one of the green lights. "Twenty minutes. We can stay out of range until we get there."

I nod and tap my fingers against the arms of my chair. "Have you thought about how you're going to get the *Fairwell* running again?"

She gives me a sly look. "It's already running."

"It was dead in the water." I glare at her through narrowed eyes. "How did you fix it? Why is everyone lying to me?"

"Engineering is my secondary—and more traditionally useful—specialty. I couldn't tell you we'd fixed it until we got Coppelia and the rest of the family back. For you, this mission was about the ship. For me, it's always been about rescuing my family. If we could have flown out of here two days after landing on the *Fairwell,* you would have insisted on it."

I wrinkle my nose. "Maybe. But if you'd trusted me—told me about your family—"

"You might have left me and Vlad on the ship to do it ourselves, but you wouldn't have helped."

"You don't know me well enough to draw that conclusion. I have a heart. And a lot of leeway when it comes to scope. If you'd been up front and simply asked..."

Zwani heaves out a sigh. "I couldn't risk it. But now that we're here —thank you."

I flick a hand at the forward screen. "We aren't done yet."

We ride in silence for a while. No more fireballs hurtle toward us, so I drop our altitude as we approach the first location. Lush green landscape stretches as far as the eye can see. A body of water appears on the horizon, and the ground below changes from forest to plowed fields. I spot a trebuchet with people scurrying around it, but we're still too high, and they don't bother firing.

"I wonder why the garrison is on that nasty barren plain when all of this is here." I wave a hand at the beautiful valley below us.

Zwani shrugs. "Maybe they don't know it's nicer here?"

"Surely they would have surveyed the whole planet before building a base."

Someone clears their throat, and I spin, heart pounding. I'd almost forgotten the pilot and leftenant were back there. The pilot is still out, but the officer stares at us over the tape stuck to his face.

I rise and go to the back, carefully staying out of range. "You have something important to say?"

His head wiggles side to side, as if he's not sure how important we think it will be. I stretch out my arm and pull the tape from his mouth with a ripping sound that makes me wince.

Internally, of course. I never show my emotions on my face.

He whimpers and tears form in his eyes, but he blinks them away. Drawing in a deep breath, he licks his painfully red lips. "It all used to look like this."

"The whole place was green and lush? What happened?" I lean against the bulkhead.

"Originally, this was a colony—they tried to break away from Lewei. Government quashed them. That area where the garrison is—that whole plain was denuded in the war. The fortress was already there, so the government used it as a base. Eventually, the colonists all went into hiding. Then Lewei started sending prisoners here."

"So, these prisoners we're rescuing—they're living with colonists who've been on this planet for generations?"

"Maybe." The guy shrugs. "Or maybe the prisoners killed off the locals decades ago. We don't come over here—ain't safe."

"This keeps getting weirder and weirder." I turn to Zwani. "How are we going to know if it's safe to land?"

She shifts uncomfortably in her seat. "We won't. Unless they figure out a way to communicate with us."

The klaxon blares again, and the ship jinks. But this time, it doesn't stop. I lunge forward, slamming into the seat backs and bulkhead as I stagger against the ship's unpredictable lurches. I finally reach my seat and drop into it, smacking the controls. "What is happening?" Squinting out the forward screen doesn't help—we're jerking around so much I can't focus on anything. A bright light flashes, dazzling my eyes. Then the ship shoots into the sky.

CHAPTER THIRTY-FIVE

We stop as quickly as we started, halting with a spine-wrenching snap. "Status!" I cry.

"Ouch." Zwani rubs her neck and squints at the controls. "I guess we're nominal?"

I peer at my side of the dash but don't see any flashing red lights. "Huh. We need expert help." I push out of my seat and head to the back again.

"What did you do?" the young leftenant whines.

"Shut up." I rip the tape from the pilot's mouth and plaster it over the officer's. It won't stick for long, but it gets the idea across. Then I kick the pilot's booted foot. "I know you're awake."

The pilot sighs and opens his eyes. "I was hoping you'd forget about me."

"Not likely. What was that?"

"I think someone messed with the ship's calibration sensors."

"Someone aboard? Is that a real-time thing, or can it be done in advance?" If I were prone to anxiety, that thought would send me into a spiral. I look at Zwani. Maybe she can fix it.

The pilot shakes his head. "Real time. On the ground. It's easy to do, if you know how."

"That seems like a stupid failing in a combat vehicle." I drop into the last seat in this row, leaving two between me and the two prisoners. If that happens again, I want to be seated.

"This isn't a combat vehicle. And not too many people know about the weakness. Plus, it was fixed in most of the fleet's ships." His lips press together in disgust.

"They didn't bother with the Luna Dark ships?" I arch a brow at him.

He scowls and shakes his head.

"So, how would one do this? Theoretically? Is it something random colonists would be able to put together?"

The pilot coughs. "Sure. If they know how. All it takes is a flux gravitic laser and a mirror."

I consider him for a long moment, then lean forward to look around him at the other guy. Without saying anything, I raise my brows. He nods in agreement.

With a sigh, I rise, then I move closer and pull the tape from the officer's mouth. "What are your names?"

"I'm Simuthenicalian." The young leftenant lifts his shoulders in a self-deprecating squirm. "Most folks call me Sim."

"Paolo." The pilot runs his tongue over his teeth as he gives me a once over. "You aren't from Lewei."

"Why? Because I don't carry a flux gravitic laser in my back pocket?"

He jerks his chin at me. "Because red hair is not common in Leweian people. And it's considered a curse, so most people dye it."

"Dye?" I finger a strand of my straight, coppery hair and frown. When did my PVD cut out? I flick my holo-ring to check. Power: zero. Great. I set it to recharge. "Maybe I am cursed. How do I evade the flux laser?"

"That's the genius of it—you can't. If they can get a line of sight on you, they can take you down. It takes some tight flying to keep them from getting a fix."

I wrinkle my nose as I consider Paolo. "Can *you* avoid it?"

"Maybe?" He sits back in his chair. "You'd trust me to fly?"

"Depends. Are you as terrified of Chief Ji as everyone else?"

His face goes white even as he straightens his spine and scoffs. "She's an old woman. How terrifying can she be?"

With a smirk, I cut the slip tie around his wrists. "Get up there. Zwani, let him have the left seat. I'll take right." We squeeze past Zwani and settle into the pilots' chairs. "Don't try to touch communications—I know how to open the airlock at altitude."

His returning color washes away again. "Yes, ma'am."

"I want you to land over here." I tap a point on the navigation screen that is at least an hour's walk from their current location. I can cover that distance easily with my grav belt in a fraction of that time.

"You want to land? Where those people are trying to take us down?" Paolo gulps.

"We're here to rescue at least part of them—they just don't know it yet. Get used to it—we've got another landing before we head back to the camp."

Paolo closes his eyes and sucks in a deep breath as if grounding himself, then leans forward to flip a few switches. The ship drops like a stone, turning a hundred and twenty degrees in a dizzying spiral. He takes us through a terrifying series of turns, jinks, swoops, and even a partial loop before landing in a clearing beyond a small copse of trees.

I jump up and motion at the co-pilot's chair. "Zwani. Come up here and watch him. I'll go get your family."

She takes the stunner I pass her and settles into my vacated seat. Lifting my helmet over my head, I mentally inventory my weapons as I head to the airlock.

"Hey, Vanti!"

I stop with my helmet halfway on.

"You think we should wait up there instead of down here?" She points up, then down.

"This boat got any defensive weapons?"

Paolo twists to look around the tall back of the pilot's chair. "Sure. It might not be a combat vehicle, but it's still a military ship. They're most effective at altitude."

I shrug. "Your decision, Zwani. I think you'll be fine. Whoever was jamming us is at least thirty minutes away. I should be back before they can reach you." I salute her with my index finger and close the airlock behind me.

The system cycles and I hit my accelerator. My grav belt propels me out the hatch and into the sky in a single, graceful arc, leveling out right above the treetops. Using the navigation system in my holo-ring, I take a direct path toward the blinking green lights.

Which are headed toward me at a faster clip than I expected. Their path is not straight, so they're likely running through the trees. I pull closer, then drop through the thick canopy to hover above the underbrush. The foliage blocks most of the sun's rays, making it difficult to see in the dim, green twilight. I pull my mini stunner from my pocket and set it to the lowest power. Momentary incapacitation, which should be more than enough for me to attack or escape.

I don't have to wait long. A pair of scruffy men crash through the underbrush, sweating and swearing. A big, shaggy dog lopes alongside, tongue lolling in a goofy canine smile. Loud breathing and unhappy cries in the distance indicate the others trailing behind. Making sure my PVD is operational, I swoop dramatically through the trees and stop a few meters from the two men who've stumbled to a halt. "Hey."

They both stare, mouths open, chests heaving. The chunkier one doubles over, hands on his knees, while the other points at me. "Who are you?"

"I'll ask the questions." I brandish my weapon. "Who are you?"

The thinner one props his fists on his hips and glares at me, silent.

"I'm Ricard," the older guy gasps between deep breaths. "And he's Hingan."

Hingan smacks Ricard's arm. "Don't tell her anything!"

"She came from the shuttle. The one with the family crest painted on it." He looks up, still doubled over and struggling to breathe. "You came from the shuttle, right? Who are you with?"

"You recognized Zwani's symbol?"

Ricard snaps upright, his face shocked. "Zwanilda came to get us?

Zwanilda Serevdoba?" His tone—surprised and kind of challenging—puts me on alert.

"How many Zwanildas do you know?" Flicking my holo-ring, I play the vid Zwani recorded. She appears in my palm, and I stretch the image larger so they can see it easily, then turn up the sound.

"Coppelia, Ricard, family, I've come to retrieve you. Yivan and Ris are safe on the *Fairwell*. This is Vanti. She will bring you back to the ship."

The younger man swings around to face the elder. "I told you! I can't believe Zwani—this is bad."

I drop a little closer. "What's the problem? Don't you want to be freed?"

Hingan spins to confront me. "Of course we want to be rescued. But at what cost? So we can be indebted to Zwanilda for the rest of our lives? This place ain't so bad. I could become a farmer and stay on here. There's that pretty little gal down at—"

"Your wife might not appreciate that." Ricard has recovered his breath and advances on Hingan. "Besides, you don't want to be trapped on this planet for the rest of your life. And the locals will never let you into their clan." He spits on the ground. "Why you'd want to ally yourself with those—"

"*Hey*!" The two men break off, turning to face me. Beyond them, the bushes rustle, and I catch glimpses of several more people lurking. Lifting a little farther out of range, I spread my arms. "Do you want to get off this rock or not? I don't care if you stay or go, but I'm leaving." Without turning my back on them, I start rising slowly toward the thick, leafy canopy. I point toward the shuttle. "That way. About five klicks. If you run, you can get there in half an hour or so. Or we can land closer. If you can guarantee our safety."

The two men exchange a look. "Safety?" Ricard asks.

"You hit us with a flux gravitic laser earlier. We evaded easily, of course—" No point in letting them think they can hurt us. "But you damaging our ship—even minor damage—is not something I'm prepared to allow."

"That wasn't us." Ricard glares at his companion. "That was Hingan's precious locals. Another reason to have no truck with them."

"They thought it was a ship from the garrison." The younger man straightens up to look down on the older man from his half centimeter advantage. "They were protecting themselves."

"Doesn't matter why," I say loudly, drowning Ricard's retort. "What matters is we don't want them doing it again. I guess you'll be walking. Or running would be better. If they're hostile, we need to get away before they att—"

A rock swishes by my head, deflected by the personal force shield integrated with my grav belt. I launch upward, dialing my defensive power to high and blasting through the trees over my head, leaving a smoking hole in the greenery.

CHAPTER THIRTY-SIX

Back at the ship, I land in the airlock and slap a hand against the hatch control. The second the external hatch indicator turns red, the ship lifts off like a rocket, straight up into the sky. I let my knees bend as the speed of the ship overcomes my grav belt's altitude limiter and my feet hit the deck. Turning off the belt, I stagger through the interior hatch and drop into a chair.

We hit a thousand meters and the ship shudders to a stop. Zwani spins her seat to face me. "Now what?"

"They're your family," I retort. "And they don't seem happy to see you."

"I told you there are some hard feelings. I wasn't trying to hide anything."

"When your family says they'd rather stay on Xinjianestan than go home with you, that's more than just hard feelings. That's serious conflict." I push out of the chair and stalk to the front of the ship. "Your move."

"I can't believe you ran because they threw a rock at you!" Zwani sneers.

I cross my arms and lean against the back of Paolo's seat. "I'm smart enough to know impact to my brain caused by a dense object is detrimental to my wellbeing, regardless of what that object is made from. It had significant velocity and mass. I've already risked my life more than I intended on this trip. You need to fix this, or we leave them—and maybe you—here."

"Cut her out," Paolo says.

We both spin to look at him. "What?"

"The problem is these people think they'll owe you for the rescue, correct?" Paolo gestures at Zwani. When she nods, he goes on. "Tell them she is here as part of your team, but you are responsible for the rescue. That's the truth, right? You seem to be in charge." He raises his brow as if he's not sure.

I glare at him. "Yes, this is my mission. And if Zwani hadn't been with us, we still would have undertaken the rescue—we're doing it for Ris and Yivan, not her. But I'm not sure how to convince them."

Her mouth opens, then closes with a snap. She nods jerkily. "How about I do another vid? I can tell them they will not owe me anything. That the rescue is at the instigation of the CCIA and has nothing to do with me."

"You think that will work?"

She raises both hands. "I don't know. It's all I can think of."

"I hope Zharo's family isn't this much trouble." I peel away from the chair I've been leaning against and flick my fingers at Zwani. "Let's do it."

She records another vid, and we drop closer to the surface. I leave them hovering out of trebuchet range and zip closer to the blinking green dots on my nav screen. They seem to have stopped in a small clearing. I drop close to the green treetops, then skim forward lying horizontal. When I reach the clearing, I slow to a crawl and stop where I can hear but not be seen.

"She might not come back." Ricard's rough, deep voice is easy to identify. "You threw a rock at her, and we told her we didn't want to go. You might have cost us our rescue! Now you'll be stuck with us."

"We aren't stuck with anyone. We can shun you." The reply is higher and has a heavy Leweian drawl. "Fenniston will decide."

"You let a woman make all of the decisions? That's not very

Leweian of you." This voice is female, similar to Zwani's. Probably her half-sister Coppelia.

"We are not Leweians. Not anymore. We are Xinjianestani and we have our own rules."

A soft chorus of agreement answers her statement. Based on voices, there are eight people in the clearing—the two men I met earlier, the two women who followed them, and four more who must be locals. At least it should be easier to negotiate with them if their leader is not a Leweian man.

I clear my throat and ease forward a half meter to wave. "Hello."

The group below jump to their feet, some yelping in surprise. The dog launches into a volley of barking. Ricard hushes it. Two of the women dart back into the undergrowth.

"May I come down? I mean you no harm." I cringe internally at the cliché phrase, but they don't comment.

One of the two remaining women waves her upturned hand at the clearing. "If you are unarmed, you are welcome." She keeps her other hand behind her body, as if hiding a weapon.

"I'm never unarmed, but I have no reason to use my weapons against you." I raise both hands near my face to show they're empty. They have no way to know my ability to injure or kill is not dependent on any external equipment.

The woman points at a boulder in the center of the clearing. "Have a seat." She waits for me to settle my butt against the warm stone, then drops onto a log about five meters away. "I am Headwoman Penniston, chieftain of this province."

"I'm Va—Linds. I'm an operative from the Commonwealth, and I've come to... retrieve Coppelia and her people."

"You are welcome, Valinds. How did you get a naval shuttle?"

Ooh, coming right to the point. "It's a long story."

She makes a rolling motion with the rock clutched in her hand.

I hide a smirk at the crude weapon—I know for a fact how dangerous rocks can be, but my grav belt shield is still on. Keeping an eye on the others—no reason to let them sneak around behind me—I make a show of relaxing on the warm stone. The boulder is surprisingly comfortable. "I came from the Commonwealth to check on an abandoned ship in Leweian space. We found two children aboard and came to retrieve the rest of the family."

A short, round, dark-haired woman who must be Coppelia hurries past Fenniston and skids to a stop in front of me. "My children are safe?"

I nod. "Eating cookies and playing with the cats."

She frowns, confused.

"They're fine." I glance at Hingan. "But your… companions seem to be conflicted on the next move. Let me clarify the situation. I'm here to take you back to *Fairwell* and help you leave Leweian space. I have others to retrieve, so you have about five minutes to make a decision. Then I will leave, with or without you."

Coppelia draws breath, but before she can say anything, I turn and point at Fenniston. "And I'd appreciate if your friends would stop trying to shoot down my ship. We aren't with the Leweian Garrison. In fact, we've eliminated them. If you want to stay here on Xinjianestan, you can. If you want to leave, I can take you to the *Fairwell,* but you'll go to the Commonwealth. If you want to stay here… well, there seems to be a coup brewing. Are you familiar with Ji Shinwa?"

Fenniston gasps. "The Shade of Lewei?"

"How does everyone but me know that name?" I grump. "Yes, I suppose. She's planning on taking over the *Houjian,* and I have no doubt she'll move on to bigger and better things from there. You might want to check in with her before she leaves. I'm not saying you should throw in on her side, but—"

"Can you take me to her?" Fenniston leaps to her feet, the rock falling to the ground.

I pull back in surprise. "You want to meet with her?"

"Absolutely. Ji Shinwa is legendary. Legions of Leweians have been waiting for her to make a move. Now is the time for all good Leweians to come to the aid of their country!" Her voice rings out in challenge.

The others exchange wary glances, and Hingan cheers weakly.

"Great. I tell you what. I have to—" I point past her with both hands. "I've got more passengers to pick up. You folks head thatta way, and I'll make sure Ji knows you want to meet up before she heads upstairs."

They all break into arguments, but I hold up both hands. "My shuttle is not large. I have Coppelia and her family members, plus four of us already aboard. I need to pick up two more people, which puts us pretty close to full. So, you'll have to get there on your own."

Fenniston snaps her fingers, and one of the men behind her darts into the woods. A piercing whistle rings out, and something screams, like a cross between a cat and a bird of prey. A shiver runs down my spine, but I ignore it.

The man returns leading a—

I squint at the huge creature. "Is that a griffon?"

CHAPTER THIRTY-SEVEN

FENNISTON and her supporters mount the big beasts that up close look less like griffons and more like enormous pigeons. Their beady eyes—each the size of my fist—goggle at me as they hop from claw to scaly claw. The Xinjianestani slide their feet into stirrups, clench their knees around the birds' iridescent gray necks, and slap the creatures on the back. The startled birds launch into the air, nearly taking out the tops of the trees, then bumble across the sky exactly like the feathered rats they resemble.

I stare, mouth open, until one of the birds lets loose with a wet splat. Looking away with a shudder, I catch Coppelia's gaze. "What the heck?"

She nods solemnly. "They call them Magna Columbasteed. Weird, aren't they?"

"And they're useful for transportation?"

"The really well-trained ones are." She shrugs. "Faster than walking or riding a *kuda*. But they require years of training, so only the headwoman and her minions ride them. It'll take a few hours to get to the mountains, and they can't fly high enough to get over the pass. They'll have to hike from there."

I close my eyes for a second and take a deep breath. Rideable pigeons. What next? Rising, I point at the shuttle. "Are you coming?"

RETRIEVING Zharo's parents is much easier. We circle overhead and drop a stack of paper Ji printed from a file Zharo gave her. They include a picture of the younger Zharo and an encoded message. With the leaflets away, we rise beyond projectile range and wait. Soon, a trio of lanterns pierce the growing darkness—the signal Zharo told us to expect.

Paolo lands the ship outside the village, and we wait. As the last of the sun's rays disappear from the sky, a trio appears on horses—or *kuda,* as the locals call them. Two dismount and hand the reins to the third who turns and leaves without a word. The couple trudges toward us, stepping into the circle cast by the shuttle's external lights.

A quick facial recognition program confirms the couple's identity: Vedalia and Ternin. I shoot a blast of Arun's PVD disruptor just to be sure, but they pass. Using the ship's external speakers, I ask the three confirmation questions Zharo provided, and they answer appropriately.

"Open the hatch." I nod at Paolo, then move to the interior side of the airlock. When it opens, I wave our newcomers to seats in the front row. "Please, make yourselves comfortable. We'll be back at the garrison in a moment." I wait for them to strap in, then drop into a jump seat. "Hit it, Paolo."

The ride back to the garrison is quick and painless. As we swing over the prison, the glowing blue force shield opens like a clamshell. Paolo drops us into the enclosure with an ease I envy. As we drop, I catch sight of a glimmer of white hull beyond the building: the *Ostelah*.

Our shuttle settles to the dusty stone courtyard, and Paolo opens both hatches. Zharo's parents rush down the steep ramp, followed more slowly by Coppelia and her family. They've studiously ignored

Zwani throughout the flight, and only Ricard slows long enough to whisper "Thanks" as he exits.

"Glad to help," I say loudly.

The others cast furtive glares at me and mutter under their breath as they stomp down the ramp.

"What's their deal?"

Zwani lets out a breath. "Same old, same old. We don't get along. Despite your reassurances, they're afraid I will hold this over them forever. You know, typical family drama. Did you see the *Ostelah*?"

I nod.

"When we didn't hear from them, I was afraid something had happened."

I don't acknowledge that, but a constant trickle of fear I hadn't recognized dropped away when I spotted the ship. "Let's check in with Ji, then head home."

We follow the others into the garrison's main room. Ji has rearranged the room forming a kind of dais on one end. She sits atop it in a large recliner relocated from the commander's quarters. Arun, Elodie, and a blond man who might be Leo stand behind the dais, shifting uncomfortably. The four guards from the *Houjian* lurk on either side of the door, closing in behind us as we enter.

The trickle of fear returns.

Leaving Zwani to watch Sim and Paolo, I stride across the room as if I own it. When I reach the end of the little stage, Andreeva steps in front of me. "Empress Ji Shinwa requires your attendance."

I stop, falling back into a defensive stance. "Empress?"

From her seat—obviously a throne now that I know the context—Ji cackles. "What do you think, Vanti? I like the sound of it. Empress."

"I think—Vanti?" The trickle of fear becomes a rushing torrent. How does she know my name? I told her to call me Linds. I've worn the PVD most of the time, and she shouldn't have any way to recognize me anyway. I'm an agent. I struggle to keep my emotions off my face. Forcing a slight chuckle, I say, "I'm Linds, remember? They say memory is the first thing to go."

For a fraction of a second, the anger on her face sends my heart into high gear. This woman just mowed down a garrison of soldiers without a thought. I don't fear many things, but the Shade of Lewei causes an instinctive reaction I have to fight every time. And I've learned to trust my instincts. Her expression clears so quickly I almost think I imagined it.

Get a grip, Vanti.

"Please, dear, I've always known who you are. Lindsay "Vanti" Fioravanti. CCIA. I was expecting you. Why do you think I let you get the drop on me back on the *Houjian*?" Her pleasant tone doesn't completely hide the steel beneath.

I stare at her, speechless. After a long moment in which we size each other up, I find my voice. "You *let* me stun you?" I bark out a derisive laugh.

"Of course. Aretha told me you were coming."

My mind goes blank. I can't begin to comprehend what she said. My handler—my supervisor in the Colonial Commonwealth Intelligence Agency—told a Leweian naval chief and potential revolutionary that I was coming. She sent me to investigate a stranded Commonwealth ship but somehow knew I'd end up infiltrating a Leweian naval ship. None of this makes sense.

"Aretha always sends me the best." Ji smiles a self-satisfied smirk.

Aretha? That snaps me out of my stupor. "You've worked with Aretha before? Are you saying she's a double agent?"

Ji laughs long and loud. She doubles over in her chair, as if this is the funniest thing she's ever heard. Andreeva approaches with a glass of water, but Ji waves her off, still cackling. Finally, she wipes her eyes and straightens to look at me. Her gaze seems to burn into my brain. "Don't be ridiculous. Aretha is completely loyal to the Commonwealth. But occasionally our interests align, and we work together. She told me you were in the area and might be of use."

"She didn't tell me squat." I cross my arms and pull back my shoulders. "Which makes me highly suspicious of your claim."

Ji waves a negligent hand. "Doesn't make a bit of difference to me what you believe. You have been useful, and I thank you. Now, unless you want to participate further in my..." She trails off and gazes at the ceiling, a finger tapping her chin. "Let's call it my return in triumph. I would accept your assistance, of course, but don't require it." She snaps her fingers.

Andreeva abandons the glass of water on a side table, scurrying to her boss's side. "Yes, Empress?"

"Escort our friends to their ship." Ji turns back to me. "Tell Aretha I appreciate your help. Now I suggest you leave Leweian space. I can't guarantee your safety here."

I snort. "Like you guaranteed it before." I rub the back of my head, recalling the wild laser attack.

"You're still alive, aren't you? That's more than a lot of people can say." Her genial expression drains away like water in a desert. "This is your only opportunity to depart."

Arun, Elodie, and Leo stumble to a halt beside me. At least I have been assuming the blond man with terrified eyes is Leo, but there's something not quite right about his gait. Arun wears his most supercilious top-lev expression of disdain and bored amusement. The tightness around his eyes betrays his concern for our safety. Even Elodie is subdued.

The guards close in around us, herding Zwani and her family into our wake. Once we're assembled, Andreeva leads us across the compound to the *Ostelah*. Our escort stops at the outer hatch. Leo takes Coppelia and her family through the airlock while we wait outside for it to cycle. Since we're in atmosphere, Arun could pop both ends of the lock, but requiring us to cycle through allows him to maintain a degree of control.

It seems to take forever. Finally, the external hatch pops again and the rest of us tromp up the ramp and inside. Andreeva and her guards stand at the base of the ramp, watching until the hatch closes behind us.

Everyone starts to talk at once, but I raise a finger to cut them off. We wait as the airlock cycles, then stumble into the ship's corridor when the interior hatch opens where the blond is waiting.

I point at Arun. "Run a scan. We need to find their bugs." I follow him toward the bridge. "Everyone else—only talk about mundane things." I engage my internal audio and call Arun. "Where's Vlad?"

He smiles a little as he strides beside me. He jerks his chin at the blond man in front of us. "That's Vlad. Did you think it was Leo?"

I chuckle. "I'd kind of forgotten about Vlad. Leo's still on the *Fairwell*?"

"I wasn't going to risk him or the kids. I tried to get Elodie to stay with them, but she insisted I needed another pilot."

I lift my chin. "You certainly wouldn't want to be stuck with anyone substandard."

"Vanti—"

I swipe my hand to cut him off. "It's fine. She was right to insist."

He nods curtly as he places his palm on the panel beside the bridge door. The screen goes red, and he leans forward to present a retina scan and whisper a code phrase. "I don't know if they had time to break through all this security."

Arun and Elodie take the pilots' seats and Vlad grabs one of the jump seats. I wait until the hatch shuts behind us, then engage a jamming program. "Hard to say. Ji is obviously skilled in data extraction, but that doesn't mean she could break through your security. I have no idea what Andreeva's skill set includes. She's still a cadet, though, so probably not extremely proficient. Did you leave a cam?"

Arun throws a quick glare over his shoulder as he works through his checklist. "Who do you think you're dealing with? Vlad, check the feeds. See where they went."

"On it, boss." The blond man dissolves into Vlad's dark visage. He catches my glare and shrugs. "He was the boss while you were gone."

I lift both hands. "Fine with me. I prefer to work solo."

The system hums, then the engines spin up. Lights on the control surface flicker from red to green. We all strap in, and Arun uses the intercom to warn our passengers to do the same. The compound seems to swing away, then dwindles below us as the ship lifts off. We spin a few degrees, then blast into the sky, the pressure shoving us back into our seats with a comforting feeling of escape.

CHAPTER THIRTY-EIGHT

As we fly back to the *Fairwell,* Arun and I run every scan we can think of and a few he invents on the fly. We find dozens of bugs planted by Ji's team—so many that I begin to wonder how she acquired so many. They can't be printed quickly and are unlikely to have been in the prison's stores. Which means she brought them with her on the *Houjian*'s shuttle. She and Zharo must have hidden them on the shuttle while I was waiting on the outside. I spare an impressed thought for the old woman's efficiency and strategic planning.

The long trip back to the *Fairwell* takes forever. The *Ostelah* was built to carry up to eight passengers comfortably, plus two crew. With Zwani, Coppelia, and the others, plus Vlad, Elodie, Arun, and me, we're at capacity. Not to mention the dog, who, fortunately, is terrified of Apawllo and stays in the family's assigned cabin.

Still, the family is loud and mistrustful of Zwani's intentions. They barely speak to her and ostracize Vlad entirely, but that doesn't stop them from holding loud discussions *about* them at all hours of the day and night. Arun and I stay mainly on the bridge and in our cabins, joining Elodie in hers for meals. Vlad, who is camping in Leo's compartment, never appears.

We finally dock with the *Fairwell.* Yivan and Ris hurtle out of the hatch and throw themselves at their parents. Noelle strolls aboard the *Ostelah,* ignoring the dog who cowers in a corner, then slinks away into the ship.

When Leo appears in the FlexLock, Elodie cheers. "We've missed you!" She flings herself at the Leweian, closing her arms around him in a fierce hug.

He chokes back a little whimper. "Can we please go now?" His drawn face and ragged fingernails reveal he didn't find the wait relaxing.

"Let's get these folks back on their ship, then we're out." Arun turns to Zwani. "Are you staying with us or going with them?"

She looks at her sister. Coppelia, with an arm around each child, stares back, suspicion written across her face. Zwani's shoulders slump. "It's up to them. I'd like to spend a little time with my family. I'm not due back to work—" She glances at Vlad.

He smiles grimly. "We can stretch the mission as long as Vanti allows." They both turn to look at me.

I purse my lips as I stare at them. We deserve a little time off. "I won't report back to Aretha until we're home. That gives you four days. Then you'll get the customary post mission break. That's the best I can do."

Zwani raises her brows at her sister. "I really just want to spend time with you. And the kids."

"Isn't Aunt Zwani coming with us?" Ris asks. "She taught us how to play vuolo!"

"She did?" Coppelia's lips press together. "That's probably a good reason to say no."

"Please?" the kids whine in concert.

The smile she was fighting to hide breaks through. "Fine, Zwani can come with us. Without her, we'd still be on… that planet."

"You mean Xinjianestan?" Yivan pulls away from Coppelia's arm. "The prison? You'd still be incarcerated if it weren't for her and Vlad."

Vlad puffs out his chest. "Kid's right. That was a big deal, gettin' you outta there. You kinda—"

Zwani smacks the back of her hand into his stomach. "They owe us nothing. It was Vanti's mission and her skills that saved us." She glares at her step-brother.

Vlad nods slowly. "You're right. Without Vanti, we wouldn't have succeeded."

"I appreciate the praise, but we need to speed things up." I make a shooing motion. "You heard Ji. We are no longer welcome in Leweian space. You need to get that ship moving."

"Right." Zwani extends her fist to us. "Thank you for your help, Vanti. I can never repay you." She touches my knuckles, then moves on to Arun. "Or you. If there's ever anything I—" She glances at her sister.

Coppelia steps forward. "If there's anything *we* can do, you contact us. The Serevdoba family owes you a debt that will not be easily repaid."

Arun waves a hand. "It wasn't that big—"

"Thank you." I glare at Arun. "If we can ever use your help, we will contact you."

Coppelia nods again, then pivots toward the FlexLock. "Ricard, Hingan. Get Zwani and Vlad's things. They're with us." She stalks away, ignoring Vlad and Zwani's surprised exclamations.

The two men disappear for a few minutes, then reappear carrying Zwani and Vlad's packed bags. The entire family thanks us again, then they disappear down the FlexLock, and the hatch shuts behind them.

"Did that seem a bit... rehearsed?" Elodie asks.

"You mean how they had everything packed up and ready to go?" Leo heads up the corridor toward his cabin. "I need to make sure they didn't take anything of mine. By accident, I'm sure."

Elodie laughs and follows.

Arun swivels toward the bridge. "Time to fly."

By the time we get strapped in, the *Fairwell* has started easing away from us, making her way toward deep space. We'll follow, using Vlad's jump bender to take us back to Sally Ride. Arun runs another bug scan while we wait for the *Fairwell* to give us maneuvering room.

"That one came up clean." He flicks off the last scan and swipes away the programs. "I've run everything three times and can't think of any other things to try."

"I guess we'll have to hope we got them all. And take the usual precautions." I flick my jammer on, then drum my fingers on the arm rest of the co-pilot's chair. I swallow down my nervous energy and take a deep breath. "Do you think you could help me get better at flying?"

Arun turns to look at me, his eyes warming as he takes me in. A matching heat builds in my chest in response. Coming back here—just the two of us on the bridge—feels like coming home. When he doesn't answer, I raise a brow. "Please?"

He grins. "Of course. You're already very good for a student. It's all about building flying hours and experiencing the unexpected."

I let out a breath, blowing my hair away from my face. "I'm definitely good at finding the unexpected."

The *Fairwell* pushes past us, the larger ship seeming to go on forever as it steams away. It would have been faster for us to move first, but Coppelia and her team were too anxious. Fair enough—they've been stranded here a long time.

The engines slide past us, leaving stars and the curve of Xinjianestan in the distance. Arun puts in a heading on an angle from the *Fairwell*'s and engages the engines. Then the comm system bings.

We exchange a surprised look, then Arun shrugs. "Vlad probably discovered they forgot something." He taps the unidentified incoming message.

A string of jibberish appears in the holo, letters and numbers that make no sense and switch to others as we watch. It looks... familiar.

"New form of encryption?" I ask.

Arun shrugs. "Not anything I've ever seen." He swipes a few settings. "Certainly not on the *Fairwell*. And there's no indication of origin."

The characters flicker in and out, like each one is on a rotating wheel moving at different speeds. As we watch, some of the letters stabilize, and it all finally stops moving, resolving into a text message:

I see you. I'm coming.

"That's the same message Leo got." I swipe my ring to pull up the copy I saved. "How did they track from his Leweian account to us?"

Arun shakes his head, silent.

"I don't like this." I drum my fingers on my leg. "Don't respond."

He gives me a disbelieving glare. "You think I was born yesterday?" Arun pushes the message away, then scrolls through his interface. "Maybe I can block it."

I grab his arm. "That will confirm we reached them."

Another message appears. This one is different—a small blue icon in the shape of a ship. The kind of message that comes in the regular system.

"You think it's the same people?" Arun's finger hovers near the icon.

"How could it be? If they knew how to reach us through normal channels, why bother with all of the drama?" I circle my hands vaguely.

"But we shouldn't be getting messages through the normal channels." He pokes the icon.

I'm coming!

My eyes meet Arun's.

"That's not creepy at all." He taps the voice reply. "Who is this?"

A clear, high tone rings through the ship. Not a mechanical sound, but a woman's voice, singing a wordless "ahh." It changes to words, and the voice pops up to an ear-piercing note on the final syllable.

"'Tis I! Helva!"

THANKS FOR READING *Dark Quasar Ignites*. Obviously, the story doesn't end here. If you want to find out when the next book is published, sign up for my newsletter. You'll also get access to a bunch of short free stories and learn about my other books.

If you haven't read the original Space Janitor series—or the follow on series, you should check them out.

NOTES AND ACKNOWLEDGEMENTS
AUGUST 2024

Thank you for reading *Dark Quasar Ignites*. If you enjoyed it, I hope you'll consider leaving a review on your retailer or Goodreads or Bookbub. Reviews help other readers find our books.

This series is exists because readers told me they wanted more Vanti. She was a supporting character in the Space Janitor books, and you (and she) demanded more. So here it is.

The caat, Noelle, appeared suddenly in a short story I wrote for my Krimson Empire Kickstarter Campaign. My beta readers warned me Vanti would have to keep the caat, but I already knew that was going to happen. In fact, I suspect Noelle will have an even larger role in the next book.

To learn more about Hadriana Caats, read *Krimson Empire* and if you join my newsletter, you can download the short story A *Sprinkle of Krimson* which is a Christmas crossover between the *Space Janitor* books and *Krimson Empire,* and Noelle's first on-page appearance.

Okay, that's enough sales talk.

In case you were wondering, Vanti is completely wrong about

Botany Bay. If you're interested in what really happened to prisoners sent to Australia, there's some really good information here. Thanks to Jenny Avery for providing that link.

As usual, I have a host of people to thank. My alpha reader and sister, AM Scott and my editor, Paula Lester, helped me keep the characters in line, the story consistent, and the grammar correct. If I left any holes or errors, that's my fault, not theirs!

Thanks to my sprint group. I've been writing (virtually) with this group every weekday morning from nine to noon since mid 2019, and without them I wouldn't have published 28 books. Thanks to Hillary, Paula, Marcus, AM, and Lou. A few others have come and gone, but this core crew has seen me through so much. You guys are amazing.

Thanks to my beta team, who find any remaining typos and plot holes: Jenny, Paul, Barb, Anne, and Larry. You make my stories better!

My deep appreciation to Les at GermanCreative for the stunning cover. And my apologies for putting out a watermarked version on the early ARCs!

Thanks to my family, especially the Support Husband, Dave, who takes care of my advertising, reminds me to post on social media, updates my computer, travels with me to author events and conferences, and supports me in so many other ways. You are everything!

And thanks to the Big Guy, who makes all things possible.

ALSO BY JULIA HUNI

Space Janitor Series:

The Vacuum of Space

The Dust of Kaku

The Trouble with Tinsel

Orbital Operations

Glitter in the Stars

Sweeping S'Ride

Triana Moore, Space Janitor (the complete series)

Tales of a Former Space Janitor

The Rings of Grissom

Planetary Spin Cycle

Waxing the Moon of Lewei

Tales of a Former Space Janitor (books 1-3)

Changing the Speed of Light Bulbs

Sun Spot Remover

Friends of a Former Space Janitor

Dark Quasar Rising

Dark Quasar Ignites

The Phoenix and Katie Li

Luna City Limited

Colonial Explorer Corps Series:

The Earth Concurrence

The Grissom Contention

The Saha Declination

CEC: The Academy Years (books 1-3)

The Darenti Paradox

Recycled World Series:

Recycled World

Reduced World

Krimson Empire:

Krimson Run

Krimson Spark

Krimson Surge

Krimson Flare

Julia also writes earth-bound romantic comedy that won't steam your glasses under the not-so-secret pen name Lia Huni

FOR MORE INFORMATION

Use this QR code to stay up-to-date on all my publishing, and get access to my free bonus stores:

Milton Keynes UK
Ingram Content Group UK Ltd.
UKHW030730291024
2435UKWH00025B/131